SHIFTING GEARS

A Crossroads Novel

By

Riley Hart

Published by:

Riley Hart

This book is a work of fiction. Names, characters, places and incidents are products of the author's imagination or are used fictitiously. Any similarity to actual persons, living or dead is coincidental and not intended by the author.

Printed in the United States of America.

All products/brand names mentioned are registered trademarks of their respective holders/companies.

Cover Design by X-Potion Designs

Cover Image by Alejandro Caspe

Edited by Prema Editing and Hope Vincent. Proofread by Jessica de Ruiter and Judy's Proofreading

Formatted by Angel's Indie Formatting

Thank you to Riley's Rebels members Joy and Shanen for letting me use your names.

DEDICATION:

To Rod Batterman. Thank you for your friendship, your support, and all the laughs. I can always count on you to make me smile.

CHAPTER ONE

Rod Nelson really wanted to fuck the man browsing the lube aisle.

This wasn't the first time sexy Brown Eyes had been there. More like the third visit in the last three weeks, and every single one of them he spent in lubrication.

Obviously, he was having a whole lot more sex than Rod was lately, which had him slightly cranky. Who knew that starting his own adult store would keep him so fucking busy?

But then...people liked sex, so it made sense that traffic at the shop stayed steady. Rod liked sex too, hence the whole reason an adult "romance" store worked so well for him. Sure there was always the Internet, and a good chunk of his sales came from there, but he realized a lot of people liked to buy their sex toys in person. There was something special about checking out the product rather than clicking a button. Plus, three quarters of his business came from spontaneous couples who wanted to add a little spice to their night. Drinking helped with that.

He watched as Brown Eyes grabbed a bottle of Easy Ride—apparently his preferred brand—before making his way to the counter. As he approached, Rod straightened from his slouched position over the counter. *Don't hit on customers; don't hit on customers; don't hit on customers.*

Please let the customer hit on me.

"Will that be all for you today?" Rod asked, as Brown Eyes set his lube on the counter—one bottle a week, just as he'd done before.

In a gravelly voice, the man said, "Yep. Just like always," and then he winked—fucking winked one of those sexy brown eyes at him. Great. Obviously the guy was a sadist and wanted to torture him.

Brown Eyes glanced at Rod's nametag and then chuckled. "Rods-N-Ends has a whole new meaning now."

He'd had the name picked out before he even applied for the loan for his new shop. It was smaller than where he used to work, but this place was his, and that was all he cared about. "I have a good sense of humor. What can I say?"

Brown Eyes nodded. He had long, thick, dark lashes, and equally dark eyes. They were mysterious which sounded like a fucking cliché, he knew, but it was true. He was taller than Rod himself, with lean, hard muscle that didn't come from the gym. Another cliché, he guessed. But Jesus, the man was pretty in a rough, masculine way that prompted those kinds of clichés.

He shook his head, making the dark brown hair that hung over his forehead move. He looked to be older than Rod was, but only by a few years or so.

"The place is yours, huh?" he asked, and Rod realized he was staring. He'd always had a weakness for pretty, rugged men, and this guy was exactly that.

"Yeah, it's only been a few months. I used to work about half an hour away from here, but some friends of mine talked me into trying to get a place of my own, and here we are." He hated to admit Nick and Bryce had been right. In a lot of ways, Rod would have been completely comfortable floating by working for someone else, but he was twenty-five and being a clerk at an adult "romance" shop probably wouldn't keep him afloat forever. So he'd decided to be a clerk at his *own* adult shop because that was a whole hell of a lot different.

Rod let his eyes scope out the aisles of the store. There was a couple in the back, but other than them and Brown Eyes, the place was empty. "What about you? What do you do?" he asked.

He held up his hands. They were beat up, but strong hands with veins running the length of them, callouses on the pads of his thick fingers. Looking closer, he noticed what looked like grease around his cuticles. It fit with his faded, slightly low-slung jeans with a hole in one of the knees. He wore a T-Shirt he'd obviously been working in as well. "Some kind of manual labor obviously. Mechanic?"

Brown Eyes smiled. "Yep. Motorcycle."

"Shut the fuck up!" Rod said and when the other man's eyes got bigger, he clarified. "No, don't really shut up. It's just that my friend, Bryce, is a motorcycle mechanic. It was Bryce and his boyfriend Nick who talked me into this place." This was too big a coincidence. He glanced around waiting for Bryce to pop up from around a corner laughing his ass off. It was something he'd do—dangle a gorgeous guy with sexy eyes and faded jeans in front of Rod before playing some elaborate joke on him.

"Really?" the man asked. "Small world. If he's hiring, tell him I'm looking. I moved here about a month back and it's been a little harder to find work than I thought it would be."

Jackpot, Rod thought, which probably made him an asshole because the guy was telling him he was out of work and Rod was thinking this could be a way in with him. "You're going to have to give me your phone number then...you know, so Bryce or I can get ahold of you...." *This is where you give me your name and phone number.*

"Landon, and you're good."

"Oh, honey, you ain't seen nothin' yet." Rod winked at him, but then he remembered he didn't really know for sure if this man was gay or not. "Are you gay?"

"Nope."

Fuck. "Me either. What a coincidence."

Landon's forehead wrinkled and then Rod said, "I'm giving you shit. I'm as gay and proud as they come and you're fucking with me too. I know these things."

Before Landon could reply, the couple walked up and Rod wanted to tell them to go away. That wasn't the best way to run a business so he grinned at them. Landon walked away, and he pretended he didn't want to tell them they were fucking with his game. He rang up their purchase—edible underwear, massage oil, and whipped cream—and they were on their way.

"Where were we?" Rod asked.

"You were ringing up my order."

Damn it. Maybe he had been wrong about the guy. He hadn't thought so, but it was a possibility. Either that or Landon just wasn't interested in him.

Rod scanned Landon's Easy Ride, the whole time mentally chastising himself for hitting on a customer. "Ten sixty-five. And listen, I'm sorry about earlier. I didn't mean—"

"Bisexual."

"Excuse me?"

"I'm bi. Do you hit on customers often?"

"No, but they're usually not as sexy as you. The last ones who were ended up being two of my closest friends though…you know…Bryce, the dude who works on bikes like you." *Hint, hint. I have a hook up.*

Landon laughed a light, earthy laugh that made Rod smile. He liked it. He wanted to hear it again.

"You're relentless."

"No," Rod corrected. "Just a hard worker when I want something. I don't give up. That's a good quality, or so I've been told."

"It can be." Landon handed Rod a twenty, and waited for his change. "I have to be honest with you…I find people a whole lot messier than lube and my hand. I'm not really looking for anything more than that right now. Friendship is okay though."

Awesome. First Landon had to put the mental image of himself jacking off in Rod's head and then had to go and tell him that he was only looking for friendship. "I can do friendship. But I have to tell you, I wasn't looking to marry you." All Rod had been thinking about was a quick fuck. He quite enjoyed fucking his way through life.

Landon nodded at him, obviously not planning on changing his mind about fucking Rod senseless.

"So what's your phone number, friend?" Rod asked.

Landon smiled, and heat pricked across Rod's skin. Damn it. Even his smile was sexy. First Nick and Bryce had to torture him with something he'd never have, and now Landon. He really had to stop meeting gorgeous men in adult stores who only wanted to be friends.

***

Landon Harrison never expected to find himself in Virginia again. If he was being honest, he hated it here. Too many memories of fighting parents, which went from the plural to singular when his dad walked out on them, leaving behind a depressed mom who waited for him to return.

He'd never felt like he fit in when he was a kid. He'd hidden the fact that he liked both men and women. Now, he didn't give a shit. If someone had a problem with it they could kiss his ass as far as he was concerned. It had taken leaving to get to that place.

The second he could, he'd been out of Virginia, leaving his mom and his sister, Shanen behind, but now he was back. Shanen was getting married, and she'd told him their mom had been acting strange lately. She was worried about her, which caught his attention. Depression had always been something his mom struggled with on and off. She'd broken down when his dad left. She didn't handle big changes well and he figured since Shanen had stuck behind when he left, it was his turn to help out.

And he was going out of his goddamned mind. Living at home after twelve years away made him feel like he'd stepped into a time machine and woken up as that eighteen-year-old kid who felt trapped and angry.

He was bored. He needed a job, freedom, friends. He wouldn't mind throwing sex in there as well, which brought him back to thinking about the pretty guy who owned Rods-N-Ends.

He didn't need three bottles of lube in three weeks, but hell, he was attracted to the man. Rod had short, dark hair, a round face that made him look a little younger than the people who typically attracted him, but that goddamned ass of his had done Landon in. As soon as he'd walked into the store the first time, Landon had wanted him. He'd definitely be a better time than Easy Ride and his hand, but then Rod went and mentioned the job. If he could possibly help Landon work on bikes other than his own again, he really didn't want to screw things up by fucking the guy.

That left him here, sitting on his childhood bed, alone, with his mom in the next room. How in the hell did this become his life?

He looked around the room. The posters of half-naked girls were long gone, thank God. It didn't resemble the way it looked when he was eighteen, but it felt the same—stifling and lonely.

A knock came at his bedroom door, and Landon tossed the lube under his pillow like he was again that eighteen-year-old kid. Jesus, how was he going to do this? He definitely had to get a job and get his own place. He could handle living at home again, just not in the same fucking house. "Come in."

His mom pushed the door open. "Hey you. What are you up to?" She looked completely put together, with her brown hair in a bun and makeup on her face. She smiled, pulling the strap of her purse up her arm.

"Not much. You heading out?"

"Yes. Are you sure you don't want to go with Shanen and me?"

They were going dress shopping. He definitely didn't want to go. "Yeah, I'm okay."

"You can meet us for dinner afterward. Jacob is taking us out to a steakhouse." She smiled ear to ear, very happy about Shanen's fiancé. His mom had always been a romantic. She'd had these big ideas about her relationship with his dad, friendship that had turned into love. What she hadn't expected was how things had gone from there. He thought maybe she saw Shanen as a second chance.

"No, thank you. I'm just going to hang out tonight."

She gave him another smile. He wished it could always be like this, that she could always be happy this way. "It's good to have you home, Landon."

He tried to return her smile, wishing he felt it. "It's good to be home."

The door closed with a quiet click. Guilt made him wish his words had been true.

CHAPTER TWO

"I'm in love," Rod said the second Bryce picked up the phone.

Bryce laughed. "Shut the hell up."

"What? Why is it so hard to believe that I'd be in love?" He crossed his arms as though Bryce could see him pouting.

"Because I know you?"

Rod winced; Bryce's words stung. He didn't even hesitate in his disbelief that Rod might be interested in someone. But then he remembered he liked being single and getting to do who and what he wanted. He didn't need anything else. "Okay, maybe you do know me, but I could be in love if I wanted to. I could fall in love every fucking day, but this guy, I've seen him three times and I'm still in love with him."

Bryce paused for a second. "*Seen* him, seen him. Like dating? Or fucking?"

Shit. "Well, neither actually…"

Bryce barked out a laugh and Rod considered hanging up on

him—the asshole. "He's a motorcycle mechanic. Let me talk to Nick. He'll understand. He obviously has a thing for that kind of man. He'll have my back on this one."

"Well, men like me are irresistible…"

Rod heard Nick scoff in the background and realized he was close enough to Bryce to hear Rod speak. "Ooh… Did I interrupt something? Let's video chat and you can continue where you left off. You'll never know I'm there."

This time both Nick and Bryce laughed. Rod couldn't help but smile himself. He liked the men a lot. They'd become really close since the first time the couple had stumbled into the store he used to work in while looking for their first dildo. Being with each other had been the first time either of them had been with another man, and apparently Nick was very well endowed. Bryce was a lucky man.

That had been over a year ago. Nick and Bryce were out to their families now and they'd moved into a new house together, where they had Rod over for dinner every once in a while. He and Bryce enjoyed making Nick blush.

"Funny man. So what else is going on?" Bryce asked.

"Do you happen to need any help at the shop? Landon mentioned just moving here and he's looking for a job. I told him I'd ask you."

"Actually…this is perfect timing. We just had someone give his two-week notice yesterday, so we will be looking to hire. He's welcome to fill out an application. I can't make you any promises. I'll have to see what kind of experience he has and how he'll fit in, but tell him to apply. You really had a gay motorcycle mechanic come into Rods-N-Ends? I thought I was the only one."

Rod laughed. "Aww, are you feeling less important because you're not the only gay motorcycle mechanic who likes to buy sex toys from me? Does it help that he's bi? But then I guess you are too. Hmm...does it help that he only buys lube? And you were my first. You'll always be special to me."

Nick laughed loudly in the background.

"Fuck you both," Bryce said, which only made the two of them laugh louder.

Once it finally died down, they chatted again for a few minutes before Rod told them he had to go. He needed to call and save the day for Brown Eyes.

He got up and walked into the kitchen for a glass of water before he went back and sat in the living room chair. The TV was on low in the background. He had a small, two-bedroom house that he could only afford because he'd bought it with the money he got when his dad died—money he only received because his dad had probably figured leaving Rod the old house in Oklahoma would be more of a hassle than it would be worth.

He'd been sure to cut Rod out of getting anything else when he died—not that he'd wanted anything from the bastard—other than an old house with major foundation problems, that went downhill as you walked through it. That had been the least of the problems.

He hadn't wanted any part of the house or anything else, but then he figured the man owed him something for making Rod's life hell, so he'd sold it for whatever he could get, and put the money down on this place. So now he was in debt with a house and sex-toy shop. Wouldn't his God-fearing, gay-hating father be proud?

His past was the last thing Rod wanted to think about, so instead he pulled out the card with Landon's number on it and called him. He answered on the third ring. "Hey, Brown Eyes."

He was rewarded with Landon's laughter again. "That what you call all the guys or should I feel special?"

"You should feel special." Rod smiled. "And you recognized my voice."

"It's distinct and there's no one else I know who would call me brown eyes."

Rod put his feet up on the table. "Well, now I can feel special too, but I find that hard to believe. You must not be hanging out with the right kind of men."

Landon groaned through the line before saying, "You can say that again. But then, I guess I'm okay with that. I don't really believe in the right kind of partner. I don't belong to that whole, *there's one special person out there for everyone* camp."

This was getting good. He hadn't really called to get to know Landon better. Okay, that was a lie. He wanted to get to know Landon a whole hell of a lot better, but he'd been thinking sexually. Still, he wasn't going to pass up the opportunity. "Tell me more."

"What? No. I don't even like talking to people I do know. I like talking to people I don't know even less."

Didn't Brown Eyes know the more mysterious he was, the more Rod would want him? It was an unspoken rule. "I sell you lube! I talked to my friend about getting you a job. I know you like both men and women. We're practically best friends."

"You're insane. Has anyone ever told you that?" Landon asked.

"Of course." Was that really a question?

Landon sighed, and Rod couldn't tell if he was really frustrated or not. "Hey, I'm just giving you shit. I don't expect you to tell me anything you don't want to tell."

"No, it's not you." It sounded like Landon yawned. "I've just had a long day. Like I said, I just moved back not long ago. I'm still...adjusting, I guess you could say, and I'm going batshit crazy. I'm thirty years old and I live with my mom in Small Town USA, when I've been in Orlando for years. Add to that, I don't have a job and the fact that I've reverted to jacking off every day and hiding my lube under the bed like I'm a kid. Let's just say it's been a shitty month."

Rod frowned, feeling the frustration behind Landon's words. "That's understandable. Big changes."

"I had a job I loved and left it behind. It's not that I miss the place as much as the freedom in my life. Shit...how did you do that? You just got me to say things I normally wouldn't say."

The frustration was still there in Landon's voice, but not as heavy as it had been before. Crazy as it sounded, it felt good to think that maybe he'd had a hand in that. "It's part of my charm. You don't stand a chance against me, so you might as well give in now."

***

Landon wasn't sure what to think of Rod. Hell, he wasn't even sure what they were doing on the phone right now. Yeah, he'd asked Rod about a job, but it had almost been a joke. He didn't make a habit of telling people he was jobless and asking for their help. And now here they were talking and…he really should ask the man about the job again. He'd lose his mind if he didn't get back to work. "What did your friend say?"

"I think it was fate you needed lube and stumbled into Rods-N-Ends, that's what I think. Bryce said someone just gave their notice. His last day is in two weeks, so they're looking."

Landon let out a deep breath. It was as though half of the weight in his chest floated away with it. He had no doubt he could get the job if he applied. He was good. He had been trained at the best motorcycle mechanic school in the country. If someone was hiring, he'd get the job. "Thanks, man. I appreciate it."

"No problem. It's not a guarantee, but—"

"No, no. I get it. If someone needs help, I'm confident I can get the job, though. I'm good at what I do."

Rod laughed. His statement probably made him sound conceited, but he didn't care. He had faith in his ability. There was nothing wrong with that.

"I'll text you the information…. Good at what you do, huh? I bet you get all the guys with that kind of talk."

"Girls too," Landon reminded him, though he wasn't sure why.

"I can appreciate women. I don't want one. Never have and never will, but I'm not scared of vagina, so stop trying to push me away by reminding me you don't only like ass."

"That's not what I was doing." Although he was pretty sure it was. "So, how'd you get into the business of lube and dildos?" As soon as he asked the question, he wished he hadn't. He wondered why he had. He didn't know Rod. What reason did he have to chat on the phone with him? Hell, he didn't talk on the phone with anyone. He hated the damn thing.

"They say to do what you know…"

Landon chuckled. "Well, yeah, there's that, I guess." But there was more to it. He wasn't sure how he knew that, but he did.

"I needed a job when I was in college. I wanted to piss my dad off, so I figured what better way than to sell evil, dirty things? Especially if some of those things were for *the gays*."

Rod spoke like it was a joke, but Landon could hear the underlying anger in his words. He felt bad for the man. Maybe the people he'd grown up with wouldn't have accepted his bisexuality but he always knew his mom and sister would. His piece-of-shit father had been gone by the time he'd realized it, so he hadn't mattered.

"I was going to be a teacher, if you can believe that," Rod chuckled. "But halfway through school I realized it wasn't for me. So, I kept selling sin. Why not live up to my obvious worthlessness? It was stupid, staying around just to piss him off, but on the other hand, I like what I do. I'm a people person and I enjoy sex. I meet interesting customers while doing my job and don't laugh, but I'm bringing them pleasure, in a way. Nothing wrong with that. So after my dad passed, I stuck with it. Even though I liked what I did, I knew I wanted more. Took some prodding from Nick and Bryce, but finally I applied for a loan and Rods-N-Ends was born."

"I'm sorry for your loss," Landon told him. There were unresolved issues with his father. He'd made that apparent, but losing him still had to hurt. Landon wouldn't know. He had no idea if his own father was dead or alive.

When Rod didn't reply, he knew it was time to pull some of the heat off of him. It wasn't as though Landon wanted to talk about dads anyway. He had enough unresolved issues of his own to deal with. "You're doing what you love. That's what matters. I feel that way about working on bikes. I thought about opening my own shop, but I guess it's good I didn't since I ended up moving back here."

"And now you'll get a job with Bryce and do what you love again."

Landon nodded as though Rod could see him, not sure what to say next. Just as he opened his mouth to announce that he should probably go, Rod said, "I'll make ya famous."

No. He didn't just say that. *Tombstone?* Landon asked. He loved that movie.

"Yeah, it just came on. This is one of my favorites. Val Kilmer is sexy as hell in it."

"Agreed. Jesus, he used to be gorgeous. What channel?"

Rod told him and Landon turned it on. Somehow they ended up watching the whole damn movie while on the phone with each other, discussing all their favorite scenes as they watched.

CHAPTER THREE

What are you doing?

Rod tossed his cell phone to the counter after sending the text. He wasn't sure what made him message Landon, but he was bored and work was slow, and the guy had sexy eyes. So sue him.

His phone buzzed a minute later, and he looked down at it.

Sleep.

He smiled, imagining a sleep-ruffled Landon, his dark hair messy from rubbing against the pillow. Or better yet, a sex-rumpled Landon, his hair disheveled because Rod had tugged on it all night while Landon fucked him.

Shit. He really needed to get laid.

It's one. Rod texted back. He didn't open until noon. Most people who went shopping for sex toys and lube didn't do so before twelve.

Couldn't sleep. Didn't pass out until about seven this morning. Thanks for fucking up my rest.

Rod laughed just as the bell rang over the door. He put his phone under the counter and made his way to the woman who walked in. She had long, curly hair, looked to be in her early twenties, and her cheeks were bright red. *Ahh, a virgin.*

"First time, huh?" he asked her.

Her mouth went wide, making an *O.*

Oh shit. "I meant in an adult store! Not having sex." Fantastic. He was sexually harassing female customers now.

"Oh. Sorry. I should have realized that's what you meant. And yes...my boyfriend and I...it's our six-month anniversary and I wanted to get something to surprise him. I looked online, but it's different, ya know? I want to actually be able to look at the product...whatever I get."

Rod smiled, wanting to take her under his wing. She was obviously nervous as hell, shy, and a little insecure. "You're in the right hands. We'll get you all figured out. Tell me a little about your boyfriend." He nodded toward the center of the store and she followed.

"We're both in college. He plays football, but he's not the conceited jock type. I mean, we were both virgins when we met. He would kill me if he knew I told you that."

Rod shook his head. "Your secrets are safe with Rod."

She smiled. "Summer break starts soon and we live in different states. This will be our last night together."

"And a special night it will be. You said he plays football. Is he

24

still pretty active, even though it's not football season?"

She nodded.

"We'll start you guys out slow then, maybe with some massage products. You can work out his muscles and if he's a good guy, he'll return the favor. The fun stuff starts after that." Rod winked at her, and the blush was completely gone from her cheeks.

"That sounds perfect. Thank you."

"No problem." They walked side by side through the store. "After the massage products, we definitely need to hit the lingerie."

The girl stumbled at that. "No. I don't have the body for something like that."

Rod frowned. It killed him to hear things like that from people— men or women. "You're gorgeous, and he obviously feels the same way. I promise you, he'll love it." This earned him a shy nod. That small confirmation was all he needed. "Let's do this."

She shrugged. "I guess since I'm here...yeah, let's do it."

Thirty minutes later they were at the counter with a whole basketful of fun, and Alethia—she'd told him her name—wore a huge smile on her face. "Never in a million years would he think I'd do something like this. He's going to freak."

"He's going to love it," Rod told her.

He gave her the total, and she paid. Alethia made it halfway to the door before stopping and turning to him. "Thank you. I was really embarrassed to come here. This is the third time I've tried and I finally had the guts to come in. I actually think I'm even a little excited to wear the lingerie. You're good with people...and you made me feel really comfortable. I appreciate that."

This was the part of the job people didn't understand. It wasn't just about selling sex toys. It was about making people happy, making them feel good; if that made him dirty and sinful, then fine by him. "That's what I'm here for. Have fun."

She smiled and ducked out of the shop. A feeling of contentment settled in his chest. When his phone buzzed again, he remembered his conversation with Landon. Rod pulled the phone from the shelf to see three missed texts.

I was giving you shit.

Oh, I see, wake me up and then ignore me.

I'm going back to bed.

Obviously Landon wasn't very patient. **Wow...are you always this impatient or am I just special? Very important stuff going on over here. I had a shy, first timer. I saved the day in case you're wondering.**

Rod set his phone down again, somehow knowing Landon was going to make him wait.

***

His mom was doing the dishes when Landon went into the kitchen. Jesus, this was so fucking strange...being back here, living at home. "Mornin'," he said, scratching his head.

"It's the afternoon." She smiled. She was dressed, wearing makeup and had her hair down. She looked good, looked happy. He glanced at the counter and saw her pill bottle there. Her eyes followed his. "Yes, I took my medication. I've been taking it for years on my own. I'm not a child, Landon."

He frowned. He understood her feeling that way. He'd just been thinking the same thing, in regards to being home. It was a tricky situation. She'd gone through a really tough time when his dad left. She had what she called dark periods from time to time, but over the years, they'd become fewer and farther between. If the situation were reversed he knew he wouldn't appreciate being checked up on like this. "I'm sorry. I didn't mean to wonder."

"It's okay. I get it, but I promise you, I'm good. Don't think I don't know you're here because Shanen over-worries about everything. I'm not a fool, but I love having you back so I'm going to pretend you moved back to Virginia just because you missed us." She grabbed a towel from the counter and dried her hands. "It's good to see your face every day, but I hate that you felt as though you had to come back because of me."

"I'm not back only because of you." He was back because it was important. Shanen was getting married. He hadn't seen his family more than once per year since he left home.

The older he got, the more he feared becoming his dad. He fucking hated that prick too much to risk being like him.

"Then why do you act so miserable?"

Guilt swarmed him, like bees around a hive. "What are you talking about? I'm not miserable." It was strange how that was partially the truth. Fuck, he hated this town. And again, he sure as hell didn't want to live with his mother but, besides his job, he hadn't had much he loved in Orlando either. He'd been in need of a change—just not this one in specific.

"You don't want to live here. You don't want to *be* here. You've made that much obvious over the years."

Landon sat in the chair and sighed. Her words stung, but he wouldn't lie to her. "No, I didn't want to be here. Not really, but that's not because of you."

"Leaving home won't change the past. It won't change the fact that he left."

White, hot anger pierced him. You'd think after all this time, it wouldn't matter, that he could forgive him or at least not feel like burning the whole damn world down when he thought about him. "What I do has nothing to do with him."

"Sure it does. Our experiences shape us, good and bad. There's no denying that, Landon. He was young...we were both young and made our mistakes. You and Shanen both know I wasn't innocent."

Landon shoved to his feet, walking over to the fridge because he needed something to do. He sure as shit didn't want to talk about his father. "Don't do that. Don't make excuses for him." Why were they even talking about this?

"People are human. We make mistakes. If you can forgive mine, why not his?"

Landon turned on her. "Because he's not here! He left, remember? He didn't give a shit and he walked away!" She flinched and he silently cursed. "Shit. I'm sorry. I didn't mean to yell at you." Still, everything he'd said had been true.

Landon pulled her into a hug and kissed the top of her dark hair. "I missed you."

"I missed you too, and I just want you to be happy. No going through life with regrets, huh? I have enough of them for the both of us, and I'm sure your father does, too."

He tried to fight going rigid at the mention of him again.

"There are a lot of exciting things going on. New opportunities. Shanen is getting married. You're back. Who knows what else will happen?"

He wasn't so sure he wanted to find out.

"I have a confession to make…I'm looking forward to living on my own again. I haven't lived by myself since before I had you kids."

He crossed his arms and looked at her. "Um…did you forget I moved in with you?"

She patted his shoulder. "Not forever. I know you better than that. Once you get a job, you'll find your own place, which is the way it should be."

"Are you kicking me out?" Landon teased her.

"Yes?" She grinned, but he knew she really wasn't. She was giving him an escape and he was thankful as hell for it. "Just don't go too far this time, okay?"

He wondered if it had been like this for his dad before he'd left.

If he'd been looking for an escape, and his mom had provided him with one, the same way she tried to do with Landon.

CHAPTER FOUR

About a week later, Landon pulled up at the shop for his interview. It was a nice, clean place. The drive was slightly a bummer, since it was about forty-five minutes away from where his mom lived, but he could handle it. He'd do anything to be in a shop again, to spend his days working on bikes and getting grease under his nails.

He killed the engine, put the kickstand down, and pulled his leg over his bike just as a guy with a similar build to his own, and dark hair walked out. "R1, huh? She's a beauty."

Landon pulled off his helmet, set it on the bike and held out a hand. "Thank you. I'm Landon Harrison."

The other man clasped his hand in a tight grip. "Bryce Tanner. It's nice to meet you."

So this was Bryce. He'd heard quite a bit about him from Rod. It was strange, and he wasn't sure exactly how it happened, but they'd been texting each other often over the last week. It felt like such an odd thing to do, texting, with the guy who sold him lube. His conversations with men on his phone were usually done on a hook-up app, but considering he'd thought about doing more than that with Rod before he'd told Landon about the job, maybe it wasn't so strange after all.

"You as well," Landon told him before Bryce led him inside. The shop was just as clean inside as it looked outside. It was obvious that the man took pride in his work, which was incredibly important to him.

"MMI, huh?" Bryce asked him about his schooling. "If I left Virginia, that's where I would have wanted to go."

Most people who loved to work on bikes did. "Yeah, it was great. I loved it."

They made their way into a small office and Bryce closed the door behind him. "We do motocross and street bikes both."

"I have experience with both," Landon told him. "I rode moto as a kid. I don't do it as much anymore, but I can definitely work on any bike you put in front of me. I have a buddy who rides professionally, and I've rebuilt his top for him more than once."

"No shit?" Bryce asked and it was obvious Landon just scored some points.

"Beckett Monroe." What he didn't say was that Beckett was the only person he'd ever slept with who he considered a friend, and still spoke to afterward. Maybe that's because they only fucked once and Beck was one hundred percent in the closet with no plans of coming out.

"Are you fucking kidding me? He won the Monster Energy cup."

"Yeah, I know. I was there."

Bryce clapped a hand on his shoulder. "I think you're my new best friend."

Just like that, Landon knew he was in.

***

It was Friday, which apparently meant everyone had to come out and buy their sex products for the weekend. Rods-N-Ends had been crazy all day, but Rod still made sure to check his phone often, hoping for a text from either Landon or Bryce to see how the interview went today. Neither man had messaged him, which didn't make for a very happy Rod.

He liked to know what was going on, which some people in his life said was a nice way of saying he was nosy, but Rod didn't give a shit about that.

At about seven, they had a lull in customers. "I'm taking a quick break, Todd. I'll be back in a few," he told the young college-aged guy he had working with him tonight.

As soon as he stepped outside, he pulled out his phone and shot a text to Bryce. **So? How'd it go?**

You want this guy don't you? Bryce replied.

And? I wanted you and Nick too. You guys are no fun though. You don't like to share.

He walked over to his car and leaned against it.

I'm not telling you. It's not my place.

Well, what the fuck did that mean? **You didn't give him the job??**

A minute passed, then another. He was going to fucking kill the man for not responding to him. Just as Rod was about to type out his confession for the murder he planned to commit when he got off work, he heard the deep buzz of a motorcycle. He looked up just as a black bike came his way. The rider pulled to a stop in the space beside him, wearing faded jeans and a black riding jacket. Landon pulled off his helmet and ran a hand through his dark hair, those sexy fucking eyes right on Rod.

"I just came," Rod said.

Landon gave him a wide-eyed, panicked look.

"Not literally, but it wouldn't take much for that to happen. You got a spare thirty seconds? Jesus, you're sexy on that thing."

Landon shook his head as though he didn't know what to do with Rod. He was used to getting that look from people and had to admit, he liked it.

"You're crazy," Landon told him.

"I'm serious. I feel like I need a cigarette and I don't even smoke."

Landon winked at him. "I've been known to have that affect on people. Keep it in your pants, though. I came to say thank you."

A heavy weight was lifted off of Rod's chest. It shouldn't be so important to him that Landon got the job. It wasn't as though it changed his life in any way, but Landon was a nice guy. It was obvious how important it was to him that he got back to work, and Bryce was his friend. He wanted Bryce to have good help at the shop. See? It made sense. He was just being a good person. "You got the job?"

"I did." Landon nodded. "I like your friend. He seems to really love what he does. That's important to me. I think I'm going to like working with him. So, thank you. I appreciate you telling me about the job and putting in a good word for me."

"Well, you know what they say…nothing in life comes for free," Rod teased him, earning an eye roll from Landon. He shouldn't think it was cute that Landon seemed a little overwhelmed by him, but he did.

"Do I want to ask?"

"Yes, you do."

"I'm not so sure about that."

"Come on." Rod walked over and nudged him with his arm. "It'll be fun." He let it sound like he was kidding, but both he and Landon knew he was serious. He was attracted to Landon. Landon was single. Why not have a little fun together?

"Do you hit on everyone you meet?"

"Nope," Rod replied. "Just you. Actually, that's partially a lie. It's not limited to you, but I'm not a complete free for all, either."

"You're crazy."

"I'm fun."

"I'm not fucking you."

Rod pretended to be offended. He stepped back, crossing his arms and said, "I'm shocked. Who said I wanted to fuck you…? And wait. Why aren't you?" It wasn't any different than meeting someone at a club and going home with them, or looking for a hook-up on an app. Consenting adults and all, why shouldn't they sleep with each other if they wanted to? But apparently he was the only one doing the wanting.

Landon ignored his question and asked, "How about I buy you a beer or something?"

"I'm at work."

"A minute ago we were talking about fucking."

"I'd make time for sex." Beer or sex. Was that even a question?

"Then make time for a beer later."

Even though he enjoyed the banter, Rod knew he needed to get back to work. He had a good time teasing Landon, though. "Fine, if you insist. I'm off Mondays and Tuesdays. I'm going on record saying that I think fucking is better than beer, but apparently you don't agree. I'll text you this weekend."

Rod turned to walk away, but Landon grabbed his arm before he could leave. "I won't fuck you because I like you. I don't fuck people I like. Sex and friendship don't typically go together with me. Too much hassle. You're a fun guy. We could be friends, and I would like to have a few of those right now. If I fucked you, I'd stop talking to you, and I don't want that to happen. I'm telling you right now that's the only reason I'm not taking your ass. Otherwise, it already would have been mine."

Landon winked at him and then pulled his hand back. He put his helmet on, started his bike, and walked it backward before he was out of the space.

I won't fuck you because I like you.

You're a fun guy. We could be friends.

Landon's words played through his head. It was the first time in his life someone had said something like that to him. Typically when it came to attraction, hell when it came to anything, people either weren't interested in him, or they fucked each other and walked away.

If I fucked you, I'd stop talking to you, and I don't want that to happen. I'm telling you right now that's the only reason I'm not taking your ass.

Rod was still standing there sorting through his thoughts when Landon drove away.

CHAPTER FIVE

"Where are you off to?" Landon's mom asked Monday evening just before he was about to walk out the door.

"I'm going out for a beer with Rod. He's the guy I met who told me about the job."

She smiled at him. Shanen had the same smile as their mom. It was a smile that said, *tell me more. Tell me everything, so I can give you advice.* "A date? Will you be home tonight?"

She meant well, he knew that, but he really didn't know how long he could handle living here if she wanted to know where he was going, and when he'd be home every time he left. He was a grown man. He had a key. He could let himself in. That's all that mattered.

It was odd. She seemed to check up on him more now than she did when he was a kid—Where are you going? When will you be home?

"No date. He's a friend." Which apparently Rod didn't like very much. Not that Landon could blame him. "I'll be home tonight."

"It's fine if you're not. You're an adult, Landon. You can do whatever you want."

"Thanks, Ma." He winked at her, and she shook her head at him. "I really am beginning to think you're trying to get rid of me."

"You know that's not true. I love my family. Family means everything."

It did, or at least family should mean everything. Before they got onto a topic that Landon didn't want to talk about, he said, "See you later," and walked out, closing the door behind him.

Rod lived between Landon and the shop, along a scenic route where Landon could take the back roads. He'd looked up directions after Rod gave him the address, hoping he could stay off freeways. If he could, he always took side roads, just him and his bike without cars and people all around him.

A little over twenty minutes later he pulled up at Rod's place. He was surprised to see he lived in a small house, in what looked like a family neighborhood. He wasn't sure why he expected something different, but he had. It looked more conservative than what he imagined for the man who Landon saw as free-spirited.

He parked his bike, got off, and then walked to the door. He knocked twice before Rod answered, and holy shit did this feel like a fucking date. Landon wasn't a dater, never had been and never would be. "This is weird. We should have met there."

"Why?" Rod's dark brows pulled together.

"This feels like a date."

"No offense, but that sounds like a personal problem to me.

We're friends—as you told me. We're going to have a beer. Friends are allowed to ride together."

Okay, well now he felt like an ass. "I know. I just...you mentioned the sex and—"

"Hey! Don't blame this on me. I mentioned sex on Friday night. It's Monday. I'm over you." Rod crossed his arms, giving him a cocky grin. Landon bit back a smile.

"Over me already, huh? That was quick."

"The heart is fleeting."

"Apparently so is the ass."

"Apparently." Rod stepped outside and Landon backed up so he could have space. "There's a bar not too far from here we can go to. I'd suggest a restaurant, but then you might hyperventilate thinking it was a date. I only give mouth-to-mouth to willing participants and since you're not, I'd hate to have your death on my hands."

"Stop trying to make me feel like an ass."

"Is it working?" Rod asked and again, Landon found himself wanting to grin. There was something addictive about Rod. Physically, he was definitely attractive. He was smaller than Landon—shorter and leaner. He had a kind smile and sharp, blue eyes.

Landon had to admit, he wasn't typically into men with tattoos, but on Rod they weren't bad, and he only had a few of them—a tribal design on the front of both of his forearms.

He wore eyeliner the first time Landon had seen him, but he

hadn't had it on Friday or today. He missed it. It gave Rod's eyes a sexy, smoky appearance that Landon liked on him. Not that he should care how good Rod looked or didn't look, which was exactly why he wasn't going to mention his ass.

"I'm taking your silence as a yes." Rod took the stairs on his small porch and went for Landon's bike. "I've never ridden before. Is it as big a rush as you'd think?"

That question right there was enough to get Landon's dick hard...and make his pulse hammer down. Most people who hadn't ridden before were nervous. Rod's excitement made Landon like him even more. "It's the best feeling in the world."

"You obviously haven't had enough sex."

He'd had plenty of sex and as good as orgasms were, bikes were a whole lot easier and less messy. Landon grabbed the second helmet and tossed it to Rod. "You'll see what I mean when you ride. It's the best fucking high there is."

He couldn't wait to show Rod what he'd been missing.

***

Rod held tight, his arms wrapped firmly around Landon's waist. Wind rushed by them. They'd passed the bar a long time ago, left the city behind, as Landon took them down twisting, tree-lined roads. Energy buzzed inside him. It radiated off of Landon as well, little jolts of electricity transferring through him and lighting up Rod's insides.

Riding motorcycles was definitely a rush.

He squeezed tighter as Landon leaned, taking a curve. His heart jumped into his throat, beating wildly. His fist knotted in Landon's jacket as he righted them again, picking up speed on the straightaway.

It was fucking incredible.

He didn't know how long they rode. His pulse sped too fast the whole time. Eventually Landon turned around and made his way back to town. He pulled up in front of the bar Rod had told him about, killed the engine, and put the bike on the stand.

Rod pulled off his helmet and stood. His legs shook. They felt like they had no bones in them. He must have nearly gone over because Landon reached out, and wrapped an arm around him. "You good?" he asked, concern in his voice.

Rod's legs were starting to come back to him, so he pulled back. "I'm fucking great. That was amazing. Jesus Christ it was almost as good as sex. Wow... I never..." He wasn't sure what to say. He never really thought riding a motorcycle would be his thing, but damn, it was like... "It's almost like you're not tethered to the earth anymore. You're just flying, nothing but space around you."

Landon cocked his head, little wrinkles forming on his forehead before he gave Rod the biggest smile he'd seen from the man. "Yeah...you took the words out of my mouth. That's how I feel about it, too. I'm glad you love it. There's nothing like it. We'll take a day ride sometime if you want. Just fucking go for as long as we like. I'll show you what she can really do."

Landon's voice shook with excited energy. Again it jolted Rod, hitting him in the chest. He nodded. "That'd be great." He liked the idea of spending more time with Landon.

"Great. I can't tell you how glad I am that you liked it. I'm looking forward to taking you out."

He almost made a joke there about it sounding an awful lot like Landon was talking about a date, but he didn't. Landon made it perfectly clear he wasn't interested in dating Rod. He wasn't sure why that made his gut twist. He didn't want to date Landon either. He just wanted to sleep with him. "My stomach is a mess. I'm scared if I put anything in it, it's going to come up again. It's like I'm high or something."

"Best kind of high there is." Landon winked. "You'll be okay though." He swung his leg over the bike, and then they made their way toward the building. Landon pulled the door open for him, and Rod went inside.

"I feel badass now. I'm a biker dude."

Landon let out such a loud laugh, he looked like he surprised himself.

"I'm wondering if I should be offended. Is there a reason me being a badass biker is funny?"

"Nope, not at all." Landon grinned. "We should probably be on my Harley and not my sports bike for that. We'll take the Harley out next time. It'll be more comfortable for you to ride on anyway."

He nodded at Landon and then spotted a table in the corner. Rod led him over, and took a seat. It wasn't extremely busy since it was a Monday night, but there was definitely a crowd. It was the only gay bar relatively close that was a spot to just hang out rather than having dancing and go-go boys. Not that he had a problem with go-go boys. He quite liked them. He just wasn't sure it fit for tonight.

"I know five minutes ago I said I couldn't eat, but now I'm hungry. Is food okay or is that too much like a date for you?"

Landon rolled his eyes, but Rod could tell he wasn't really angry. "Eat, and stop giving me shit."

"I'm just wondering what part of wanting to have sex with you made you think I wanted to date you anyway?" It wasn't as though Rod was looking to settle down. He wasn't capable of that kind of thing.

"I didn't say that. I don't think it either. All I said was I like spending time with you. Sex and emotions fuck things up, even if it starts out as just having a little fun."

"I think you're sleeping with the wrong people. Let me guess, you're a heartbreaker? You never want to settle down and everyone you're with falls madly in love with you? You seem like the type."

Before Landon could reply, the waiter approached them. "I'll take fries and a Corona," Rod told him. Greasy food and beer was exactly what he needed.

"I want a burger and something dark." The waiter went through their dark beers with Landon. Once he chose, the man walked away and Landon continued where they left off. "What do you mean I seem like the type?"

Hell, he shouldn't have said anything. Rod shrugged. "Gorgeous,

44

confident, nice."

"Those qualities make me a heartbreaker?"

"Maybe." He leaned back in the booth. "I'm not trying to bust your balls. I'm just trying to figure you out." Which honestly was a bit of a surprise to him. Rod loved people, loved to talk, but it was rare someone interested him the way Landon did. He had this quiet urge, a faint whisper inside him that wanted to get to know Landon better. Not just superficially, which should have set off a shit ton of warning bells. Rod was good at ignoring things when he wanted to.

Landon let out a deep breath and now he could tell the guy was getting a little frustrated. "There's nothing to figure out." He leaned back against the brown booth seat.

"I just don't believe in love. Look at the fucking divorce rate and tell me how anyone can. It's a lie people try to sell you. I don't believe people are capable of completely giving themselves to someone else. See? Nothing exciting. I'm just a cynic." Landon didn't look as relaxed as Rod thought he wanted to. He had his right arm stretched out, his thumb tapping on the table. His dark eyes had a far off look to them, his voice rough, irritated. There was more to it than he shared, and damn it if Rod didn't want to know more. Who was he to dig into Landon's pain? He was just the guy who sold him lube and told him about a job.

So he leaned back as well and wondered if he pulled off the relaxed look he thought Landon sought. "Again, what does love have to do with sex?"

"Nothing, I guess. Not always. If I downloaded a hook up app right now, met some guy in a hotel and fucked his brains out, that's one thing, but it's different when you know someone. There's the possibility for all the other shit to get in the way."

Rod sighed. He guessed he could see where Landon was coming from. "I get what you're saying. It's not that I don't believe in love. I look at people like Bryce and Nick and I have to believe. Hell, they're fucking crazy about each other. They'd never been with men before. They changed their whole worlds for one another, but I know how to draw the line. I know that's possible for them, but it's not possible for me. So yeah, I agree in that I don't see some guy falling head over fucking heels for me, but I also don't let that get in the way of getting off."

"You said falling for you."

"Huh?" Rod asked.

"You said you don't see a man falling in love with you, not the other way around."

Rod hadn't realized that's what he said, but he also didn't doubt it. He didn't believe someone would fall in love with him, and he was okay with that. "So? We were talking about you and how you have this whole thing backward."

"Who says I'm the one who has it backward?"

"I believe I just did."

The previous tautness in Landon's body seemed to have disappeared. His right arm was loose beside him, his hand maybe in his lap. His shoulders weren't tense, and his eyes sexy and playful like they were those times Rod had seen him in the store.

With the left side of his mouth slightly tilted up, he leaned forward. "Yes, you did." The waiter came back and handed them their beers. When he walked away again, Landon held up his glass. "Different strokes for different folks, I guess."

Rod clanked his glass together with Landon's. "For you, I guess. I'm not satisfied with just stroking. I want the real thing, thank you very much."

"What am I going to do with you?" Landon took a drink of his beer, his eyes holding Rod's the whole time.

"I'm sure you'll think of something." He took two long swallows of beer, that little whisper inside him hoping that Landon stuck around long enough to figure something out.

CHAPTER SIX

Landon sat on a stool as he looked at the engine of the bike in front of him. It was a nice bike, but it had a bent crankshaft, which wasn't good.

"How's it going?" Bryce walked up to him and stood on the other side of the bike. Landon had been working with him for two weeks. He liked the guy. He was funny, smart, and knew what he was doing when it came to bikes.

"The customer isn't going to be happy, but it's nothing we can't fix. We just can't fix it for cheap."

Bryce nodded. "All that matters is that it can be fixed."

"True."

Bryce looked behind Landon and Landon saw a pleased smile spread across his face. "Hey, baby. What are you doing here?"

Landon turned around to see a tall, dark-haired man he assumed must be Nick. He'd heard plenty about the guy but had yet to meet him. He met Bryce at the back of the bike and Bryce leaned in pressing a quick kiss to his lips.

"I came to see you. I brought you some food."

"Potatoes?" Bryce asked.

"Of course."

They kissed again and then Nick's eyes landed on him. "Oh, hey. You must be Landon. Bryce and Rod have both told me about you. I'm Nick."

He held out his hand to shake, but Landon showed him the grease on his. Nick just shrugged. "Are you kidding me? I'm with this guy. A little oil from a bike is nothing new to me."

Landon chuckled. Yeah, he guessed not. He stood, wiped his hands on his work pants and then shook Nick's hand. "Nice to meet you." Only now he was wondering what Rod had said about him to Nick. Knowing Rod, it could be fucking anything. Maybe he really didn't want to know. No, who was he kidding? He wanted to know. It excited him that he never knew what to expect from Rod, or what would come out of his mouth.

"Nice to meet you too," Nick told him, just as Bryce grabbed his hand and tugged.

"We'll let you get back to the bike. I have something I need to show Nick in my office." Bryce winked at Landon and he let out a loud laugh. Yeah, he bet Bryce had something to show Nick, and he had a feeling Nick would like seeing it.

The two men disappeared down the hallway, and all Landon could think about was his conversation with Rod last week. Maybe Rod had been right. He really needed to get laid. On the one hand, his reasoning for not sleeping with Rod made perfect sense...but on the other? The other he was just fucking torturing himself, dangling something he wanted in front of himself and then denying himself that very thing.

He wasn't into that tease and denial.

He wanted Rod.

But he enjoyed their growing friendship too.

He couldn't stop focusing on Rod. The man had taken up residence in his brain and it was starting to drive Landon a little crazy.

About forty-five minutes later, Nick said goodbye as he snuck out of the office. He hadn't made any fucking progress since he'd disappeared with Bryce, so he forced thoughts of Rod out of his head—thoughts that shouldn't be there in the first place—and focused on the bike in front of him.

Landon finished out his workday, washed up in the bathroom, and then got on his bike, ready to go home...only he didn't feel like going home. Shanen was going to be there while she discussed wedding plans with their mom. Sure, he could sequester himself in his bedroom, which happened most of the time, but that's not what he did.

Twenty minutes later, he pulled up in front of Rods-N-Ends. It was pretty sad that he had nowhere to go other than a sex store to hang out with the guy who owned it. *Can I really not find somewhere else to go, or do I want to be here?*

Rod was busy with customers when Landon got inside. He wandered around by the front registers feeling like an idiot for being here. What did he expect to do? Hang out with Rod half the night, while the guy flirted and sold dildos to people? This was a stupid fucking idea.

"Look who it is," Rod said when he made his way to the counter.

Landon nodded at him, letting him finish ringing up the customer. When the guy left, he told Rod, "I just thought I'd come by and say hi."

Rod had his black eyeliner on again. He had to admit, he'd never been into a guy who wore make-up before. Not that he had a problem with it at all, to each their own. And not that he was into Rod either because the guy was his friend. His friend who made no secret of the fact that he wanted Landon to fuck him, and who Landon was also fiercely attracted to, but his friend all the same. Still, he found himself oddly happy that Rod wore the black eyeliner today.

"Hi." Rod smiled at him and leaned against the counter. "Miss me or avoiding your house?"

Shit. Rod had gotten good at reading him. "Both?"

"I'm wearing you down, Landon Harrison. Sooner or later you will be mine...at least once. I don't ask for much. I only expect one night."

Landon opened his mouth to argue with him, but Rod cut him off. "Oh. I almost forgot. I have something for you." He bent down and rifled around in the cabinet beneath the cash register.

Less than a minute later he stood and handed a box to Landon. He opened it up and said, "I'm going to fucking kill you."

"What?" Rod looked at him with puppy dog eyes, as though he was innocent. "I'm just trying to help. And it's not like I went out and specifically got it for you. When companies make new products they sometimes send us a sample. No one used it."

"It's not a new product. I have a FleshStroke at home, thank you very much."

"Yes, but this one is new and improved. It's even more realistic. Feels just like a—"

"Yeah, I get the point. You don't need to explain it to me."

"I'm just trying to help." Rod grinned and the motherfucker had Landon smiling too.

"I don't need your help. Plus, I prefer a hand."

"I have two of those as well." Rod held his hands up.

They both started laughing. Landon's gut hurt, he laughed so hard. Jesus, the man was crazy, and damned if Landon didn't enjoy that about him. "What the hell am I going to do with you?" This wasn't the first time he'd muttered those words to Rod, as though he had to do anything with him at all.

"You'll get tired of me sooner or later." Rod winked at him, but something about the curve of his lips, and the sudden dullness in his eyes, told Landon that he really believed that. It was the first hint of real vulnerability he'd seen from Rod.

"Nah, you keep things exciting. You're a good friend. That's why

I won't fuck you, remember?"

Rod sighed. "Thanks for reminding me." Just then the door opened and more customers came in. With a straight face, Rod looked right at them. "Welcome to Rods-N-Ends, your orgasm headquarters. What can I do for you today?"

Landon nearly had to bite his tongue to keep from laughing.

***

They played cards. It was a deck with penises on them that Rod pulled out when Landon continued to hang around. In between customers, they played poker and Gin Rummy on the counter.

Around eight, Landon ran across the street and got them both a pizza for dinner. It was a weekday. Rod's help had left a while ago, leaving just Landon and him when he didn't have customers.

He was surprised that Landon seemed to plan on spending his entire evening at the shop, but he wasn't disappointed. At eleven on the dot, Rod turned out the "Open" light and locked the doors.

"I should probably head out," Landon told him.

"You don't have to." He didn't want Landon to leave. He wasn't sure how he felt about that. Maybe that's why he wanted to have sex with Landon so badly. Well, besides the fact that he was sexy as hell, but for Rod that would put things in perspective. People knew Rod was up to fuck, so they often fucked him and then that was that. He was used to screwing people and then being on his way. He wasn't really used to having someone refuse to sleep with him, because they valued his friendship. It made waters...murky for him. Like he couldn't see through things to know the outcome and he didn't like that.

Landon sighed and ran a hand through his hair. "It makes me feel like shit, but I almost fucking hate going back to that house every day. I'm pretty sure that means I'm an asshole."

"No it doesn't."

"Actually, it does. My mom and Shanen are both so happy to have me home. Things were never easy growing up, but there was never a time in my life that I doubted my mother's love for me, so yeah, the fact that it's hard to be around her makes me a dickhead."

Every single part of Rod wanted him to ask Landon why—why things hadn't been easy on them. Why he hated going home, but then, did he really want to open that can of worms? Did they really want to trade sob stories about their childhoods? Rod sure as shit didn't want to talk about the daddy who hated everything that Rod ever was. Rod had put this behind him a long time ago. He had a feeling Landon wouldn't want to have a heart-to-heart about it either.

"Well, I happen to like dickheads. They're fun. You can come hang out at my place, if you want."

"No." Landon shook his head. "I don't think that would be the best idea."

"Afraid you won't be able to keep your hands off of me?"

Landon rolled his eyes.

"Then shut the hell up and come hang out at my house. We can watch a movie and then retire to separate bedrooms and stay awake all night thinking how much better it would have been just to have sex and get it over with." He winked at Landon.

"You're relentless."

"You know I'm just giving you a hard time, right?" It wasn't that he didn't really want to have sex with Landon, because he did, but he also didn't want to push the guy away before he was ready to leave. "I really do respect your boundaries. I just like to tease you and your reaction is fun."

"Yeah...yeah, I know." There was a brief pause and then Landon continued, "So what do we need to do before we can get out of here?"

That was exactly what Rod wanted to hear. "You sit. I'll work. Oh, I need to stop by the store and grab some pizza chips and chocolate milk first. I can't watch a movie without them."

"Wait. What? Pizza chips?"

"Chips that are pizza flavored. I love them."

Landon crossed his arms. "Really? They don't taste like pizza, you know?"

Rod walked to the register and Landon followed, staying on the other side of the counter.

"I invite you to my home and you insult my taste in food? And yes, people like them. I like them. You will too. I'll convert you."

Landon frowned. "Convert me into someone who eats pizza flavored chips with chocolate milk. I don't think so. You really are insane."

"You'll see." Rod winked at him. "Now be quiet so I can count the drawer down."

The smile on Landon's face made warmth flood Rod's chest. He liked making Landon smile. He decided he'd try to do it more often.

CHAPTER SEVEN

"Young Kiefer Sutherland was so fucking sexy."

Landon nodded at what Rod said. "And Emilio Estevez. He's badass. That makes him even sexier."

"They're all gorgeous, every fucking one of them. I can't believe you like these late eighties, early nineties westerns too. I thought I was unique." This wasn't the first time in the past two weeks they'd ended up on Rod's couch, watching movies while Rod ate pizza flavored chips and drank chocolate milk like he was twelve years old. Contrary to what he said, Landon still wasn't a fan.

He huffed at what Rod said. "I think you're the most unique person I've ever met."

"Thank you." Rod shifted on the couch, then laid down and put his head on Landon's lap, just put his fucking head there like it was the most normal thing in the world.

He almost said something, but then decided to keep his mouth shut. At first he thought the guy acted the way he did because he was just really fucking horny. Now, he wondered if it was something different. It was almost like he needed the attention, which was why he was so outspoken. It wasn't that Landon thought Rod was the type of guy who wanted to be the center of everyone's universe, but it was like he needed something he didn't have, yet he wasn't sure how to get it. Like he was looking for comfort or validation through affection.

He didn't think Rod was as confident as he seemed. Which honestly, was a good reason for him to keep his distance—another reason, that was. That had been a large part of the problem when it came to his parents. Jealousy and lack of confidence, which resulted in a competition of one hurting the other before the other hurt them.

Still, Landon put his feet up on the coffee table and didn't say a word as Rod used his thigh as a pillow.

"Chip?" Rod held up the bag for him, but Landon waved it off.

He looked down at Rod, studied the curve of his face. The cut of his jaw, and how smooth he was. He'd obviously shaved this morning. Rod wasn't what he would call a twink; though smaller than Landon, he was too big for that. Everything about him seemed softer than Landon was, though.

Rod set the bag of chips on the floor. "You want me. You're watching me instead of Emilio."

Landon rolled his eyes. "I was trying to figure out how to get your big head off my lap." He really shouldn't be here. He wasn't quite sure why he was. All Landon knew was that he enjoyed Rod's company and that was that.

"Ugh, fine." Rod started to sit up, but Landon put a hand on his shoulder.

"You're okay. I wouldn't want his majesty not to be comfortable."

"Oh, I like that. You should call me that all the time. It can be your pet name for me."

"I already have a pet name for you. It's Delusional. It fits well, don't you think?"

"You're a funny guy. Now be quiet. I'm watching young Kiefer." Rod didn't move from his spot for the rest of the movie and Landon didn't ask him to. They were friends. It wasn't a big deal, he told himself. Still, he couldn't remember ever watching a movie with someone's head in his lap before.

The longer the movie went, the antsier he became. Rod didn't seem to notice. If he did, he didn't say anything. Finally the movie was over, and Rod sat up. Landon made the decision that he should definitely head home. He opened his mouth to tell Rod, when he asked, "Who do you sleep with more often, men or women?"

"That's not why I'm not having sex with you."

"I didn't say it was. I'm just curious about you. We're friends, right? We better be otherwise this celibacy thing really needs to go out the window."

Landon leaned back against the seat. He hadn't realized he'd gone tense until now. "I don't know. It started out mostly women. I lost my virginity to a girl and—"

"How old were you?" He pulled his feet under himself and sat cross-legged on the couch.

"Um...seventeen."

"That old?"

"What do you mean that old. How old were you?"

"Fifteen. I don't recommend it," he said as though Landon going back in time and losing his virginity earlier was an option. "Boys at fifteen don't know what they're doing. It hurt like hell."

His chest squeezed at the thought of someone hurting Rod. "I'll keep that in mind. As I was saying, I knew I was bisexual even then, but coming out in high school wasn't an option for me. My mom found out the typical way, because of porn, but her and Shanen were the only people who knew."

"What about your dad?"

Landon worked his jaw so hard it hurt. His sperm donor was the last thing he wanted to talk about. "He wasn't around. I don't want to talk about it."

There wasn't a pause, wasn't an awkward silence as Rod asked a different question. "How did she take it?"

He appreciated that about him, that he didn't push. "She was okay. My mom's got a romantic streak a mile wide. She's always looking for love in everything she does. She was hypnotized by the whole forbidden love thing. She just knew I was going to fall in love with some boy and lose him because of society."

Rod's forehead wrinkled and he definitely understood the reaction.

"So, yeah, women at first. I left when I was eighteen with no plans to come back. It was pretty equal—men and women for a while, but then the last few years, it's been mostly men."

"Men for me in case you're wondering."

No, he hadn't been. The guy was a nut. Landon picked up one of the couch pillows and threw it at him.

"What? How do you know I haven't been with a woman?"

"Have you?"

"No, but you couldn't have known that."

Landon nodded because he was right. "Fair enough."

"Strictly top or do you bottom?"

"Ah fuck." Landon rubbed a hand over his face. "Are we really going to do this?"

"We're getting to know each other, *friend.*"

Knowing Rod, the man wouldn't stop until Landon told him. "Mostly top but I do bottom from time to time. You?"

"Mostly bottom but I do top from time to time."

See? His answer seemed to say: *We'd work perfect together in bed.*

And they would. The relentless attraction that Landon felt for him went into high gear. He definitely needed to change the subject or who knew where Rod would take it? "Do you have any family?"

Rod's body language changed. He frowned so swiftly that

Landon wondered if he realized he did it. "No. My mom died when I was young, no siblings and my dad passed a couple years ago."

The mood in the room darkened, became heavy. This was definitely a sore spot for Rod, when he tried to make everyone believe he didn't have any. He understood that. He had those painful wounds inside him as well that he wanted to forget existed.

Landon reached over and touched Rod's leg. "I'm sorry."

"Eh." He shrugged. "Such is life. I wasn't old enough to really know her and he hated me anyway." His voice was light, too light, and Landon knew that it bothered him, even though he tried to pretend it didn't. How could thinking your own father hated you not bother you? But his dad had stayed. That had to mean something.

"I'm sure he didn't hate you."

"Oh no. He did. There's no question about that. But it's fine. I've had a lot of years to get over it. I'm tired. We should hit the sack."

He couldn't imagine someone disliking Rod. He was electric, magnetic.

"Are you staying?" Rod stood. Landon looked up at him and nodded. It didn't matter that only a little while ago he'd planned to tell Rod that he was going to go home.

Rod jerked his head toward the hallway and Landon stood. Words teased his tongue but he didn't know what they were. He was afraid to open his mouth because he wasn't sure what would come out. He wanted to know what happened. Maybe part of him wanted to share his own history with Rod. Or hell, maybe he just wanted Rod to know that if his dad did hate him, that it was his loss and not Rod's.

None of those things came out.

Rod turned off the TV, and then the lights. Landon followed him down to the end of the short hallway. The bathroom was on the left side—next to it one bedroom and across the hallway another.

"You're in there." Rod pointed to the room on the right as though Landon didn't know. He'd used the spare room a few times over the last two weeks.

Landon nodded, still not trusting his fucking tongue. What in the hell was wrong with him?

"Goodnight."

Rod went to walk into this room, but Landon reached out and wrapped a hand around Rod's wrist. He tugged him closer and then pressed his lips to Rod's forehead. When he pulled back, Rod had his eyes closed. "Don't do that. Please don't fucking do that unless you plan to go with me to my room. I don't know what we're holding out for. Just once…" Rod opened his eyes. "Just once and then it'll be out of your system. We'll fuck then be friends. Friends who have fucked. I like it."

Landon smiled, but felt almost sad for some reason. He didn't like the way Rod said that Landon would have him out of his system after they slept together. Which technically should be exactly what he was going for, but it felt wrong the way Rod said it.

"No. We're friends who will be good friends. Good night." He walked in the room and closed the door. He spent the whole night doing exactly what Rod said he would do two weeks ago—lying awake and thinking about how much better it would have been to have sex. He wondered if Rod was doing the same thing.

CHAPTER EIGHT

It was the next afternoon when Landon climbed off his bike at home. As soon as he opened the door he smelled sauce cooking. He made his way into the kitchen to see his mom standing in front of the stove with an apron on. "Smells good. Is that for me?" He grinned at her.

"No, but you can have some."

He looked at the large pot on the stove... "You feeding an army?" She'd used the biggest pan in the kitchen. It would take a month for the two of them to finish it and that was if they ate it every night Landon was home.

She laughed. "No. I joined a club for people over fifty. It's a place to meet friends, get out of the house, stuff like that. It's a Meet Group...? I think it's called." She waved her hand at him. "I can't remember, but we're having a potluck tomorrow and I'm making pasta and sauce."

"A meet group for people over fifty? That makes it sound like you guys are old."

"We are old," she said and Landon laughed. "Here, make yourself a plate."

Landon did as she suggested before making one for her. The two of them sat at the kitchen table when she said, "I'll probably be busy a lot with the group. They have a lot of activities. I want to be more active in my old age." She winked at him.

He liked this playful side of her, and he liked the idea of her getting out of the house and meeting people. It was almost as though she decided Shanen getting married was time for a new start for her as well. "Good. I'm glad. That sounds nice."

"How was your day at work?" she asked.

"Good. How was your day?" He took a bite of his food and then a drink of ice water.

"It was nice. Shanen has finally decided on her colors for the wedding. She's going with lavender and silver. It'll be pretty."

Landon nodded. As ridiculous as it sounded, there was a part of him that was surprised Shanen was getting married. She was a year older than him. She'd been roommates with their mom until she moved out a few months before. She'd focused on college and her career, and he'd always assumed that's what it would be for Shanen the same way it was for him. Cut out the tears and the fighting. The *I love yous* that turned to *I hate yous,* before they became declarations of love again.

But she was doing it. She was really fucking doing it and it was hard to be happy for her the way he should. He just wanted her to be okay.

"Sounds nice," he said, remembering that he should probably answer his mom.

"It will be. So what's going on with you? Were you with Rod again last night?"

Shit. The last thing he wanted to do was talk to her about Rod. "Yeah. He has a spare room and he lives closer to the shop."

"That sounds convenient." He didn't have to look at her to know she was smiling. Christ, this was awkward. "I'd like to meet him sometime."

That made him snap his head up. "What? Why? He's a friend."

"I've never met any friends of yours. You left so young and you rarely came home."

Guilt burrowed deep inside him. Yes, he'd left. He left her and Shanen both, but he hadn't disappeared. He could never do something like that. "I know, and I'm sorry. It's not a reason to have Rod over for you to meet him though. We've only known each other for a few weeks."

"You seem close..."

"Can we not do this? I'm a little old to have these discussions with you."

She sighed and then nodded. "Fine. I'll share my life with you instead then. I'm thinking about doing in-home caregiving again. It was painful but rewarding work."

"If you think you're up for the emotional toll, I think that's a great idea." It had always been hard on her and he understood that.

"I think it's important work. I'd like to make a difference. What better way than taking care of people's loved ones?"

Before he could reply, she continued, "Have you put anymore thought into getting your own place?"

Where the hell had that come from? Not that he didn't want his own place, because he did. "You're really trying to kick me out, aren't you?"

"No. You know that's not true, Landon. I know you don't want to live here though. And that's okay. Shanen was okay with it, but that's not you. I guess…life is short. I want you to be happy. I want all of us to be happy."

"I'm fine, Ma. It's nice to stay with you again."

She didn't look anymore convinced than she had a second ago. But at least he'd tried.

"You know I love you, right, Landon? You and Shanen are the most important people in my world. I might not have always shown it the best way. It's true what they say, we hurt the ones we love the most. That doesn't mean we don't love them."

Discomfort slid down his spine. Landon set down his fork and looked at her. "What's going on? Are you okay?"

"No, no. I'm fine. I promise. I didn't mean to scare you. And thank you for trying to make me feel good, but I know I hurt you. It was never intentional, but I did. I hurt both of my kids, and your father. Neither of us were innocent."

Landon grinded his molars to dust. "Don't compare yourself to him. You stayed."

"Landon—" He looked at her, trying to tell her with his eyes that he didn't want to go there. "Okay, fine. I've said my piece. I'll let it go."

The look she gave him said, *for now.* He wanted nothing to do with this conversation again. "I might stay at Rod's place a little more often, if he's okay with it. It'll give you your space without letting you kick me out all together." He tried for light and it worked.

She smiled at him. "Whatever you want, Landon."

Whatever he wanted. Too bad he didn't know exactly what that was.

***

Rod smiled when Nick and Bryce walked through the doors of Rods-N-Ends. It was the first time they'd made it besides opening day when things were a mess.

"We figured we'd come check out the new digs," Bryce told him with a smile.

"It's about time. I assume you're both a little more familiar with the products now… You won't be needing my help. I mean, I'm glad to offer my assistance. I have new favorite products."

Both men laughed, Nick looking a little more embarrassed about it than Bryce was. That was Nick and Bryce—Nick would always be a little more under the radar than Bryce was.

"It looks good." Nick looked around the building.

"Looks fun." Bryce wiggled his eyebrows and Nick wrapped an

arm around him, pulling him closer.

"I agree," Rod told them.

It was Nick who replied. "It's dangerous to get the two of you together."

"I'm going shopping in a minute. We can stock up on fun stuff." Bryce winked at Nick and then looked at him. "So what's up with you and Landon? I can't get a read on him."

"What do you mean you can't get a read on him? He's a good guy," Rod said, suddenly feeling defensive.

Bryce grinned. "Simmer down. That's not what I meant. I just didn't know if something was going on with the two of you. He's mentioned coming from your place a few times."

Landon had stayed at Rod's place four of the last seven days. He'd asked if Rod minded, Rod told him no, and that was that.

He'd offered Landon the keys so he could go there when he was at work, but he always refused them.

There was a chair at the end of the counter now, because he spent evenings here with Rod.

He didn't know what in the fuck it meant. Landon still slept in the spare room every night. Apparently Rod was good enough to use his house but not good enough to have sex with. "We're *friends*. He stays at my place because it's closer and easier."

The second Bryce opened his mouth, Rod knew the kind of words that would come out of it. "Nope, not even the kind of friends who get off with each other. I tried. Believe me, he won't do it."

"It's sex. Hell, I'd never had a guy before and I was excited as hell about the chance to fuck Nick."

"Jesus, Bryce. I'm going to kill you," Nick said, his cheeks flushing. "Can we not talk about our sex life every chance you get?"

"What?" Bryce looked shocked. "It's Rod. Have you forgotten our very first conversation with him? We're past being coy when it comes to him."

"Yes, no need to be coy," Rod said. "I'd be willing to suffer through the two of you sharing even more with me if you wanted to." Rod winked at them. Nick shook his head and Bryce laughed. "But yes, I agree with you. We enjoy each other's company. Neither of us wants a relationship. Why not get off with each other? Apparently he just doesn't enjoy sex." At least not the thought of it with Rod.

"Is there something wrong with a man who doesn't want to fuck any and everything in sight?" Nick asked.

"Yes," Both Bryce and Rod said at the same time. Bryce was a man after his own heart.

In reality, he respected the right to be more open about sex, and also those who chose not to. Whatever floated your boat. It wasn't as though he thought all men only wanted sex, but teasing was the only way he knew how to deal with what he was experiencing.

"I didn't want to fuck anything that walked," Nick reminded them. Nick had only been with two people in his life—his ex-wife, and Bryce.

"I know," Bryce said. "But you wanted to fuck me so that's

different. You were holding out for me."

"Well, apparently Landon isn't holding out for me."

Unfortunately for Rod, that bothered him more than it should.

CHAPTER NINE

Landon was horny.

This was the longest spell he'd gone without sex since he left home at eighteen. Stroking one out wasn't working anymore, so he figured it was time to do something about it.

It was his day off from the shop. He wished it wasn't because at least when he was at work, he had something to do to keep him busy. Sitting here in an empty house while his mom was out for the day left him downloading a stupid fucking app to his phone.

An hour later, he sat in the same place talking to a man about two miles away from him who was looking for a quick hook-up.

I want to be fucked, the guy said. Jesus, he felt like such a cliché.

Still he replied with, **I can do that.**

Good. I'll be naked when you get here. My address is—"Hey, Landon. What's up?"

Landon fumbled his phone at the sound of his sister's voice. He hadn't even heard her come in. He exited out of the app, feeling pretty fucking awkward that he'd been planning to screw a stranger when his sister walked in. He really needed to get his own place, to keep accidents like this from happening.

"You look like you're up to something. Is that Rod? Our mother keeps talking about him."

"Aw, fuck." He tossed his phone to the couch just as Shanen sat on the other side of him. "Why is she talking to you about him? She won't stop, and it's driving me crazy."

"Are you dating him?" she asked.

"No. Not that it's any of your business. He's a friend. I've told her that a hundred times."

Shanen sighed. "I think she just wants so much for both of us to be happy in ways she never was. But then, I worry that it might hurt her at the same time. You know how she is. She doesn't do well with change, and she's afraid to be alone."

Yeah, yeah, he knew that. "She keeps telling me she thinks I should look for my own place. I have to tell you, Shan, it's really fucking tempting."

"I know." Shanen leaned her head on his shoulder. "It's hard. I've done it all my life."

Guilt cut off his air, threatening to strangle him. He knew Shanen hadn't said it to make him feel that way. She'd only spoken the truth.

"I'm sorry."

"Don't be. You made the right decision for yourself. I made my own choices as well. If you feel like you should go, go. It'll work out. She's joined this group and she has plans. She's happier than I've seen her in a long time."

And she was. He enjoyed seeing it. He wished she could always be this happy. "We'll see. I'm not sure what I'm going to do yet."

She sat up and poked him in the side. "Even if you stay, that doesn't mean you have to be here all the time. You can still stay with your boyfriend sometimes too."

Landon rolled his eyes at her. Shanen was just like their mom in some ways. She'd never give up on this Rod thing now.

"He's not my boyfriend."

"You can have one, you know?"

He nodded. "I know." But did he really? Shanen believed that, but Landon was pretty sure he didn't.

"You can bring your boyfriend to the wedding too, if you want."

His first thought was that Rod would like Shanen. They'd get along well. Both his mom and Shanen would like Rod. "Shut up."

Shanen winked at him. The people in his life were going to drive him crazy.

When she left, Landon found himself deleting the app from his phone, but refused to let himself think about why.

***

"Just so I can get this straight, we're not going on a date, right?"

Rod asked when Landon showed up at his house on the Fourth of July. He knew this wasn't a date, but he loved giving Landon a hard time. When he dropped his head back and looked up at the sky, Rod knew he'd hit his target.

"Nope, not a date."

"So we're just two gay guys, spending the day together on your bike, and then watching fireworks?"

Landon groaned before tossing the helmet to him. "Put this on and shut up."

"Whatever you say, sir. Ooh, that's kinky. I've always wanted to try and role-play that master/boy stuff. What do you think? Want to order me around? Make me strip for you?"

He could see Landon trying to bite back a smile, which was exactly what he'd wanted. Landon had seemed a little down lately. Rod knew if he asked, he wouldn't say why, so he decided just to try and cheer him up instead. "You can tell me to get on my knees and suck your cock. I'd do it for no other reason than to experience the sub fantasy."

Landon grabbed his own helmet off the bike, and unlatched the straps. "Oh you would, huh? Sounds like a real hardship."

"No one said life was easy."

"Shut up and put the helmet on, *boy*."

Heat shot through his body. "Oh fuck. That was actually kind of hot. Huh. Who knew? Maybe next time I go out I'll look for a guy who wants to order me around."

Landon's jaw tightened in an unfamiliar way. "No. Don't do that."

"Why?"

"Because." He fiddled with the straps on his helmet. "Just because."

"Just because?"

"Can we go?"

Rod would much rather find out what that because was about. He stood there without a word, and it only took a few seconds for Landon to groan again. He obviously knew Rod well and knew he wasn't going to let this go. "Because there are a lot of creeps out there. That's not the kind of thing you just look for with some random guy at a club, or on an app."

Well shit. That wasn't the response he wanted. "You don't think I can take care of myself? I'm not stupid."

Landon looked at him with puzzled eyes as if he really did suddenly think Rod was dumb. "I never said you were stupid or that I think you can't take care of yourself. You're obviously doing a fine job of that. I just don't think it's smart to play around with that shit unless you're experienced. That's all. You don't need some random asshole to tell you to get on your knees for him. You're better than that—and before you say anything, it's not because I give a shit that it's a hook up. Hell, everyone I've ever fucked has just been a hook up, so I'm not anti-fucking who you want. I'm not anti-Dom/sub either. I just...just don't do it."

It was obvious the conversation was over when Landon pulled his black and orange helmet over his head. He strapped it without a word and Rod stood there watching him.

You're better than that. I just...just don't do it.

He wasn't sure that anyone had ever told him he was better than anything. It felt...strange. Strange, but good. "Yeah, okay. Jesus, I was only talking out of my ass anyway."

Landon didn't respond. He only got onto his bike and started to back it out of the driveway. When he got onto the street, Rod put on his helmet, climbed on the back of Landon's Harley, and they were on their way.

CHAPTER TEN

They rode for hours.

They stopped once about an hour and a half in. Landon needed to stretch out his legs, and arms, so he'd pulled over at a gas station. They didn't really talk. Rod had made a trip inside to go to the bathroom, and then they were on their way again.

Landon wasn't sure what in the hell made him lose his shit on Rod the way he had. Why the fuck did it matter to him who Rod had sex with, and if the guy ordered him to his knees or not? It had nothing to do with him, so he should have kept his fucking mouth shut.

But the thing was, he couldn't really take back what he said. He didn't want Rod out there getting topped by some motherfucker who thought he had the right to tell him what to do. Some guy who didn't know him from Adam. There were a lot of messed up people in the world. All you had to do was turn on the news at night to see that. Rod was his friend. He just wanted him to be careful. There was nothing wrong with that.

So now here he was pouting on the drive they were supposed to be enjoying. He'd wanted to take Rod out for a real cruise for weeks, and now that they were doing it, he was tense the whole damn time.

He was stuck between Rod's sex life having nothing to do with him, and maintaining that it was okay to care since they were friends.

Landon told himself he was done acting like a fucking psychopath. He'd forget the conversation. Rod could do whatever he wanted. They were just going to have a good time today.

He pulled into the parking lot of the bike show.

He'd been glad when Rod had agreed to come with him. He knew Rod seemed to like riding with him, but walking around and looking at bikes for hours might not be his thing. The good part was that's not all that was here. The whole block was lined with different celebrations—the bike show, a farmers' market, a tattoo exhibit and more.

When they finally parked, he waited while Rod got off the bike from behind him. When he was out of the way, Landon got off as well. The second he looked at Rod he said, "It won't happen again. I should have kept my mouth shut."

"No." Rod shook his head. "You shouldn't have. It's…it's important that you care. That's what that was, right?" He glanced at the ground looking more unsure than Landon had ever seen him.

"Yeah…yeah, that's what that was."

Rod looked up, a thank you in his eyes. "Let's go. Show me

bikes. I like to watch you get hard when you talk about them."

Landon rolled his eyes. Only fucking Rod. "Let's do it then."

It took a few minutes for them to make their way inside the gate. When they got there, Landon paid for both of them. There was no use in them paying separately since they were there together.

He was glad when Rod didn't mention it because he had a feeling it would just get him annoyed again.

Their first stop was the tent full of tricked-out bikes. Landon loved looking at these. It wasn't something he would really want for himself, but it was pretty amazing what people could do with a bike.

"Look at this." He kneeled in front of the custom-built motorcycle. "Do you see the chrome work on this bike? It's gorgeous. I don't like how low it is to the ground, but it's fucking beautiful."

He knew Rod didn't really care, but still, he knelt down beside him and looked at what Landon showed him. "That's cool. Do you do stuff like that?"

"No." Landon shook his head. "Maybe I'd like to get into body work one day, but right now I just do mechanic work. It takes a lot of skill to do shit like this."

Rod nudged him. "You could do it. You'd make beautiful bikes."

Landon smiled, feeling a little silly that Rod's compliment hit him in the chest. "Thanks. I appreciate that. Now quit sucking up."

"What am I sucking?"

Crazy fucking man. "Be good." Landon pushed to his feet and

Rod was right behind him. "Let's keep looking." And he tried to forget the fact that he wished he didn't have to be good when it came to Rod.

***

While Landon looked at bikes, Rod looked at Landon. He enjoyed seeing Landon in his element like this, and it was obvious that's exactly where he was. His passion radiated off of him, seeped into Rod's pores and made him feel passionate about this as well.

He'd ask questions from time to time about different makes and models, what was good and what wasn't. He waited for Landon to get frustrated with him about it, but he never did. Jesus, his father hated the fact that Rod couldn't care less about cars and shit like that when he was younger. It was like he didn't deserve his penis because he'd rather do just about anything than fix stuff. His dad loved fixing things, everything, and he'd wanted that to rub off on Rod.

Landon seemed to enjoy answering his questions though. It made him excited to ask more of them. It really was interesting. "Maybe I should get a motorcycle…"

"I just came."

Rod let out a sharp laugh, making a few people turn to look at them. "Sorry," he said and then looked at Landon again. "You stole that line from me."

"So? It's true. And really?"

Rod shrugged. "Maybe. It's a fucking rush to ride with you. Maybe I can learn to ride. I'll be a badass biking motherfucker."

Landon rolled his eyes with a smile. "I can teach you to ride, if you're serious. If not, no worries."

He was serious. He didn't realize it until just this moment, but he was. "Thanks. I appreciate it."

"You don't have to thank me—Oh hey, look at this." Rod was shocked when Landon grabbed ahold of his hand and led him to some more bikes. He saw a few people glance their way, but then Landon was rambling about throttles and speed and all sorts of other stuff, making it impossible for Rod to pay attention to anything else but him.

A little while later, they were finished at the bike fair. They made their way to the food stands to grab a bite to eat before going next door.

"I'll pay for the food," Rod told him. He figured that was fair since Landon had paid for them to get in.

They each ordered cheap beer, fries, and burgers before they found a spot to sit in the grass. It was a little out of the way from where most of the people congregated, filling up the tables and walking around.

"We'll start you out on my Switchback to see if you even like riding, but in reality it wouldn't be a good first bike for you. You'd need something a little smaller with less power." Landon popped a fry into his mouth and Rod nodded at him.

"Sounds good. Did you always know you liked riding?" he asked.

Landon glanced away, then at his fries before popping another into his mouth. "Yeah, my dad used to ride. He always had bikes. He started me out on motocross when I was five."

"That's fantastic." He didn't have stories like that with his own father. They had nothing to bond over, and his father had hated him for that. "I bet he's proud of you." It was then that he realized Landon rarely spoke of his father. He talked about his mom, and sister, but not his dad.

"Eh, not really. He's an asshole. I don't know why I brought him up." There was a raw sort of sadness roughening Landon's voice. Rod wanted to know more, wanted Landon to let him in, but he wouldn't ask for it. He couldn't.

"Yeah, mine was too. They're good at that."

Obviously done with the conversation, Landon said, "You're not wearing your eyeliner."

Rod wasn't sure if he was supposed to respond to that or not. Landon hadn't asked him like it was a question. Hell, he wasn't even sure where it had come from.

"No, I'm not. I don't always wear it. Only sometimes. I didn't feel like this was the right environment for that."

Landon's features went hard. His eyebrows furrowed. "Fuck that. If you wanted to wear it, you should have. If someone has a problem with it, they can kiss our asses."

His pulse throbbed against his skin. The anger in Landon's voice enticed feelings in Rod he wasn't used to. Feelings that had no business coming out, but they did because Landon was on his side. It wasn't often he'd had people on his side in his life. "Both of ours?"

Landon didn't seem to notice the astonishment behind Rod's playful words. "Yeah. I hate shit like that and I wouldn't hesitate for a second before telling someone that."

Oh, he was in trouble. He was starting to like this man. Rod wasn't supposed to like him that way. Hell, Landon wasn't even interested in sex with him. There wasn't a chance this was going anywhere. "Thank you for hypothetically defending my honor."

A second later, he almost choked when Landon said, "It's funny because I've never really been into that before. Eyeliner looks good on you though. Not as though that matters." He shrugged, but it mattered to Rod. He was so incredibly fucked.

CHAPTER ELEVEN

They went to the tattoo expo next, which was located in the next indoor facility over. Landon didn't have any ink himself, but he thought Rod might enjoy it since he had a couple of tattoos, though according to Rod, what he was looking forward to the most was the fireworks tonight.

The tattoo expo was even busier than the bike show had been, with people at booths getting tattooed and people waiting. "Do your tattoos mean anything?" Landon asked him as they made their way around to tent after tent. He'd been curious about it for a while now.

Rod glanced at him and frowned, as though he hadn't expected the question. "The one on my left arm is for freedom, my right is for happiness. They're Maori. You don't have any do you?"

Freedom and happiness, Landon liked that. "No."

"Do you want one?"

Did he? He didn't think so. "I don't know. Not right now, if that's what you're asking."

"You're no fun," Rod told him, as he approached a stand that said, Peace, Love, Tattoos. There was a woman working who had just finished a tattoo for another lady. "I'm getting one."

The artist smiled. "I'm Eliza."

"Rod."

"Do you know what you want?" she asked.

"His name on my ass cheek."

Eliza's eyes went big but Landon found himself putting his arm around Rod's shoulders. "You're such a fucking nut. He's kidding. He's not getting my name tattooed on him. He's trying to freak me out, but I know his games now."

Eliza gave them a kind smile. "I wouldn't have a problem with it." She laughed. "I just didn't expect it. Here, look through this first. You should check out some of my work."

She handed Rod a binder, which he set on the counter in front of them. Somehow Landon ended up behind him, with one hand on each of Rod's shoulders, looking at the book over him. It took him a few minutes to realize what he was doing, and when he did, he let go. "You do beautiful work," he told Eliza. "Your shading is incredible."

"Thanks," she replied just as Rod said, "I agree. Not everyone can shade well."

Landon didn't know that part, only that he liked what he saw.

He listened as Rod told her what his other two tattoos meant, and Eliza had some ideas about something similar. The new tattoo was a symbol for strength, which he planned to get on the inner area of his left bicep.

While Eliza prepared to tattoo Rod, Landon sat beside him, his chair reversed. "Why freedom, happiness, and strength?" He leaned on his arms, which rested on the back of the chair.

"Childhood trauma, why else?" Rod winked at him, but Landon didn't play into it. He waited for Rod to continue. "Because I spent my teen years wanting my freedom. Since then I've fought to be happy, and we could all use a little strength."

Landon thought about his own life—his anger toward his father for leaving him, for walking away, and his mom's struggle being on her own. "Yeah, yeah we can."

They were quiet then, as Eliza began tattooing Rod. Landon watched him, thought about him. Rod intrigued him. He'd never particularly found himself intrigued by anyone before, not in the same way he was about Rod, at least. It was as though he wanted to know everything about him, wanted his secrets, but those things frightened him at the same time.

He'd never really been afraid of anything like that before and the knowledge that he was now didn't sit well in his stomach. It made him feel seasick. Like he didn't have his legs under him, which only served to intensify his worries. That annoyed him more.

Less than an hour later, Rod was bandaged up and they were leaving the booth.

"She did a fantastic job on it," Landon told him, trying to avoid the thoughts that plagued him while Rod was getting his ink.

"Thanks. I like it. Tattoos make me feel badass." Rod winked at him.

"You are so fucking badass. I don't know how you contain your badassness." Landon noticed the corner of the wrap covering Rod's tattoo peeling up. He stopped them and pushed the corner down again, trying to keep it secure.

"Thanks," Rod told him. They were close. Too fucking close. He could see gold flecks in Rod's lively, blue eyes. He needed to back the hell up and he needed to do it now.... but he didn't. Instead he focused on Rod's penetrating stare and wondered what he was thinking; reached up and cupped his cheek, wondering what he was doing.

"Fucking faggots."

Landon went rigid at what was mumbled from the man who walked past them.

"Excuse me?" he turned toward the asshole who'd spoken. When he did, Rod grabbed his arm, but Landon ignored it. "What the fuck did you say to us?"

"He's a dickhead, Landon. Just ignore him," Rod said. Those words got the man's attention.

"What did you say to me, you fucking queer?" The bald guy turned on them quickly, hate in his dark eyes.

"He said you're a dickhead." Landon didn't stop until he was nose to nose with the guy. He smelled beer on his breath and sweat on his body. "But I think that's too nice for you because as you pointed out, I like dick." He couldn't deal with homophobic bullshit like this. He hated fighting, he really fucking did. He'd seen the fallout over stuff like this, but he also couldn't sit by when someone said something like this asshole did.

"Are you really going to do this? Fuck him, Landon. Let's go," Rod said.

Landon didn't back away, didn't respond in any way. He didn't take his eyes off of the prick in front of him. He could feel people around them stopping, staring.

"So you're the girl? You let him give it to you? Maybe I should take this up with your man." The guy laughed. Landon heard someone else chuckle behind him. He glanced up to see the guy had a friend with him. He'd seen them both when they were at the motorcycle show and had fucking known they were trouble.

"Landon," Rod said again.

"Listen to your man."

"Fuck you," Rod told the guy.

"You can shut the hell up, you queer piece of shit."

Anger shot through him hearing the guy talk to Rod that way. Landon shoved him. He stumbled backward into his friend. They both looked at him with hate spewing from their dark stares.

Logically he knew he should walk away from this, but there wasn't a bone in his body that could handle that. *Come fucking on,* he thought. Just as they were about to come at him, another voice cut in. "Is there a problem here, gentlemen?"

Three security guards approached them. Landon didn't speak, didn't turn away from the men, his fists clenched.

"No, no problem at all." Rod tugged gently on Landon's arm.

The homophobic bastard's friend added, "Everything's fine. We were just leaving, weren't we, Tom?"

Landon could see that the guy didn't want to walk away, and neither did he. If there was one thing he always swore to himself, it was that he'd never take shit from anyone.

"Tom. Let's go," the tall guy behind the homophobe said.

"Yeah. Everything's fine," he finally said. "Let's go." The two men walked away, but Landon still didn't move. His chest heaved in and out, his nails digging into his hand.

"Other way, gentlemen," security said to them.

"Landon, come on. Let's go."

Landon's fists loosened slightly when Rod grabbed his arm again. He pulled away, turned and led them both toward the gate.

***

Rod fucking hated fighting. That didn't mean he would take anyone's shit, but he would do whatever he could to avoid violence. It surprised him that Landon had been so...willing to partake? He hadn't really seen that coming.

"We can head to wherever we're going for the firework show. Might as well get a good spot. We can just hang out for the last couple hours until it starts."

"No," Landon said shortly.

"No?" Rod eyed him, surprised by his reply.

"I need to get the hell out of here."

Just like that? They were going to leave because some asshole couldn't keep his mouth shut? "Really?"

"Really."

Rod tried not to be disappointed...but he was. As crazy as it sounded, he'd never watched a fireworks display with anyone before. "Come on. Let's not let that asshole ruin the day. We drove three hours."

He didn't want to leave. He wanted to enjoy this day with Landon. He'd been looking forward to it since Landon mentioned it.

"I'm tired. It'll be late when we get home anyway. Let's just go." He handed Rod his helmet without another word. Rod watched as Landon put his on before swinging his leg over the bike. A second later it roared to life. Landon didn't turn to look at him, and after standing there for another minute, Rod knew he had no choice except to put the helmet on and get behind Landon.

As soon as he had his feet on the pegs and his arms around Landon, he sped out of the parking lot.

He hated this, hated that their day had gotten screwed up. It had been...hell, it had been pretty fucking incredible. He'd never spent a day with another man like this, doing things that were very close to dating territory, even though both of them knew that's not what this was.

Rod was okay with that. He wanted it that way. There was no way a guy like Landon would really be interested in him anyway.

That's why he didn't understand why Landon hadn't just fucked him and left already.

It was nine when they pulled into Rod's driveway. He expected Landon to say he had to go, but he turned off the motorcycle, then removed his helmet. "I'm tired, and I work in the morning. Can I crash here?"

"Yeah...sure...no problem."

Rod unlocked the house, and Landon closed and locked the door behind them.

"I'm going to take a quick shower, if you don't mind."

Rod nodded at him. Landon went to the spare room and then came out with the small bag of stuff he left here. He never unpacked the bag, just wore and washed the clothes before putting them back inside. Still, he left it here. What the hell were they doing?

Rod screwed around in the kitchen, washing the few dishes in the sink while Landon showered. It wasn't very long before he heard the water shut off and Landon came out with wet hair, in a pair of basketball shorts and nothing else. He could see the outline of Landon's dick through the soft material of the shorts. Fuck, this guy was trying to kill him. He'd always had a thing for guys in basketball shorts.

"Do you need help cleaning your tattoo or anything?" Landon asked.

This was the shit that was going to drive him fucking insane. It just confused the hell out of him when Landon was so *nice* to him—

helping with the tattoo, letting Rod sit with his head in his lap, which he'd done more than once now. Hell, just spending so much time with him and planning today, even though it got shot to hell. But then he refused to sleep with him and kept his distance in other ways. He felt like a yo-yo, never knowing what to expect.

"It's fine. No worries. I got it. I'm going to take a shower."

"I'll probably go to bed."

Yes. Of course, because he could sleep here a few nights a week, and keep a bag here, because Rod was good enough to give him a place to crash, but that was it. "Great. Sleep well."

He walked out of the kitchen and went straight into the bathroom, anger simmering beneath his skin. Rod did his usual routine—minus the shower because he didn't want to risk messing up his tattoo. Instead he washed up. He was horny as hell, and wanted to jack off, but then something made him hurry instead. Okay, so it wasn't just something. It was Landon. He let his feelings get hurt when he shouldn't have. It wasn't Landon's fault he wasn't interested in him. Maybe he could catch Landon before he went to bed and they could...watch a movie, or hell, watch a fireworks show on TV. It wasn't the same, but it was something.

Rod left the bathroom. He pulling the door open and said, "Hey, Land?" before he realized all the lights except for the one in the hallway were off.

Fuck. He'd missed him. Rod hit the hallway light. He'd never be able to sleep tonight.

CHAPTER TWELVE

Landon couldn't sleep. He was also a fucking dickhead, so he probably didn't deserve sleep. There was no reason he and Rod couldn't have gone to watch the show, and no reason they couldn't have gone to the local one when they got home. He'd been pissed and pouting and had taken it out on Rod, even though he knew Rod was looking forward to it.

He was starting to understand Rod. The guy was sarcastic and fun. He liked to laugh and liked to make other people laugh, but there was more to him than that. Landon thought he might be lonely...thought things might affect him more than he let on. He thought maybe Rod needed a friend more than he'd originally realized.

Hell, he probably needed one too, which was why he was so fucking thankful for the guy. Which was why he didn't want to do anything to screw this all up.

Landon rolled over and glanced at his phone. It was after midnight. He'd listened to the fireworks earlier and wondered if Rod had gone out to watch them. He'd almost gotten up to look, but instead he just continued to lie in bed, tossing and turning for hours.

He was pissed at himself for ruining the night—for screwing up the day twice, if he was being honest.

Landon's right leg twitched. He started to rock it, antsy. He looked at his phone again. It was one in the fucking morning. He needed to get his ass to sleep, but his brain wouldn't stop running. He knew there was no chance he would go to sleep until he tried to talk to Rod.

Which, he had to admit, was worrisome. Was what happened today really that big a deal? He didn't know; he just knew he'd been a dick. He'd been completely aware as they stood in the kitchen that Rod had been hurt, and he needed to make it okay.

The bed creaked when he got out of it. The sound echoed in the small room. Landon walked over, and quietly opened the bedroom door. Rod's door was cracked open a sliver. He didn't usually sleep with it open. Maybe he was still awake.

Landon took the short few steps across the hall, quietly sliding the door open. "Hey...you awake?" The blinds were open, the light from the moon spilling in the room, a spotlight on the bed. The bed where Rod lay on his side, top leg bent, his hand behind him, sliding a toy in and out of his ass. "Oh fuck," rushed out of his mouth. Rod laid there, wide eyes taking him in.

He should walk out. Walk the fuck out of the house. He needed to turn away and leave right now, but instead his dick instantly went hard. He opened his mouth to say he was fucking stupid for walking in and that he was sorry, but what came out was, "Don't stop."

There was a brief flash of surprise in Rod's eyes. "I wasn't planning on it. Don't leave."

"Not a fucking chance."

Jesus this was a mistake, a colossal fuck up, but Landon couldn't walk away. *It's nothing,* he told himself. They were adults, and they were going to watch each other get off, because there wasn't a fucking chance Landon wouldn't get off at the sight of this. He'd been fucking horny for months and seeing Rod laid out like this...fucking his own ass with a toy? Yeah, he was surprised he hadn't come in his shorts already. But this wasn't a big deal. They could do it and then get back to the way they'd always been.

"You going to turn on the light, or what?" Rod asked, and damned if Landon didn't smile. He flipped the switch. His eyes burned when the room lit up, but fuck, the second they focused on Rod, an aching throb shot through his cock.

He was sexy as hell—lean muscle, hairy thighs, and his dick, long and hard with pre-come leaking onto the blanket.

"Jesus you're fucking hard, tenting your shorts. Let me see you, Landon. Let me see what I've been pretending is fucking my ass."

Landon's body went rigid. His cock flexed, strained to be free. He glanced over to see a bottle of Easy Ride on the bedside table. He walked toward it, walked toward Rod, rubbing his swollen, aching prick with the palm of his hand. "Lay on your back and pull your legs up. If you get to see my dick, I want to see your hole."

Rod immediately did what he said, rolling over, thighs against his chest as he slid the life-like dildo in and out of his ass. "Jesus," he hissed. "So fucking pink. It's sexy as hell watching you swallow that cock."

His legs almost went weak, so he sat on the edge of the bed. He leaned up enough to pull his shorts down. He stopped when they were partway down his thighs, not having the patience to go any farther.

Landon was ravenous with desire, his want for Rod eating through his logic. "Look at me. See what you do to me?" He held the root of his dick, so Rod could see it.

"Oh fuck," he groaned. "Look at that thick, fucking meat. It's just as big as I hoped it'd be."

"Christ." Landon tightened his fingers around the base of his cock to keep himself from coming. He reached over and grabbed the lube. "You pretend it's me?"

"Yes...fuck yes. Wouldn't have to pretend if you weren't such a prude."

Landon laughed. Leave it to Rod to make him laugh at a time like this. "Shut up and show me how you like to be fucked. Do you say my name?"

"Yeah."

"Then do it. Let me hear you. I want to hear you say my name when you blow."

His balls hurt. They wanted to fucking explode. Landon squirted some lube into his hand, wrapped it around his swollen cock and started to stroke. "I'm going to come so fucking hard. My nuts are already full and achy."

Landon eyed Rod's balls. They were tight, big, and hairy. He wanted to push them out of the way so he could see Rod's hole easier. Or better yet, fill his mouth with them, but instead he pumped his hand up and down his dick. Rod pulled the dildo almost all the way out before pushing it back in again. He rocked as he went, easily holding his legs up so Landon could see his pretty hole.

"I'm flexible. I could do this all night."

That sounded perfect to him. "My name. I didn't hear you say my name." It was fucked that he wanted to hear his name on Rod's lips so badly.

"Landon…" Rod kept fucking himself, kept gyrating his hips. "Landon…yes. So goddamned good."

Landon squeezed his dick tighter, stroked faster. "You're so fucking gorgeous, your hole all stretched out for my dick." He wanted it to be him. As much as he enjoyed the show, he'd rather be the one pounding into Rod.

His eyes tried to drift closed but Landon popped them open again. There was no way he was going to miss this. He wanted to fuck Rod, fuck him long and hard. Fuck him deep. Fuck him all night until he got him out of his system. Maybe that's what they needed to do. Rod could be right. They just needed to get this shit over with, and then they could continue being friends. But then…what if they were wrong? What if it screwed everything up?

"I'm losing you. Why am I losing you, Land?"

Rod's words jerked him out of his thoughts. "You're not," he lied. "Look at that hole. You have such a sexy ass." It was made for fucking.

"Love having it full." Rod picked up the speed.

"Can you come like that? Just from anal stimulation?"

"Yeah."

"Do it. Let me see you come all over your stomach just from fucking that pretty hole. I'll jerk myself off, wishing I was buried in you."

"You could be," Rod said, and then his eyes went down to Landon's prick.

You could be... He could, but something was holding him back. This was different, he told himself. They could do this instead, but in some ways it was different and in others it was the same.

He stroked faster, played with his balls with his other hand, the whole time watching that dildo slide in and out of Rod's tight ass and pretending he was buried balls fucking deep. "Rod..." he said, feeling his orgasm creeping up on him. Balls tightened more. He strained, fought off coming because he wanted this to last.

"Again, say my name again."

"Rod." Landon let his name pass his lips, then again, and again, and again.

"Oh fuck, Landon. Fuck, right there. Right fucking there." Rod's dick jerked, flexed against his stomach as he shot his load. It flew up his chest, ran down his abs, and damned if Landon didn't want to eat it.

Landon saw stars. His balls let loose, the first jet shooting from his cock and running between his fingers. He kept jerking off, kept coming, kept rubbing the thick cream through his fingers until he was milked dry.

His fucking bones melted. He wanted to collapse on the bed and never get up.

He looked over and saw Rod staring at him, the damn dildo still lodged deep in his ass.

Jesus. What the fuck had he done? "Shit. I'm sorry. I shouldn't have barged in like that."

"I didn't complain, and if you apologize to me again for that, I'm going to kick your ass. We watched each other masturbate. That's it. Something was bound to happen anyway."

Landon nodded. Rod was right. He knew he was right. *I want your friendship. I don't want to lose it. I don't want this to fuck everything up.*

Landon leaned toward the table to grab a tissue to clean up the mess when Rod reached out and grabbed his wrist, pulling Landon's fingers to his mouth...and Landon let him. He watched him as Rod licked the come from his hand, and between his fingers. And then, damned if he wasn't leaning over, licking the thick, bitter fluid from Rod's chest, tasting him, fucking feasting on him, savoring the heat of his flesh and the muscles beneath his skin. His prick twitched, teased with the idea of getting hard again, but it didn't happen.

Neither of them spoke for a minute. It was so different being with someone he knew, someone he considered a friend, other than Beck, and they'd fucked before they'd become close. Landon didn't trust himself. He'd seen what being in love had done to his parents. Seen the back and forth, how they both tried to hurt each other, both tried to one up each other. He didn't want that. Ever.

"I should...I should go to bed."

"Okay," Rod replied.

Landon stood, walked to the door and stopped. "Do you want me to turn out the light?"

"Nah, I should probably do something with the cock hanging out of my ass first."

Fuck. No shit. What was he thinking? He was acting like a green-behind-the-ears virgin. "Makes sense. Coming screws with my brain." Jesus. What was he saying? He needed to shut the hell up. "I'll see you tomorrow. Good night." And then before he could do anything else stupid, Landon walked out of the room and closed the door. He hoped like hell he hadn't just made the biggest mistake of his life.

CHAPTER THIRTEEN

Rod wanted to fucking kill Landon.

There was more than one reason too. At least he had a good motive. It wasn't as though he'd snap in the heat of the moment and kill without proper cause. The first reason being the fact that he couldn't get the man out of his goddamned head.

Jesus Christ he had a pretty cock—thick and long and full of veins that he wanted to taste. He would trace each of them with his tongue, suck the mushroom head into his mouth until he drove Landon as crazy as he'd been the past week and a half.

Yep, that was right. It had been a fucking week and a half since he'd seen Landon, and that was his second good reason for wanting to strangle him. What were they? Eighteen? Embarrassed and shy because they'd masturbated together like they weren't two grown-ass men who both enjoyed sex and were both one hundred percent okay with enjoying it with other men?

He didn't fucking get it. Had he done or said something that made Landon think he wanted to live the American dream with him?

Maybe get married, adopt a few kids and join the damned PTA? Nope. That wasn't what he was after. He wanted sex. Wanted sex with Landon. And Landon wanted it with him. He wasn't dumb enough not to see that now. He also wasn't dense enough to think that it would ever be more than that even if he wanted it to…which was why he didn't. See? Landon was avoiding him for nothing, and keeping them both from having the sex they both wanted.

Rod crossed his arms. He'd been right all along. The man was a sadist.

"Sir? My boyfriend said you carried Easy Ride? I don't see it on the shelf," a young guy with blue hair said to him.

"Don't get him Easy Ride. Men who like Easy Ride are assholes. Buy another lube just to spite him."

"Excuse me?" The guy's brows pulled together. They were blond, not blue.

"Never mind. It's in the back. I'll go get some for you." Obviously he didn't have to worry about being a dickhead to Landon by making him think he didn't carry his favorite lube, since it didn't look like he'd ever see Landon again.

Rod went to the back and grabbed a bottle of Easy Ride before heading to the front of the store again. As he rang the customer up, Blue Hair asked, "Guy problems?"

"No. In the last thirty seconds I decided I never want to see him again anyway. If he can't admit he wants me, then I definitely don't want him." It was sex for God's sake. Why was Landon being so ridiculous about this?

Blue laughed. Rod didn't see what was so funny about the situation.

After paying he said, "Glad I don't have to deal with that shit. Good luck, dude," before heading for the door and it took everything Rod had in him not to throw something at his head.

If Landon was done with him, he'd just go out and find someone else who wanted to spend a night with him. If there was one thing Rod had never struggled with, it was finding a guy who wanted to fuck him senseless for just one night.

***

"Someone run over your dog?"

Landon looked up at Bryce. What the fuck kind of question was that? "Huh?"

"Your dog. Someone run him over? You've been mopey lately."

Landon set down his wrench and looked at Bryce. "Do you know me well enough to be able to tell when I'm mopey?"

"Are you mopey?"

Yeah. Yeah, he was.

Without Landon answering, he said, "See? Obviously I do. Nick has me all in touch with my emotions now. It's fucking weird. I'm here, if you want to talk. Or we can just work on bikes and drink a beer sometime, which will probably help more than talking would."

Landon couldn't help but chuckle. It felt good to laugh. He'd been a surly bastard the past two weeks and he knew it. He was also being fucking weak, maybe a little immature, and definitely ridiculous, but he ignored those thoughts.

"Sure, working on bikes and having a beer sounds good sometime." It wouldn't hurt for him to meet more friends. Rod was the only person he'd spent any time with outside of his family since he moved back. Considering he only saw his family when he was at his house, that made it even sadder.

Bryce kneeled down beside him and looked at the bike. He ran his finger over the rear fender and then turned to Landon. "Looks good. Nick and I are having a barbeque this Sunday. I'm running the grill and Nick's making the rest of the food. He's a chef. He makes potatoes that are so fucking good they get me hard."

Landon's eyes darted to Bryce at that. He couldn't help but crack a smile. Bryce just shrugged his shoulders like it was no big deal.

See? He could make friends other than Rod. He wasn't a total asshole.

"And Rod's coming, I think. You two can probably ride together."

And here he was being weak, immature and ridiculous again because Landon opened his mouth and said, "I forgot, I have to help my sister with something on Sunday."

He didn't know what in the hell was wrong with him. He'd never actively avoided someone he'd screwed around with before. Most of the time, it had never been a problem. They were random hook-ups or people looking for the same thing as him. If they changed their tune on that, he still didn't actively avoid them. He couldn't control how other people felt, yet it was different with Rod, and he couldn't put his finger on why.

The fact that he actually missed Rod was different for Landon as well.

CHAPTER FOURTEEN

"Why did I never think of working at a sex-toy store? That literally sounds like the best job in the world. Bryce, will you take me? I've never been to an adult store!" Bryce's best friend Christi batted her eyes at him.

"That look doesn't work with me, Chris. You're going to have to find someone else," Bryce replied to her, and she crossed her arms to pout.

"Are they always like this?" Rod asked Nick. He couldn't believe this was the first time he'd met Bryce's friend. He'd heard a lot about her, though.

"Always," Nick replied.

"Oh, you love it. I take him off your hands sometimes. I could always ask you instead, hot live-in boyfriend Nick."

Nick laughed.

Bryce growled at her.

Rod smiled. "I like her!" Then to Christi he said, "He is hot, isn't he? I thought I hit the jackpot when they came in, but then they started looking at each other with googly eyes, and I knew they wouldn't be up for a third. I've tried to get them to let me watch, but no luck."

"Can you two stop?" Nick said.

At the same time, Bryce added, "I asked Nick. He said he's thinking about it."

Both Rod and Christi's eyes bugged out of their head as they looked at Nick and Bryce. Nick started choking on his beer and Bryce slapped him on the back as he cracked up laughing.

"What about me?" Christi asked as Rod said, "Don't tease me like that! I'm going through a dry spell and I hate it."

He knew Bryce had been giving them shit. He was way too possessive over Nick for something like that, and Rod only teased as well. Yes, they were both beautiful men, but they were the best friends he had. Pretty much the only real friends he had. He'd thought Landon would become that as well, but obviously not.

Jesus. Was he thinking about Landon again?

"No luck with Landon, huh?" Bryce asked.

He'd had a little bit of luck with Landon. Not nearly enough, but as much as he teased, he also wasn't going to tell anyone his and Landon's personal business.

Rod shrugged. "I'm over that. He's not really my type. We don't talk much anymore."

Rod wasn't sure why, but his eyes were drawn to Nick. He

looked at him intensely, deeply, like he could tell Rod was lying, and thought if he looked hard enough he'd be able to tell why.

The thing was, Rod had never had a problem with people coming in and out of his life. Most people came in and left soon afterward. He didn't typically get close to anyone and that worked fine with him. Like he said, Nick and Bryce were his only real friends, and that wasn't a new thing for him.

But this thing with Landon...he couldn't get the fucker out of his head and it was pissing him off. Maybe it was because he was in a dry spell. Hell, he hadn't even gone home with anyone when he went out the other night. Or maybe it was because Landon obviously got hard for him, but held himself back with talk about friendship and stuff that Rod had known would never last anyway. And obviously he'd been right.

Rod turned away from Nick, hoping his thoughts didn't show on his face.

"That sucks. Want me to fire him?" Bryce asked and Rod rolled his eyes.

"No." He knew Bryce wouldn't anyway.

"I'm glad because he's good as hell at what he does. I guess it's good that he couldn't come today though."

"What?" Rod sat straight up from the way he'd been leaning back on their couch. "You invited him?"

"Yeah." Bryce nodded. "He seemed interested but then he remembered he had something to help his sister with."

"Bryce can you come help me with something in the kitchen?" Nick asked.

"Uh oh," Christi added.

That piece of shit, immature asshole. Was Landon avoiding him? "Did he remember the sister thing before or after you told him I was coming?"

"Um..." The look on Bryce's face said he was starting to put two and two together. "I...can't...remember...?"

Murder was looking more and more like a possibility. Landon went on and on about how messy people were and yet he was the one who didn't have the balls to even be in the same room with Rod because what? They'd seen each other naked? The guy was a real piece of fucking work. "Never mind. You don't have to say anything. I already know the answer." Rod changed the subject. "I'm hungry. When are we going to eat?" Nick, Bryce, and Christi looked back and forth between the three of them, and Rod felt like that kid he'd been when he was growing up, the one who was left out of things.

***

Landon sat on the living room couch, his mom in the chair. She was watching some crazy reality TV show that didn't look like any kind of reality he knew or wanted to know.

"What is it with this stuff? Why do you like it?" he asked and she shrugged.

"I don't know. I guess it's fun seeing people who are more screwed up than I am." His mom winked at him.

"You're not screwed up."

But she had been before. Maybe she would be again. Landon himself was screwed up. Maybe everyone was.

"You're sweet, Lando, but we all know I have my problems. Most people have problems, but things feel good now. You never know what the future holds."

He jerked slightly when his phone buzzed in his pocket. The only people who called or texted him were Shanen, his mom, and Rod, but then Rod had stopped since Landon was such a prick and didn't talk to him the way he used to.

He pulled it out of his pocket and wasn't surprised that it was Rod's name on the screen.

Get your ass to my house, or I'll show up at yours. We both know you don't want that.

"Fuck," he groaned quietly. His mom looked at him with a brow raised.

"Problem?"

"No. Rod just needs my help with something. I'll be back in a bit." There wasn't a part of him that thought Rod wouldn't show up at his house, even if he had to break into the shop and steal Landon's address from his file.

His mom smiled. "No rush. I might head out to take care of something this evening. Don't do anything I wouldn't do!" She winked at him and he could do nothing but close his eyes and shake his head. *Jesus, his life was odd.*

"He's only a friend."

"You're boring."

"Thanks, Mom."

"Anytime!"

Coming. Landon texted back. And the truth was, he wanted to go. He missed spending time with Rod. But he also still stood firmly by the belief that they were friends, and they shouldn't fuck around. Look what had happened already. Sure it was Landon's own damn fault, but that didn't change the fact that it happened. Fault wasn't always what mattered, and he knew himself well enough to know he'd get itchy feet and run.

He had to find a way to make Rod understand that...and not lose him. Jesus, he didn't want to lose their friendship.

I'm too pissed to make a joke about that. Thanks for fucking up my sense of humor.

Landon chuckled. The man was definitely insane. He grabbed his stuff before going out and climbing on his bike. He let it idle for a second as he latched his helmet. Kickstand up, he backed out of the driveway and then pulled away.

He knew this had something to do with the get together at Bryce's house. He'd probably mentioned that he invited Landon, and that he'd decided not to come.

Twenty minutes later he was at Rod's place. He put his bike on the stand, and was pulling his helmet off his head as he walked to the door. Landon held his hand up to knock when it pulled open.

Fucker. He was wearing the eyeliner. Why did he have to wear the eyeliner?

Flashes of their last night played in his head—Rod laid out on the bed, the dildo in his ass, the feel of his mouth as he sucked Landon's fingers into it, cleaning him up.

The taste of Rod on his tongue as well.

Rod stood in the doorway, one hand on the jamb and the other on the door, blocking Landon's entrance.

"Oh, nice of you to show up. You really fucking ditched Bryce and Nick's house because I would be there? Is this high school? Two adults can't be in the same room with each other after they screwed around and got each other's cooties?"

Well...when he said it like that... "Can I come in or not?" Landon pouted.

"I don't know. Are you sure you can handle it? I mean, I've seen your dick. I think that means we're supposed to pull each other's hair and call each other names."

Rod was right, and he felt like a fucking idiot for it. "I can pull your hair if you want. Might be fun."

Rod gave him an evil eye. Apparently now wasn't the time for jokes. Landon let out a deep breath. "Just...just let me in. There's something I want to tell you." Something he'd never talked to anyone else about, but he knew he needed to share it with the man standing in front of him right now.

CHAPTER FIFTEEN

Landon looked to be wrestling with a hundred different emotions. His mouth was tight, those sexy eyes that Rod loved, heavy-lidded. There was a part of Rod that wanted to tell him *fuck it.* He didn't need to know whatever Landon wanted to talk about as long as the guy pulled his head out of his ass.

But then there was another part of him, maybe a selfish part, that wanted any piece of Landon that Landon would give him. Rod liked spending time with him, liked talking to him. There was no two ways about it. He just plain liked Landon.

Rod stood back and signaled for Landon to come inside. "Do you want a drink?" he asked while closing the door.

"Nah, I'm okay. Thanks." Landon pulled off his motorcycle jacket and set it on the small table in the dining room before heading straight for the living room. He looked comfortable here. He should be, Rod guessed. He'd spent enough time in Rod's home before his meltdown.

He followed Landon over, both of them sitting on the couch

before he looked at Landon, waiting for him to speak.

Landon rubbed a hand over his face. "Say something funny. This feels ominous. It's going to be anticlimactic when I tell you what I have to say. I'm a grown-ass man. I should be over this shit."

Rod wasn't so sure about that. It wasn't as though he didn't have his own demons. "I'm not sure it matters how old you are. If something affects you, it affects you. No one has the right to say how long or in what way other people are allowed to feel things. Our emotions are our own." Rod shook his head. "Wow. I sounded really insightful just now."

Landon chuckled and Rod smiled.

He reached over and squeezed Rod's knee, and that small movement felt so fucking intimate, it nearly stole his breath.

"Thank you," Landon told him.

"No problem."

"I missed you, ya know."

His pulse ran wild. Jesus, had anyone told him they missed him before? "I missed you, too."

Landon pulled his hand away and Rod wanted it back. *Nope. Need to cut out those kinds of thoughts. Right. Fucking. Now.*

"I'm just going to spit this out and stop being so fucking dramatic about it." Landon leaned back against the couch. "My parents had a...what you call a rocky relationship, I guess. They weren't very good at hiding it from Shanen and me. I'm not sure they were very good at hiding it from anyone. They fought about everything, all the damn time. We both knew they'd been good friends before, the best of friends. They slept together one drunken night and Shan was the result of that. They never should have been together, but they tried because of her, then me soon after her."

"Not your fault," Rod told him.

"I know. Logically, I do, but knowing it doesn't always change things." He sighed. "Anyway, they were off and on, back and forth all the fucking time. When they were off, it was always about one hurting the other, showing that they didn't need them, and then deciding they did and they'd be back together again. It was a fucking disaster. Not to mention how hard it was on Shanen and me."

He nodded, getting a clearer picture of Landon's past in his head.

"They were on one of their breaks—Jesus, is this a *Friends* episode? Anyway, they were on a break. My mom went out with another guy one night. There was a storm, and I freaked out being with Shanen alone. I called Dad, he came over, and Mom showed up with her date. She flaunted him, which was wrong, but he'd done the same thing to her. The guy left. They fought. Dad walked out, and I begged him, fucking pleaded with him to take me with him. He was my best friend. He taught me to ride motocross. I wanted to go with him, and he looked at me, told me to be good, and we never heard a word from him again. I was twelve. See? I told you, anticlimactic. How many people in the world have the same kind of story?" He sat back and sighed.

"And? What do their lives have to do with yours? You live your life and they live theirs. You can't compare it." Rod truly believed that.

"Thank you." Landon shook his head, resting his elbows on his knees. "I used to think it was my fault. I called him. If I hadn't, it wouldn't have happened. And then I was just fucking pissed. He left us. He *left* me. I needed him, and he walked away from us like we were fucking nothing, Rod. He left us to hurt her. They both did too many things to count to hurt each other, but she stayed. Even when times were hard and we struggled, she stayed."

Landon's pain displayed clearly on his face. His thick lashes lowered when he closed his eyes and for the first time, Rod noticed how long they were, noticed the perfect curl to them.

"Mom struggled… Shan struggled. It was hard on them. I became the man of the house. He knew." Landon leaned forward, his forehead resting on the palms of his hands. "He fucking knew he wasn't coming back. I know it. I saw it in his eyes, heard it in his voice, and I wanted to go… Even knowing that, I wanted to go. They were there when he wasn't, and I wanted to leave them."

Fuck. The pain in Landon's voice nearly broke him apart. He ran his hand through Landon's thick, dark hair. Then touched his knee, leaned his forehead on Landon's shoulder. Landon's father had left him. Rod's had hated him. Weren't they a fucking match made in daddy issues? "You were a kid. You loved him. No one can hold you responsible for that."

Landon shook his head and sat up straight. "It is what it is. There's no changing it. But seeing that? Living with the fighting and the back and forth, and knowing their history... That's why relationships aren't my thing. You just fuck people up by loving them."

Rod wouldn't know about that. He felt pretty fucked up by not being loved.

"Well, I'm on the pill, so we don't have to worry about me getting pregnant. There's one concern out of the way."

Landon's head snapped up, his eyes pinning Rod. For just a second he wondered if he went too far, if this wasn't the time to joke, but then there was a smile in Landon's eyes. It teased the corners of his mouth too, and Rod wanted nothing more than to see it stretch across his face.

"You're so fucking crazy." And there was something in his voice... Something that if Rod didn't know better, would sound like amazement.

"I'm so fucking serious. That's one of the perks of gay sex—no unwanted pregnancies."

Landon's voice was calm, even when he said, "I'm serious."

"So am I. When did you think I was asking you to fall in love with me? You said love fucks people up, but who's asking for love? I'm not. I know you're sure as hell not. I'm not quietly pining for you to fall in love with me. You're sexy. We get along well. I think we could have fun in bed together. I want to fuck you, that's all. I've never had someone so adamant not to sleep with me before. I'm starting to take it personally." Rod crossed his arms, pretending to feel affronted.

"Shut up." Landon nudged him with his elbow. "I was so fucking hard the other night, I thought I'd lose my damn mind. You have nothing to take personally. I want you. I want you so fucking bad that sometimes it takes everything in me not to strip you bare and fuck the hell out of you. But I like you more."

Goddamn, hearing that nearly did him in. He wanted to ask Landon to say it again, all of it. How much he wanted Rod and how much he liked him, too. It was almost like he spoke a foreign language, one Rod couldn't associate with himself. Not when it came to this man.

"I just don't want to fuck up what we have. Look at what happened last time. We didn't talk afterward."

"In my defense, everything that's happened since last time was one hundred percent your fault," Rod told him.

"I know," Landon said, that damn smile teasing his lips again. "It would most definitely be my fault. Seeing what I've seen…living what I lived. It's got my wires crossed when it comes to sex and relationships. It's a fucked-up excuse but it's true."

Rod got that. He really fucking did, but damn he wanted Landon too. And if Landon wanted him just a quarter of how much Rod desired him, then there was no chance this was going away. They'd fuck, maybe fuck a few times, and then Landon would get tired of him and they could go back to being friends. The end.

"I'm going to say this once, and then I'll let it go. I won't push, won't bring it up again, and we'll pretend none of it happened." He grabbed Landon's face and held him so he had to look at him. "I want you. I want you to fuck me. I want to suck your dick. I want you every fucking way I can have you. Every person that I've ever had sex with walked away with no problem. This wouldn't be different. We get along. We have crazy-fucking chemistry and that chemistry would no doubt transfer in bed. Neither of us wants or expects anything other than friendship, and maybe getting off together from time to time. Really, if you look at it, it's the perfect situation. We get sex and friendship and don't have to worry about any of the other shit."

It was there, in the dark corners of the back of his mind, that only part of what he said was true. There was something, something deeper in the way he felt about Landon. Something that could most definitely turn into more, but this? The sex? He would make that be enough, and then Landon would leave before Rod had the chance for his feelings to turn into what they shouldn't.

He let go of Landon's face. Rod couldn't read his expression and wasn't sure if he wanted to, or if Landon could see Rod's quiet truth in his eyes. "So that's it. We go on the way we were, or we go on the way we were with sex involved sometimes. And now I'm done. Do you want to watch a movie with me?"

"No," Landon said, his voice low and grainy.

He was going to leave. Jesus, Rod couldn't believe he was really fucking going to walk away.

"Okay. Whatever you want."

Rod stood, but Landon's hand suddenly wrapped around his wrist, keeping him from going very far. "Come here," he said, quiet but firm. "Just come here." Landon tugged gently, and Rod turned and went to him.

CHAPTER SIXTEEN

Landon pulled softly on his arm again, and Rod got the hint. He kneeled between Landon's legs, with his knees on the floor. "You're determined," Landon told him.

Yes, yes he was. At least when it came to this. "Is that a bad thing?"

Landon smiled. "Hell no. You've had my dick hard since the first time I saw you. Easy Ride comes in the mail too, ya know?"

"Aww, so you came to see me?"

"Shut up so I can kiss you." The look in Landon's eyes turned dark, hungry, urgent, and he pulled Rod closer, covering Rod's mouth with his own. His tongue went straight for Rod's lips, demanding entrance, and Rod gave it easily. He tasted like a mixture of coffee and mint, like maybe he'd had a drink right after brushing his teeth.

Rod slid his hands up Landon's thighs until he got to the bulge at the apex of them and rubbed his hand over it, feeling the large bump beneath his jeans.

Landon growled into his mouth, making it vibrate through him.

He pulled back, grabbed the bottom of Rod's shirt and pulled it over his head. "I'm so damned hungry for you. This won't be slow. It'll be fast and hard."

"Were you under the impression that I wanted it slow?"

Grinning, Landon reached around and swatted Rod's ass. "Let's go to the room."

"Why move when we can do it right here?" He didn't want to give Landon the chance to change his mind. Rod reached under the couch and grabbed a bottle of lube, before pulling a condom from his wallet and tossing both to the couch.

"You keep lube under your couch?"

"I live alone. I can jack off wherever I want. Are we going to talk or do this?" But really, he liked talking to Landon, and if what Landon said was true, he liked talking to Rod as well.

"Fuck now, words later."

Hell yes. Definitely what he wanted to hear. Rod stood up to take off his jeans. As he worked the button, Landon traced a path across his stomach with his tongue. He nipped at the skin next to Rod's belly button, just enough to sting before he sucked the skin into his mouth again.

"Oh fuck." Rod's bones melted; his knees went weak.

"Get out of those pants before I rip them off of you. Want your ass."

Rod looked down at him and nodded, letting Landon know he was good to go. Finally, his goddamned fingers started to work and he got his pants unbuttoned and unzipped. Blood rushed through his ears. His cock ached as he pulled down his jeans.

Landon leaned in. "Jesus, you're leaking like crazy. Look at that fucking wet spot. I want your taste on my tongue again." And then he nuzzled his face between Rod's legs, his mouth against the growing spot of pre-come in Rod's underwear.

"Damn, I'm going to fucking kill you if you make me come too soon." Even as he spoke, Rod had his hand in Landon's hair, pushing his face closer to his aching cock.

Landon smacked his ass again, before pulling back. "Get them off."

There was a slight tingle in Rod's cheek from the smacks. "You're naughty, aren't you?" The thought just made his balls even more heavy and tight.

"For some reason, I doubt I have anything on your level of naughtiness."

Rod shrugged. "It gives you something to strive for. You can practice on me if you want."

"I'll consider it, now get your ass out of your underwear and on my dick."

Rod's cock pulsed behind the tightening fabric. "Don't have to tell me twice." He stripped out of his underwear, just as Landon pulled his shirt over his head. Rod took a second to admire the definition of his muscles, his taut, golden skin. The ridges in the cut of his abs, and the dusting of hair on his chest. He fucking loved men with hair. Loved rubbing his body all over the coarse roughness of it.

"Wait," he said as Landon began working the button on his pants. "I get to play. Do you know how much it killed me not to touch you last time?" And it had. It had hurt. He wanted his hands on Landon so badly. Jesus, he was a beautiful man.

"Then do it," Landon told him.

Rod went down on his knees again. He pulled the button free, the zipper sticking slightly as he tried to work it down over the bulging swell behind it. He loved a nice, thick cock and Landon definitely had that.

This time it was Rod who swatted Landon, his hand smacking against his thigh. "Ass up so I can get you out of these things."

Rod shoved the coffee table out of the way, and then leaned back on his haunches. Landon pushed against the back of the couch and lifted his ass, so Rod could pull his jeans and underwear down. When he got to the knees, he had to move to the other side of Landon's left leg so he could pull them off.

Landon's prick stood tall and hard, the tip glistening with pre-come. Rod wanted to suck his balls dry, milk him till he had nothing left in him, but he wanted Landon inside him too, wanted to feel a part of him in the only way he really knew how. "Jesus you're gorgeous." He looked up at Landon. "I can't believe I get to play with you."

Landon gave him a strange groan, his brows pulled together as though something Rod said confused him, but then his eyes fluttered and he groaned out, when Rod wrapped a hand around his cock and stroked.

"You're going to make me lose my load before I'm inside of you." Landon's hand wrapped around Rod's stopping it, but it didn't put a halt to Rod's hunger. He leaned in, tonguing Landon's swollen sac— all that soft skin covering the tight balls beneath it.

He couldn't stop touching him, tasting him. He wanted to do it all because this might be the only chance he got. There was a pulsing need inside him, an urgent hunger that wouldn't go away. It just kept spreading, multiplying, growing.

He sucked Landon's heavy balls into his mouth.

"Oh fuck, that mouth of yours. I knew it would be good," Landon said and pride swelled in Rod's chest. If there was one thing he was good at, it was sex.

"Come here," Landon pulled Rod's mouth off of him, pulled Rod to his lap and Rod went easily.

They attacked each other's mouths. He felt Landon's teeth bite into his bottom lip. Not enough to make him bleed but enough to make his dick threaten to explode right then.

They kept kissing, kept eating at each other's mouths as Rod heard the bottle of lube open. He straddled Landon's lap, leaning up slightly to make it easy for Landon to wrap his arm around Rod and finger his hole.

He shuttered with the first brush of Landon's finger against his pucker. "Fuck yessss," Rod hissed, gyrating his hips. He really fucking needed something inside of him.

"I jacked off to thoughts of you more than once," Landon said before pushing a slick finger inside him.

Rod's eyes rolled back. "Yeah?"

"Yep. Wanted to know how hot and tight you are. Wanted to feel you from the inside. At first, I kept seeing that dildo sliding in and out, but soon it was my cock. Me filling you and making you moan. I came all over my hand more than once a day thinking about this ass."

There was a part of Rod that tried to block out the words. They were sex talk, things you said when you fucked someone, but then...they almost sounded different coming from Landon. Maybe it was because they were friends. Rod had never slept with someone he considered a friend before. Jesus, what if Landon was right? What if his fucking libido put crazy thoughts in his head and he screwed this up?

"Landon..." His previous thoughts were gone when Landon pushed his finger in deeper, curved it, rubbing his insides. "God*damn*. Fuck me. I want your dick." He grabbed the condom and ripped it open. He didn't need that one finger, two fingers, three fingers bullshit. He just wanted Landon's prick. He loved cock and wasn't ashamed of it. There was no changing that. There was never a chance of changing anything about who Rod was.

He rolled the condom over Landon's erection as Landon used both hands to squeeze his ass. He spread Rod's cheeks before kneading them.

"Lean forward." Landon grabbed the base of his cock, before scooting down on the couch so they could get a better angle. "Ride me."

Rod did as Landon's husky voice told him to do. He went up on his knees. Landon squirted more lube in his hand, rubbed it on his erection and then added more to Rod's tender hole.

And then he lowered. Landon kept ahold of his dick and Rod slowly sat on it, let it stretch and fill him the way he loved to be stretched and filled. "Finally." He smiled when he spoke, trying to keep the mood light.

"Took you long enough to come around," Landon teased back.

"I'm stubborn and ridiculous. What can I say?" And then he sat all the way down, the back of his thighs on Landon. Landon's cock buried as deep in Rod's ass as it could go.

"Don't move." Landon grabbed his hips, leaned forward resting his forehead against Rod's chest. "Don't fucking move. Not yet. Jesus, you feel even better than I thought you would."

That's what he wanted to hear, what he needed to hear, and finally, when Landon started to guide his hips, Rod was ready. He rode Landon hard—up and down, he let Landon's cock fill him before pulling almost all the way out of him again.

He felt the familiar stretch of his ass, the pressure that made him come so fucking hard.

Landon thrust up into him, a deep breath gasping from Rod's lungs every time he slammed home. Rod stayed up on his knees, letting Landon run the show for now, letting him fuck fast and hard the way he'd promised.

"Jerk yourself off. My balls are gonna explode any second. Let me feel your ass squeezing me until I do."

Yes. Rod wanted that very, very much. He rubbed his swollen cock. Each stroke sent another bolt of pleasure through him—his cock and ass both in fucking heaven right now.

Landon's hand slid up to his throat. He almost lost his rhythm for a minute, but relaxed when he just held him there, rubbing his thumb over Rod's Adam's apple.

"You're so fucking sexy riding me like this. And Jesus, that eyeliner gets my dick hard."

Okay, so he'd wear it every damn day then.

Rod moved faster. Landon did as well. Their bodies slapped together. They were sweaty, and breathing heavy, the sounds of their sex the only thing in the room, and he fucking loved it.

His balls drew tight. His legs quivered. "Fuck...I'm gonna—" And then he did. Rod shot his load, white ribbons of come shooting up, landing on his chest, in the trail of hair that lead to Landon's dick and disappeared inside him.

He felt Landon tense. His hands went to Rod's ass and he squeezed his cheeks hard, nails biting in as he shot, coming in the condom, thrusting his way through orgasm.

Rod collapsed against him. He'd get up in a second, but right now he wasn't sure his legs worked.

They were slick, their sweat mixing together, Landon's dick still buried in his ass when he said, "What took us so long to do that?"

"You…it's all your fault," Rod said between breaths, and hoped like hell they would be able to do it again.

CHAPTER SEVENTEEN

Rod's reply made Landon feel like an idiot but also made him smile. Rod was absolutely right, and now that he'd had him, he was even more frustrated at himself for holding out so long. "Always busting my balls."

"Always making it so easy," Rod replied, still straddling Landon's lap. Landon had his arms wrapped around him, holding his ass. It was a nice ass, tight and firm, and so fucking hot. "That was fun." Rod grinned at him, and damned if Landon didn't feel another one tugging at his lips as well. He was good at that—being funny and quirky to the point where it was impossible not to have a good time when you were around him.

"Yeah...yeah it was."

"My ass is sticky." Rod stood up, grabbed his underwear and pulled them on. He tossed Landon's to him, before going into the kitchen. It took Landon a second to realize he watched him, taking in all of Rod—his long, lean muscles. His come was no doubt drying into Rod's skin as they spoke, and Landon's dick perked up at that thought. It was more than that though. Watching him stirred unfamiliar emotions in his chest.

Landon turned, pulling off the condom before the damn thing leaked everywhere. He tied it and then tossed it in the trash. "Do you have plans the rest of the day?" he asked without thinking it through.

"No." Rod pulled a jug of orange juice from the fridge. "Want some?"

Landon nodded. "I'm tired. Mind if I hang out here?" Part of him knew there was no reason he couldn't go home. It wasn't *that* far, but then, he had just come like a fucking geyser and the plan was to continue on as friends the way they'd always been, so there was no reason he *had* to leave either.

Rod stopped pouring the orange juice and looked at him. "You're staying?" There were questions in his eyes, think lines formed along the edges.

"Um…yeah?"

There was a pause and then Rod winked at him, before pouring their drinks again. "I'm giving you shit. Of course you can stay." But something didn't sound right about the way he said it. Not that Landon thought Rod wanted him to leave, but maybe that he was surprised that Landon was staying. He had no one to blame for that but himself.

Landon took one of the cups of juice from him and then went back into the living room. He set the glass on the table before pulling his underwear on.

"We still have *Young Guns Two* that we need to watch. You

game?"

Young Guns Two. It still surprised him that he met a guy close to his age who liked the same kind of movies he did. "We're weird," Landon told him, and Rod just shrugged.

"At least we're weird together." He nodded to the hallway. "Let's lay in my bed and watch. There's more room. You're a couch hog."

"What? Me? Who's the one that's always lying down while I have to sit up? You put that big head of yours on my lap and I can't move for two hours at a time."

"That's because you're a couch hog and taking up space I want." Rod looked at him as though what he just said made perfect sense.

"Yes, but you're lying down and I'm sitting up."

"Because you have my space."

"But—never mind. You win. There's no sense in arguing with you."

Rod smiled, raised his glass like they were going to toast, and then took a drink. "You keep that attitude and you and I will get along just fine. Let's go watch sexy men roll around in the dirt and shoot each other." Rod went for the hallway, leaving Landon standing there wondering what in the hell he was going to do with the man.

Landon turned the living room light off and then followed Rod to his bedroom. Rod already lay sprawled out on the bed, his head on the pillows, the remote pointed at the television.

He was sexy, Jesus, he was sexy, but in a comfortable way if that made sense. He was the guy who drew people to him, but maybe didn't realize that he did. He'd joke and tease, but Landon wondered how much of that might be a smokescreen for other things that were going on with him.

As Landon stood in the doorway watching Rod set up the movie, studying the rise and fall of his chest, the trail of hair that dipped below his boxer briefs, and the slight smudge of black liner under his eyes, he realized he wanted to know those things. Wanted to know if there was more to Rod than he showed the world. He wasn't sure if he'd ever wanted to know someone else that deeply before.

"You want to fuck me again, don't you? Give me a little while and I'll be ready for you. I've heard once with me usually isn't enough."

That jerked Landon from his thoughts. Leave it to him to say something like that. "You're so hot, Rod. I don't know how I ever keep my pants on around you." Landon walked over and climbed onto the bed beside him.

"Hot Rod? I like that. You can call me that from now on if you want. It can be our code to let me know when I get your engine running."

A light, airy feeling loosened up some of the tightness that always sat in his chest. "That was corny, and you're crazy if you think I'm calling you that."

"I thought it was creative. You're no fun."

"Never?" Landon cocked a brow at him.

"Okay, sometimes. Maybe you used all your fun for the day when we had sex. We might have to wait until tomorrow before I can enjoy you again."

Landon opened his mouth to reply, what he was going to say, he didn't know, but he figured a comment like that required some kind of response. Before he got the chance, Rod said, "Shh. We'll talk later. The movie is on. I'm going to cover us up. You can't watch a movie in bed without being covered up. I turned the AC up, so we won't be too hot."

Christ, Rod was crazy. He went a hundred miles per hour all the time, flip-flopping from one subject to another and never saying what Landon expected him to say.

Never doing what Landon expected him to do either.

And he liked that. Liked it more than he'd realized until this second. "Don't be a blanket hog." He tugged on the corner of the light blanket, and then they settled into the movie to do just as Rod said, watch sexy men roll around in the dirt and shoot each other.

An hour and a half later, Rod was passed out, his breath floating over the hair on Landon's chest, his head resting on Landon's arm. "Rod? Wake up. The movie is over." When Rod didn't reply, he added, "Hot Rod?" just to see if he was playing him.

After waiting a minute, and Rod didn't stir, Landon sighed, thought about staying, but instead forced himself out of Rod's bed. He turned everything off and then made his way to the room across the hallway. He wasn't there thirty seconds before he wished he'd stayed in the other room.

CHAPTER EIGHTEEN

Rod was bored.

He'd been at Rods-N-Ends most of the morning, working on paperwork and other parts of the job that weren't as fun as selling sex toys. This part of it always bored the hell out of him—the sitting still, going over paperwork, and running numbers. On the other hand, it made him feel good. It didn't matter that he ran what some people wouldn't consider a reputable business, the kind of place his father would have hated, but wouldn't be surprised that *someone like Rod* appreciated it. He still ran a fucking business and that made him proud as hell. A few years ago, he never would have seen that for himself.

He was a disgrace after all. Not the kind of son any man would want, so working in a dirty store might be something he could handle, but not running one. It didn't matter that he'd graduated both high school and college at the top of his class, that he'd done it by himself, because his father sure as shit wouldn't help him. It didn't matter that he'd accomplished things in his life his father never had.

Rod was dirty.

Rod was a faggot.

Rod ruined his father's life and his good name.

Why the fuck was he thinking about that right now?

He usually did a pretty good job at keeping all that shit in the past, where it belonged.

Since he was done with paperwork for the day, and it was technically his day off, he had nothing to do. Landon and Bryce were both at work. Nick was busy today, and since the three of them were the only people he spent any time with that meant he was shit out of luck.

That also meant Bryce and Landon would be forced to keep him entertained between cleaning carburetors and playing with their tools.

He wouldn't mind playing with Landon's tools, but he was pretty sure Landon wouldn't sneak away to Bryce's office with him. It had been over a week since they fucked and Rod had fallen asleep during the movie. He hadn't seen Landon since, but he knew Landon had been busy. They'd spoken on the phone every day.

They were practically married. He wasn't sure why Landon didn't realize that.

He made the drive to the shop, making a quick stop at a coffeehouse, up the street where he got iced drinks for himself, Landon, and Bryce.

He pulled up to the small building with a sign that boasted that they would work on all makes and models, foreign and domestic, parked and then got out carrying the drink holder.

"I'm bored and you guys are my only friends, so you're stuck with me."

Landon's eyes snapped up from where they'd been focused on a blue bike. He smiled, and that damn smile made his cock start to wake up. Or at least made it aware that Landon was here.

"Can you believe he thinks we're his friends?" Bryce said to Landon.

"No shit. That's what I was thinking," Landon replied and Rod stopped walking.

"Fuck you both. I'll take my coffee and go."

"Hey! No! Don't do that!" They both called him back and Rod smiled. It was Landon who stood and walked over to him first.

"One of those for me?"

"Nope."

"Funny guy." He pulled one of the cups from the holder and then turned to hand it to Bryce. He took the next for himself before saying, "Let me get you something to sit on. Thanks for this. I appreciate it. It's hot as hell out here."

"No problem. Like I said, I was bored so I thought I'd bribe the two of you."

Landon winked at him and then walked away. Rod watched him go. There was a smudge of black on the ass of his faded jeans. They were worn, frayed edges at the bottom, curving around his ass just the right way, having many wears to take shape.

"You're drooling," Bryce said.

"Fuck you."

"He's all right. He's no Nick but…"

Rod shook his head at Bryce. "He's sexy, that's all there is to it."

"Never said there was more to it."

Damn it. He was right. Why had Rod added that part?

"Here you go." Landon walked back into the room with the chair from behind the desk. He set it close to the door because Rod wasn't technically supposed to be where they worked on the bikes since it was a liability.

He hadn't had his ass in the chair for five seconds when Landon said, "Oh shit."

Rod looked over his shoulder to see two women walking toward them. One was in her late twenties or early thirties with a familiar smile. The older woman had eyes he'd know anywhere. "Oh shit," Rod repeated what Landon said. "That's your mom and sister, right?"

The women both smiled big, his sister looking like she was trying to speak out of the corner of her mouth so no one could see, but she wasn't doing a very good job of it. He had no idea what in the hell she would be whispering that she wouldn't want anyone to know about, but it was definitely something.

"She's smooth," Rod said and Landon chuckled.

"Can I help you?" Bryce asked, obviously unaware that they

were Landon's family. Apparently this was the first time they were here. Of course it would be when Rod stopped by.

He'd never met the family of someone he was fucking before, and he had a feeling it would make Landon act like Rod had asked for his hand in marriage again.

"It's okay, Bryce. I got it," Landon said just as the two women approached them.

"Hey, what are you guys doing here?"

"We were doing some shopping, so we thought we'd stop by and see where you work," his mom said.

Landon's sister picked up right after with, "Who's your friend?"

So obviously they'd heard about him, what he didn't know was what in the hell that meant.

***

"Subtle, Shan, real fucking subtle." He took a drink of the iced coffee Rod brought. He hadn't planned on doing this whole awkward-meet thing, but they were all here now, so he decided to make the best of it. He wouldn't have a problem with his family meeting Bryce, Nick, or anyone else, so why should it matter if they met Rod? "Mom, Shanen, this is my friend Rod. Rod, this is my mom, Joy, and my sister, Shanen the Subtle."

Rod held out his hand, and said, "Hot Rod, nice to meet you."

Oh fuck. Leave it to Rod. Shanen and his mom smiled as bright as the fucking sun and Landon just dropped his head back and looked up at the sky. He was so fucking screwed.

"Hi, Rod. It's so nice to finally meet you." His mom used a sugary, sweet voice that told him she'd decided she liked Rod already.

"I've heard wonderful things about you."

His mom waved a hand at Rod. "Oh, there's no reason to lie. I'm sure Landon hasn't said a word about me and that's okay."

Actually, Mom, I told him about what happened. He knew more about Landon than anyone, which was kind of sad because he didn't feel like there was a whole lot to actually know.

"No, he does. I'm not lying. Are you kidding me? I'd get him in trouble if I could, but he told me about the group you joined and how you've been making extra meals for them." He looked at Shanen, fitting in with them the way Rod could fit in with anyone—or at least play it off well. Landon envied him that. "And I know you're getting married soon. Congratulations by the way."

"Thank you," Shanen replied as his mom looked at Landon as though she'd needed to hear what Rod said. He was suddenly glad that Rod had spoken.

"What am I? Chopped liver?" Bryce asked from the background and everyone laughed. Jesus, he couldn't believe he'd forgotten the man was there.

After their second round of introductions, Bryce went back to work on a bike, and Rod said, "I just stopped by to say hi. I should get going."

When he looked at Landon, he could have sworn he almost saw

a flash of disappointment in his eyes. Landon frowned. "You don't have to go. I'll be working, but I'm sure Bryce won't mind if you hang out."

"Don't leave on our account," his mom said before Rod could reply. "We don't want to chase you off. We really just stopped by to say hi. We're heading out in just a minute."

Rod hadn't answered yet and Landon knew he would say no. Surprising disappointment curled low in his gut.

"That's okay, really. I have paperwork I need to get done. I was stopping by as a way to procrastinate. It was nice to meet you both. I'll talk to you later, Lando." He nudged Landon with a smile that didn't reach his eyes.

His car was only a hundred feet away. There was no reason he couldn't walk by himself, but still Landon found himself saying, "You guys can fight over the chair if you want. I'm going to walk Rod to his car. I'll be right back."

Rod had already started to walk away. Landon jogged to catch up with him. "Hot Rod?" he asked.

"Maybe it was overkill. All they had to do is look at me to know I'm hot."

The words were definitely something Rod would say, but they still didn't ring true. "Are you okay? Sorry if they were being strange. That's the first time they've met...one of my friends."

"Special friend?" Rod smiled.

"You're such a crazy bastard." But he sounded more like himself

144

now. "You really don't have to go. Or you can come back once they're gone. Maybe they're tracking you. It's a big coincidence that they showed up when you did." Or he just had really shitty luck.

But the thing was, it hadn't gone as bad as he assumed it would. It hadn't been as awkward as Landon envisioned that kind of situation. It was just his family meeting a friend of his, someone who was important to him. Another truth? He realized he didn't want Rod to go. It made him feel good that Rod had stopped by. He wanted to see him.

"No, I need to head out." Rod shook his head. "I need to get some work done."

Landon nodded, understanding the need to get back to work. "Okay... Thanks for stopping by and for the coffee."

"No problem. I'd kiss you goodbye, but I don't want you to get the wrong idea."

Cracking a smile, Landon reached out with his left hand and briefly touched Rod's waist before pulling his hand back. "So fucking crazy."

"Oh great. Now you just ruined it by touching me. Your family is going to think you're in love with me, and I'm having a hard time not agreeing with them. You have no one to blame but yourself." Rod winked at him, got in his car, and drove away. He was always leaving Landon at a loss for words when no one had ever done that to him before.

With a sigh, and definitely not mentally prepared for dealing with Shanen and his mom, Landon went back for the shop. Bryce was talking to them but excused himself when Landon approached.

"He is very nice," his mom said.

"He is. I like working with Bryce."

She rolled her eyes. "I wasn't talking about Bryce and you know it."

"He'll be crushed to discover you don't think he's a nice guy."

She huffed and Shanen laughed. "Lay off him, Mom. He's an adult. He's not going to talk to you about Rod and if they're dating or not."

He'd never loved his sister more than he did in that moment.

They stayed and talked to him for about five minutes, about their shopping trip, and other wedding crap that could have been discussed when he wasn't at work. They left just as Bryce came out again.

"This is driving me crazy." Bryce sat at the bike again. Landon was about to apologize for having people stop by, but just one look at Bryce told him that wasn't what he was talking about. He'd seemed a little on edge here and there throughout the day.

"Is everything okay?" Landon headed back over to his bike. He needed to get the carburetor out and clean it.

"Yeah...I think. Nick is with his mom and youngest sister, Michelle, right now. They're the two who took it the hardest when we got together, as though two people loving each other is something that anyone should take hard." He shook his head. "Anyway, his sister's husband is a real piece of work and didn't want

Nick around the kids. This will be the first time he's seen them since we got together."

"Are you shitting me?" Landon's gut clenched. He couldn't imagine that. No matter what, he'd always known his mom would accept whoever he was with. "They won't let him around the kids?"

"Yeah, I guess they think being gay is a virus they can catch or something. It's been fucked all the way around. It's hard on him, and it pisses me off that I can't be there to support him. I don't want him to know it bothers me, because it will make him angry at his sister. I just want them to have a relationship. That's the most important thing."

Bryce's eyes were firmly on the engine of the bike in front of him. He figured it was probably easier to talk that way. Landon understood that. "Hell, man, I don't know what to say. I'm sorry the two of you have to deal with that."

"Yeah," Bryce said. "Me too."

"His family has never accepted him being gay? Or bi?" Landon wasn't sure how he identified.

At that, Bryce looked at him. "Neither of us had been with a man before each other. We'd never been interested in men before each other. We couldn't explain it, still can't, but we give each other something that no one else can. That's all we know and it's enough for us. Not everyone has come around quite as easily as we did."

Now that he thought about it, he remembered Rod telling him a little about how they'd gotten together. Still, it was different hearing it from Bryce himself. "Wow...that's wow..." He didn't know how to respond. For Landon, he'd almost always known he was interested in both men and women. There had never been any surprises. It's who he was, but there were people, both gay and straight, who didn't get it. They thought he had to be one or the other, that he couldn't make up his mind or whatever the hell other excuses people used. Landon knew differently, so whatever happened between Nick and Bryce, that was their thing and he believed it. He didn't think it had to be one or the other.

"Yeah, it's been a wild ride. We're good, solid. I just want this for him. Want it so fucking much I can't stand it. I'd do anything to fix this for Nick. I need today to go well. No one deserves it more than he does." The strength of Bryce's love for Nick hung on every word, every fucking syllable. It was in the tone of his voice, and his posture. It was a pretty incredible thing to witness. When he looked at them, he couldn't imagine the two men trying to hurt each other the way his parents had done. He couldn't imagine one of them walking away.

Bryce went quiet after that, and Landon could tell he didn't want to talk about it anymore. That didn't stop Landon from thinking about it.

CHAPTER NINETEEN

"Got any Easy Ride?"

Rod turned when he heard Landon's voice behind him. He'd been stocking the shelves and hadn't paid attention when he heard someone come in, so it was a surprise to see Landon standing there. "Still giving your hand a good workout? I'm beginning to get my feelings hurt."

"You? Not a chance." Landon crossed his arms and leaned against the shelf. "Did you get all your paperwork done yesterday?"

Actually he'd gotten it done before he'd gone to the shop and seen Landon, but since he hadn't told the truth about that, he just nodded and said, "Yeah. Do you really need more lube?"

"No. Do you realize how much I'd have to jack off to go through all the lube I have? You've kept me in good supply."

"You know me, I'm your go-to guy for anything sex related. It's my specialty. Only thing I'm good at." Rod winked at him and Landon frowned. "What's the frown for?"

"It's not the only thing you're good at."

Rod smiled at him. "I was joking, but maybe I should pretend I wasn't so you can make me a list of all the things you think I'm good at."

Landon leaned closer to him. Rod smelled soap, like he'd washed his hands well after getting off work, but he smelled like fresh air too. It was almost as though the outside air seeped into his pores when he drove, the scent clinging to him. Those pheromones that drove Rod crazy. "Always looking for a compliment," Landon said next to his ear. His breath brushed across Rod's cheek, making him shiver.

"You're being different. Sex loosens you up. You should have it more often. Getting off with me has kept you going for over a week, unless you've been with someone else since then." He shrugged as though it wouldn't matter, but his gut felt like it was suddenly full of cement.

Landon got that wrinkle in his forehead that he got every time his eyebrows pulled together. "I haven't been with anyone else and I'm not being different. I'm just in a good mood."

He liked Landon in a good mood. Landon in a good mood was fun, and a little sweet. And he should probably stop thinking shit like that because they were only *friends.* Friends who had fucked, but friends all the same. "Is that why you stopped by? Because you're in a good mood?"

"No, I came over because I have an idea."

"Your first one?" Rod asked. "I'm happy to share this moment with you."

"There you go again, always bustin' my balls."

"It's fun."

"Fun for you. I'd rather you did something else with my balls."

Rod's cock liked the idea of that. The rest of him did as well. He could think of a hundred different things he'd like to do with Landon, his balls, and every other part of him. "Is that what your idea is about? If so, I think it's a great first idea. I'd definitely be willing to help you out with that."

Landon grabbed one of the Big Daddy vibrators from the box and put it on the shelf for him. "No, that's not my idea. I mean, sex is always a good thing but motorcycles are too. I was thinking when we're both off on Monday, if you're still interested, I can start teaching you how to ride."

Excitement pricked at his skin, making its way up his arms, over his shoulders to land in his chest. "You're really going to teach me how to ride?"

The corners of Landon's eyes wrinkled. "Of course. Why wouldn't I?"

People didn't always do the things they said they would. Promises were easy to make but hard to follow through. It didn't matter if they were big or small. Maybe this felt like something small to Landon, but it sure as hell wasn't to Rod. "What am I going to ride?"

"My bike. It's a little big for your first one, but I think you can handle it. We'll take it slow. If you're serious about riding, I'll start looking around for you, see if we can find you a good used bike. You'll need one eventually, anyway."

Landon's words hit him like a punch to the chest. Logically he knew they shouldn't have that kind of effect on him. It was a nice thing Landon was doing for him, and he wanted it. Wanted to learn to ride a bike and maybe have his own. He didn't really have much in his life besides the damn store. Still, he hadn't expected something like this from Landon. He didn't expect things from most people, so they didn't let him down. This was...hell, he didn't know what this was.

"Why do you look like you're going to vomit?" Landon touched his shoulder. "It's not a big deal. If you don't really want to ride, you don't have to ride. It was just a thought."

"No, I want to ride." Urgency lit fire to Rod's words. He needed to get them out before Landon took back his offer. "I'm excited. Can't wait to have all that power between my legs."

Like Rod hoped he would, Landon laughed.

"Monday sounds good, now stop talking so I can put these vibrators away."

Shaking his head, Landon grabbed another package from the box, and helped Rod finish stocking the shelves.

***

Rod stood on his porch when Landon pulled up to his house on Monday. He'd brought his Switchback because it would be easier to teach Rod how to drive. If he was being honest, he'd admit he almost backed out. The thought of someone else driving his bike, especially someone who had never ridden, scared the shit out of him. She was his baby, and he'd lose his mind if she got fucked up, but then he realized he was actually looking forward to teaching Rod. He wanted to see Rod on a bike, wanted to show him this part of himself that Landon loved so much. There was something about Rod that told Landon he needed it, that it would mean something to him, and *that* meant something to Landon.

Rod walked over to him with the helmet under his arm, "Where are we doing this?" His voice sounded off, a little deeper than his usual tone. His nerves showed in his eyes, in the tense set of his body.

Landon turned off the bike but continued to sit on it. "I was scared the first time I rode. Scared because I wanted it so fucking much." He rubbed his hand over the handlebars. The first time he rode would always be a defining moment in his life. It was the only time he'd fallen in love. "It's a rush, I can tell you that, but it's also like exposing yourself to everything around you. You're vulnerable, just you and your bike. At the same time, it's the most liberating thing I've ever done. You're going to fucking love it. Just try to let everything else go."

"You're good with pep talks."

"You're deflecting. I got your number now, *Hot Rod.* It's okay to be nervous. It's smart to be nervous."

Landon's response seemed to surprise him. The top of his nose wrinkled, and his eyes went slightly narrow as if he was expecting some kind of joke, or a *but* in there.

"You're sexy when you're sweet."

"And you're deflecting again." He hadn't realized it in the beginning, but Rod didn't take compliments very well, didn't seem to believe they were genuine.

"No I'm not." Rod shook his head and then said, "Take me for a ride first. Then we can have my lesson afterward."

"That sounds like a fair deal to me." Landon would take any excuse he could to ride. He liked that Rod enjoyed it as well. If he got his own bike, they could go out together. If not, Landon didn't mind having him on the back of his bike with him.

It took Rod a minute to get his helmet on. Landon backed the bike out of the driveway. Once Rod got on behind him, he turned the throttle and sped away.

He took back roads as he headed for Wards Creek Road. It was the long way through the county but it would be a beautiful ride. If there was one thing he loved about Virginia it was how green it was here. He'd always loved all that lush, deep green and that's about all there was for most of the ride down Wards.

Rod's arms were around him, his hands on Landon's thighs as they leaned left and right together, rounding curves and making their way away from city and homes lining block after block.

He loved this, just fucking going without having any real destination in mind. He'd done a lot of that in his life, just taken off, him and his bike.

It surprised him that Rod liked to ride so much. He liked it, having that to share with a friend.

He didn't know exactly how much time passed before he saw what looked like an abandoned industrial building to the left. The parking lot was about the size of a football field, so Landon slowed down and pulled in. He parked the bike, put the kickstand down, pulled off his helmet and said, "It's not what I had in mind, but it'll do."

"Where did you have in mind?" Rod asked.

"A high school parking lot down the street from your house."

Rod got off the bike and frowned at him. "I'm sorry. You should have said something."

"Nah, it's no problem. You wanted to ride, so we rode. I'm always up for taking a trip on the bike, but now it's time to get down to business." He didn't quite know why he was so excited to teach Rod to ride, but he was.

Landon set his helmet down and then stood next to Rod. "Okay, I know it seems obvious but I'm going to go through where everything is first."

"That's obvious?" Rod asked with a grin.

"It's not?" It had been so long since he'd learned to ride, and it had been second nature to him, what he'd been born to do.

"No, and now I'm stressing the hell out even more. What if I fuck up your bike? This is a Harley and I don't know what I'm doing. I'd never forgive myself if I downed your bike and messed it up."

"Downed my bike? Have you been looking up motorcycle terms?"

"Yes. I also know if we ride together, you'll be my backdoor because you're more experienced. I want to be the backdoor." The edge was still in Rod's voice even though Landon thought he was trying to hide it.

He felt the tension, thick waves like humidity hitting him. The truth was, he should be worried about the same things Rod was. He loved his bikes. He didn't typically let anyone drive them. Rod would be the first person to drive his Harley since he got the bike.

But he wasn't worried. He wanted to give this experience to Rod, show him this thing that he loved and that's all there was to it.

CHAPTER TWENTY

Rod had been looking forward to this, but he wasn't sure it was such a good idea. "I didn't get my license until I was twenty and I could afford to buy my own car to drive. I failed the test twice. I drove on the curb when I parallel parked."

Damned if Landon didn't smirk at him. "Parking won't be a problem on a bike. Or in an empty parking lot. Funny how that works."

Apparently everyone was a fucking comedian nowadays. "I'm serious. Let's find a bike of my own that I can buy to learn on. I do want to ride but not on yours. I don't want to fuck it up."

Landon's eyes darkened, his sooty lashes nearly blocking them from Rod as his eyes went narrow.

"Don't look at me like I'm crazy." Maybe he was suddenly acting crazy, but he just didn't think this was a good idea anymore.

"Do you want to learn to drive a bike?" Landon asked. "Do you really want it?"

There was an unfamiliar ache inside him. It burrowed deeper, digging a bottomless pit of want inside him. He really did want this. He wanted something new, something different, something else that could be his. "Yeah. I'm not changing my mind on you. I just think it's a better idea if I get my own."

"Get on the goddamned bike, Rod."

"I'm not—"

"Get on the bike. You're not going to hurt the damn thing going fifteen miles an hour in the parking lot, and if you do, oh well. It can always be fixed. I want you to learn to ride. Who knows how long it will take you to find a bike. You learn now, you'll be ready to get your license when you get your bike, and then I'll drag your ass out to ride with me."

The ache inside him got bigger, swallowed him fucking whole. It was more than the desire to learn to ride though. It was the man standing in front of him, which was a fucking disaster waiting to happen. What the hell was wrong with him? He wanted to open his mouth and say *thank you* over something as simple as Landon wanting to ride with him.

"I'm not going to say it again. Get on the bike."

Rod tried to ignore the barrage of thoughts and questions trying to drive him even crazier than he already was. "Yes, sir. I like it when you're bossy."

"Stop backhandedly trying to veer the conversation into something about sex. You do that every time we talk about something serious. Get on the bike and put the kickstand up. I want you to get a feel for how much weight she has behind her."

A hundred different replies popped into Rod's head, but he bit them back, and did as Landon said.

"If you want a Harley, a good beginner bike is a Harley 883. We might want to look for something else for you though. The Harley is better for you to learn on over my sports bike because it's closer to the ground. The center of gravity is lower so it's easier to balance."

Landon spoke with even more confidence than he usually did. It was a nice sound on him.

"Okay." Rod tested the weight of the bike like Landon told him to.

"Put the kickstand down again. The front brake lever and throttle are on the right side of the handlebar. Most of your braking is going to come from the front brake."

Rod nodded and Landon continued.

"Left lever handlebar is the clutch." He walked around the bike to the left side, and pointed toward the left foot peg. "This is your shifter. First is below neutral so you'll go down for first. Then you'll shift upward, past neutral for second, third and so on."

"Jesus, you should have told me to bring a notepad. Maybe you should quiz me on this later."

Landon shook his head at him and smiled. "You'll be fine. I want you to get a good feel for the clutch so once we get started, let off the clutch slowly, test the clutch before giving it some gas. You ready?"

Rod turned toward him and made sure his facial expression asked, *are you fucking crazy?*

"Okay, you're right. I'm rushing it. I'll go over it again."

Landon explained all of the things he'd already told Rod, adding a few more details. He talked about balance, and speed, and how to move with the bike. He worked up to turning, and how he'd need to lean in the direction of the turn, but to never brake during that time. He asked Landon a few questions, making sure he had everything down right. He was probably being a little over-cautious but he'd rather be safe than sorry.

"Okay, let's give it a try. You're not going to take off yet. You just need to feel what the bike can do. Test the clutch like I said."

His heart beat so hard, it damn near burst through his chest. His pulse vibrated through him, his stomach twisting in a mixture of nerves and excitement. He'd never done something like this before. Never.

Landon's hand came down on his shoulder and he squeezed. "You're just testing the clutch. I promise, you'll be okay. I'm a good teacher."

"You're a cocky bastard. I can do this. I'm just finding my center."

Landon laughed. "Center, my ass. You're nervous. Do it."

Rod didn't reply to him. Instead he started the bike, and did exactly what Landon had told him. He felt the initial power of it, the bike moving as he slowly let off the clutch, and then he pulled the throttle. The bike lurched forward, his body jerking with it. He panicked, clenching the handlebars tight. He thought he would go down but then instinct took over, and he put his fucking feet on the ground, since he was damn near stopped now and kept himself up.

Okay, so that hadn't gone as he thought it would. He turned to apologize to Landon. The second he looked at him, Landon burst out laughing. It was a contagious laugh, loud and boisterous. Rod was stuck between joining him and kicking his ass.

"It wasn't that funny," he said, but Landon was laughing too hard at him to reply. It made that want even stronger inside him. He wanted this. He could do this and he fucking would.

Rod repeated the process, this time not turning the throttle quite as much as he did the first time. The ride was smoother, steady as he went about ten feet or so before easing on the brake.

"There you go!" Landon jogged over to him, the laugh replaced by what Rod could have sworn looked like pride. "See? Just like that. I knew you could do it. Let's practice that a few more times and then you can really give it a go."

That easily it was as though Rod's nerves and hesitance melted away. He was going to do this. He couldn't fucking wait.

***

"Yes! Just like that!" Landon yelled across the parking lot.

After practicing stopping and going, Rod had driven the parking lot at least twenty times. He hadn't gone past first gear, but he hadn't needed to. He wasn't on the open road yet. Landon wanted him to take it slowly. They'd worked up to turns now, which Rod fucking owned. He caught on quickly, and Landon felt a large plume of pride in his chest watching him.

He waited as Rod drove back toward him. He probably hadn't heard Landon's excitement over his last ride, but he hadn't been able to hold it in.

As soon as Rod pulled up in front of him, and took his helmet off, Landon could see something unfamiliar in his expression. He almost looked dazed, his eyes wide as he held out his hand. "I'm fucking shaking. My whole body is. Jesus, it's like I'm cracking apart from the inside, but it's not a bad thing. It's almost as though I can't hold myself together."

Landon was all too familiar with that experience. Rod's excitement bled into him, his heartbeat kicking up. "It's the adrenaline. There's nothing like riding, even if it is the first time and you're cruising a fucking parking lot. It's almost like you're flying." Maybe that sounded crazy to people who didn't ride, but he knew Rod would get it now.

"Yeah...yeah it is."

Reflexively Landon wrapped an arm around him and pulled him into a half hug. "That was perfect. Jesus, I'm much more excited about this than I should be. I can't wait for us to go riding together."

Rod took a few deep breaths, as though he was trying to ground himself. Landon wanted to tell him not to, just to fucking let go and ride it out.

"Who knew you were so easy to excite? If I realized that, I would have ridden for you a long time ago."

He wasn't surprised when Rod changed the subject and deflected his compliment. Landon could understand that, though. He wasn't real fond of that kind of attention on himself either. "You're welcome. That's probably enough for today. Are you hungry? We can take a ride somewhere and grab some dinner."

"Are you asking me on a date?" Rod crossed his arms. "I don't know if I think that's a good idea..."

Landon chuckled. "Shut the hell up and get out of my seat. I get to drive now."

He was still smiling a few minutes later when they drove away.

CHAPTER TWENTY-ONE

They went out to eat at a local seafood place. Rod still felt jittery, adrenaline pumping through his veins, making everything feel magnified. He'd driven a fucking motorcycle, and he couldn't wait to do it again. Maybe to some people that wasn't a big deal, but to him it was. Who would have thought he'd be driving a Harley? Surely not anyone he knew.

Surely not his father.

The bastard had hated him, but he suddenly wished he was alive to see it.

"We can go again tomorrow, if you're free. I'll keep an eye out for a bike for you, if you want." Landon took a bite of his mashed potatoes, a big ass grin on his face. He was excited, happy. Rod didn't really get it, but a large part of him really fucking liked that this meant so much to Landon.

"Sure. I'm up for it anytime you are, and yeah, if you see a bike that'd be great. I can't afford much, maybe a couple thousand? Can I get a decent, used bike for that?"

"We'll figure it out. It doesn't have to be a perfect bike. I know a good mechanic." Landon winked at him.

"You should give me his number."

He was surprised when Landon picked up a crouton from his salad and tossed it at him. He had been a whole lot lighter lately, like he'd let go of some of whatever it was that weighed him down.

"You don't want to start a food fight with me. I don't care if we're at a restaurant. I will win."

Landon held up his hands in surrender. "I give up. I really don't want to get kicked out for throwing food."

"That's what I thought," Rod told him. They finished eating, talking here and there about little things. When the check came, Landon tried to take it, but Rod stopped him. "I'll take care of it."

Landon frowned. "What? No, you don't have to buy my dinner."

"Then we go Dutch."

"It's not a big deal. I'll get it."

He couldn't accept that. It was important to Rod. He wanted to say thank you. "You took the time out of your day to teach me to ride. You offered your bike and your gas. Let me buy you dinner."

It took a moment, but Landon nodded. Rod paid and then they were on their way again. He couldn't let Landon pay for his food. It was more than just the riding lesson too. Landon paying for him really would feel like a date to Rod, and he wanted to keep the line drawn clearly, even if it was in his own head. Rod paying for Landon was a thank you. Landon paying for Rod would feel like something it couldn't possibly mean.

A little while later they were pulling up at Rod's house. He had no idea what Landon's plans were so he pulled off his helmet and asked, "Staying or going, champ?"

A second later Landon killed the engine and pulled his own helmet off. "Champ?"

"Eh, it came out. Sometimes I say random things. It's a fun quality. Keeps people on their toes."

"You are the craziest person I've ever met."

"Thank you." Rod climbed off the bike and then Landon did the same. He guessed that meant he was staying.

"Do you have plans? You don't mind if I hang out?"

Yes, because he always had plans and he hated it when Landon came over. "No, I'm good. We can watch a movie."

"You need a new hobby."

"I have a very good hobby—sex. Soon it will be motorcycles. Doesn't a guy deserve some downtime?"

Landon shook his head, and they both went for the door. "Sex is your hobby?"

"Sex should be everyone's hobby."

Landon shut up after that. Rod knew he couldn't deny his logic.

"Can I use your shower?" Landon asked when they got inside.

"Sure. Go for it."

He went into the spare room, Rod assumed to grab some clothes and then disappeared into the bathroom. Rod made his way into the small bathroom in his room, figuring he'd do the same.

Because one could never be too safe, Rod made sure he was ready in case they had sex, showered and took care of all his business. He figured they *would* fuck. Why else would Landon want to stay? Not that he didn't stay here often, but it had been a while since they'd been together the first time and damn, the man had to be as horny as he was.

Plus, they'd had a pretty incredible day. Getting filled by Landon's cock would be the perfect ending. He figured Landon must want to get off as much as he did.

By the time he made it out, Landon was sitting on the couch, with wet, messy, dark brown hair, wearing a black T-shirt and a black pair of basketball shorts. He thought once more how there was almost nothing as sexy as basketball shorts on a man.

"What are you watching?" Rod asked as he took a seat on the couch, then just went for it and lay down with his head in Landon's lap. "The news?"

"What's wrong with being aware?" Landon asked.

"The news is depressing. I'd rather live my life blissfully unaware and happy. It's like those people who predict when the world's going to end and all that shit. No thank you. If someone said they could tell me when I would die, I'd say go to hell. Why the fuck would I want to know that? Blissfully unaware, I'm telling you, it's the way to go."

He felt Landon's laugh vibrate through him from where his head sat on Landon's lap. Rod wanted to nuzzle into him but held himself back.

"I've never met anyone like you," Landon said.

"Most people haven't."

He rolled over so he faced Landon, looking up at him. "Do we have to watch the news?" Rod could think of something better they could do. The outline of Landon's dick was right beneath him. He could lean forward, bury his face in Landon's crotch. He wanted Landon's scent to fill his senses. Landon's cock deep in his throat.

"Why couldn't you use your parents' car?" Landon asked.

"Huh?"

"You said you didn't get your license until you were twenty and could afford your own car. Why couldn't you use your parents'?"

Rod's gut clenched. Why the hell was Landon asking him this? "Mom was dead, remember? And my dad wouldn't let me use his. I'm going to see if I can find a movie for us to watch." He tried to sit up, but Landon's hand on his shoulder stopped him. Oh, fuck. Was he really going to try and do this?

"I told you about my past. Shit, I've never told anyone. You can't tell me why your dad wouldn't let you use his goddamned car to get your driver's license?"

The muscles in Rod's body got rigid, his emotions coiled tight. "Why do you want to know?" Why the hell did it matter?

"Because you're my friend," Landon replied, but that wasn't

what did Rod in. It was when he added, "I don't know why I need to know…" As though there could be more of a reason. As though maybe he could possibly be as confused as Rod was over why they spent so much time together, and why he enjoyed it so much.

Rod had fucked a lot of men—sex, blowjobs in club bathrooms, threesomes. He enjoyed sex. He was a single man. Why the hell not? But he'd never had this. This friendship the way he had with Landon. He thought if they started fucking, it would put things more into perspective. They'd be toys to each other, and yeah, still hang out, but toys all the same. He didn't feel that way though. He felt…more, and he really didn't want to.

"It's the typical gay boy story. Macho, church-going, God-fearing man, who ended up with a faggot for a son. The kind of man who wasn't good at all the shit his dad wanted him to be good at and had no interest in it either. Nothing I ever did was ever going to be good enough for him, so he only gave me what he had to. He definitely wasn't going to let me use his car. Didn't want me to fuck it up." Jesus, he hadn't meant to say all of that. He could see it there, in Landon's eyes now, the pity. The last thing he wanted was pity.

"That's why you didn't want to ride my bike?"

"The curb incident really happened when he tried to teach me, not when I took the exam."

"Rod—"

"Don't. I'm not doing this. There are a whole lot of things we can do besides talking about shit that doesn't matter. Things that are a lot more fun." Rod turned his head, nuzzling his face in Landon's crotch the way he'd thought about a few minutes ago. He tongued Landon's balls through the nylon fabric of his shorts, heard Landon suck in a deep breath.

This was what they needed, not to talk about all that other stuff. Just fucking. Afterward they could be friends again. The kind of friends who laughed at Rods-N-Ends, not the kind who wanted to find all the secrets buried inside each other.

He wrapped his mouth around Landon's sac, wetting his shorts.

"Rod…" Landon's hand gripped his hair, tried to pull him off, but Rod wouldn't let him.

"I want you. I didn't get to blow you nearly enough last time. I'll suck you good. You can fuck my mouth, if you want. Take it hard. Then you can have my ass." When Landon tried to pull him away again, he added, "Let me. Please…just let me." He hated the needy sound in his voice, but he wanted this. Needed it more than anything else.

Rod pulled Landon's shorts down, freeing his dick. He sucked the head into his mouth, heard Landon hiss in pleasure, and then, "Fuck…*fuck.* No." This time he used his strength to get Rod off him. He didn't completely push him away, but far enough that Rod couldn't reach his cock anymore.

Rod closed his eyes. Damn, he was being pathetic. What the fuck was his problem? Landon left him feeling off kilter and he didn't know how to deal with that. "Okay." Rod shrugged. "Movie then?"

Landon looked at him, his eyes intense, burrowing deep as though he could see parts of Rod he kept hidden.

"Don't do that," Landon said.

"I'm not doing anything."

Then he felt Landon's hand on his cheek, his thumb brushed against his skin, and he realized he'd closed his eyes again. "Let *me*." Landon repeated Rod's words from a minute before. "It's my turn this time. *I* want *you*. Gonna pleasure you till you can't fucking take it anymore."

Yes…please… Rod didn't speak though, just continued to lie there looking at Landon.

"Get up. I want you in a bed this time."

There wasn't a chance in hell he was arguing with that.

CHAPTER TWENTY-TWO

Landon had a million thoughts going through his head that he couldn't process. It was funny how you met someone and saw them a certain way. The more you got to know that person, the more you discovered that there are so many other hidden pieces to them that you didn't expect. He was like a gift you always got to unwrap. There were layers and boxes and hidden compartments you didn't know about.

Yeah, he was sexy and funny. He was blunt, and unapologetic and those were the things that initially drew Landon to him. The things that made him enjoy spending time with Rod, but he thought maybe Rod hurt more than he let on. That maybe there was shit going on inside him that made some of his behavior a façade.

And damned if Landon didn't want to soothe that. If he didn't want to take care of him, and *that* was the fucked up bit of it all that he couldn't process right now. He wouldn't know where to start and honestly wasn't sure if he wanted to try, so he figured he'd do the next best thing. He'd show Rod that he meant something to Landon with his body instead.

Rod turned to face him when they got to the bedroom, but Landon kept moving, kept walking until he was right in front of Rod, looking into the pools of his confused eyes.

"You're looking at me like you're going to eat me alive." Rod smiled, but it wasn't genuine. He could see that now. He knew the difference between Rod deflecting and when Rod was really happy. When in the hell did that happen? Maybe the better question was why?

"Shut up. I know what you're doing," Landon told him. Even to his own ears, his voice sounded deeper, confused.

"I'm not doing anything."

"I am. I'm going to do exactly what you said. Take off your shirt."

Rod did as he said as Landon knelt in front of him. He pulled Rod's pants down, not pausing while he slid them past Rod's thighs, he ran his tongue from the root of his erection to the tip.

"Oh fuck," Rod groaned.

"Mmm. I love this. I've always loved sucking dick. Love the feel of that soft, velvety skin and the hardness beneath it."

"Feel free to suck mine as much as you want," Rod replied, and Landon couldn't help but chuckle.

He finished pulling Rod's pants down and then nudged his thigh. "Open up your legs. I want to play with your balls. Jesus, your sac is fucking tight already." He palmed Rod's nuts, felt the hair against his hand, the heat radiated through his skin. "Farther," Landon told him and Rod obeyed. He leaned forward, head between Rod's open thighs and sucked his heavy sac into his mouth. He felt Rod's legs tremble, his right knee buckle before he stood firm again, and Landon couldn't help but smile around Rod's balls in his mouth.

He was hot, so fucking hot. Landon released him, licked the seam, then Rod's taint, before running his tongue over his balls and up to his leaking prick again.

"You're killing me," Rod rushed out, before burying his hand in Landon's hair.

"Is there a better way to go out?" Landon leaned back, palm flat against Rod's stomach and pushed him down.

"Thank God. I don't know how much longer I could have stood there." He sat on the edge of the bed. Landon ignored what he said. He didn't want to talk right now. He wanted Rod's dick in his mouth. Wanted to savor him and pleasure him until Rod couldn't take it anymore.

Landon rubbed his face between Rod's legs. Felt his rough pubic hair chafe his skin. He smelled of soap from his shower, his skin tasted clean, but still that salty taste teased him.

Landon sucked Rod's erection into his mouth, went down his length as far as he could go before pulling up again. He looked up at Rod. He had his eyes closed, head dropped back, his chest rising and falling with heavy breaths.

He was fucking beautiful this way.

While his hand played with Rod's balls, he sucked him again. Teased the head of his prick, licked at his slit, before just sucking his helmet with strong, greedy pulls. He felt that way, greedy for Rod. He wanted to devour him.

"Oh shit, I'm not going to last long." Rod's hand tightened in his hair. He wanted to taste Rod's come. Wanted to drive him crazy until his orgasm crashed into him, but he also wasn't ready to stop playing. Visions of the first time he'd seen Rod naked played in his head, the image of him on the bed with the dildo in his ass. He knew Rod liked anal play, and this had become about Rod. There was no doubt Landon would unload as well, but he felt a foreign need for this to be about this man.

"Lie down. Ass on the edge of the bed," Landon said as he opened Rod's bedside drawer. There were a few boxes of toys—his dildo, a plug, and some anal beads. They could play with those things later; right now Landon only wanted himself inside of Rod.

He heard Rod getting into position, as he'd told him. Landon grabbed the lube from his drawer. When he turned, Rod was there, legs spread and held open, his ass on display for Landon.

"We were in such a rush the first time, I didn't get to spend enough time with your pretty hole." He rubbed his finger over Rod's pucker, watched it clench and then release again.

"Please..." Rod said softly, needy.

"Please what?" Landon asked, this time using his thumb rubbing circles on Rod's hole. "Tell me what you need. Tell me what will make you feel good."

"Whatever you want...just something."

Landon pulled his hand back. Did Rod always sacrifice what he wanted for others? Was he always just willing to take what he could get instead of demanding what he needed? "Tell me what you want, what will make you feel good or I'll stop now."

It would kill him to stop. His balls ached. His cock leaked in his shorts, really fucking needing to get off. Rod turned his head, brows furrowed as he looked at Landon and it confirmed that this was the right thing to do. On some level, it was uncomfortable that he knew what Rod was feeling, that he wanted to do whatever he could to give the man what he needed, but it was there, and he couldn't deny it.

Not in this moment. He shoved those scattered thoughts away for now.

"Tell me," Landon said again.

"I want you to kiss me. Lay on me. I want your weight smothering me, your tongue in my mouth, and your fingers in my ass."

Landon wanted that too.

He moved between Rod's legs again when Rod said, "Take off your clothes first. I love your body. I want to feel your skin against mine."

Landon's dick jerked. He put some pressure at the base of it, before getting rid of his shorts, then his shirt. He squirted some lube on his first two fingers and tossed the bottle to the bed. "I need to watch for just a second," he said, rubbing his slick fingers against Rod's pink asshole. Rod shuddered as Landon played with it, first softly and then with a little more pressure.

He pushed his first finger in, watched it disappear inside of Rod, as he fucked him with it. Rod moaned, pulled his legs farther back. "Can I have another finger? And your mouth. Can I have your mouth?"

Yeah, he really fucking could. Landon worked another finger in his tight channel, before leaning over, covering Rod's mouth with his own. He fucked him—in and out, pushing those two fingers in deep, before taking them almost all the way out again.

Their mouths fused together. Their tongues tangled. Rod let out deep sounds that Landon swallowed.

He wrapped his legs around Landon, his heels digging into Landon's ass.

Rod kissed him like he was fucking starving for it, and damned if Landon wasn't just as ravenous for his taste.

He felt Rod squeeze his fingers and couldn't wait to feel Rod's hole sucking his dick the same way.

Rod's arms went around him. He thrust, rubbing his dick against Landon as they made out.

Pre-come spilled from Landon, and he pulled back just enough to watch it drip onto Rod's stomach.

"Oh fuck, that was sexy. I want your cock inside me now. Gimme your dick, Landon."

He kissed Rod again, as he held on to his own erection so he didn't come before he got inside him.

His dick was angry at him, wanting to fucking explode. Landon stood and grabbed a condom. He rolled it down his aching shaft as Rod said, "I'm going to lie on my stomach. I want you to do me from behind."

A tremble rocked through Landon, trickled down his spine. "Whatever you want."

Rod moved to the head of the bed, hands on the bars of the headboard, his tight ass ready and waiting for Landon. As he climbed on the bed, he ran a hand over Rod's globes. "This ass of yours…so fuckable…so pretty." *So mine,* whispered a quiet voice in his head that Landon ignored.

Rod wiggled it, looking back with a smirk on his face. "So fuck it then."

Landon straddled him, angling his cock between Rod's cheeks, pushing into his already lubed hole. He hissed as he slid inside, the sweet burn already starting in his balls. "Jesus, I forgot how tight you are on my dick." Especially like this. He worked his way in as Rod looked over his shoulder at him. As though he could read Landon's mind, Rod nodded and Landon slammed forward, burying himself to the hilt and the hot glove of Rod's ass.

He lay down on him, wrapped his arm around Rod's chest, his other hand covering Rod's on the headboard.

And then he fucked.

Hard. He pulled back, before thrusting his hips again. Over and over, he pumped into Rod's greedy hole. Each time he slammed forward, Rod grunted and begged for more. And Landon wanted to give it to him. He'd give him anything in this moment.

Their skin slapped together, their sweaty bodies making a smacking sound each time they met.

Rod pushed back against him. His teeth dug into Landon's arm as Landon fucked him and the sting just added more to his pleasure. "Can you come like this? Do you need stimulation to your dick?" he asked as he kept plundering into Rod.

"Oh yeah…fuck yeah. Even if your dick wasn't enough, my cock is rubbing against the bed. Harder," he gasped the last word. "Give it to me harder."

So Landon did. His jaw hurt it was so tense as he slammed into Rod with everything he had. Their loud breathing echoed through the room, blended together with the sounds of their bodies slapping against each other.

"Fuck….*fuck!*" Rod said before his asshole clenched around Landon's dick. His teeth bit into Landon's arm again, this time as he came, and it was enough to make Landon's balls nearly pop. He exploded, coming in long spurts as his balls emptied. He damn near saw double, his vision blurred as Rod's hole milked him fucking dry.

He didn't move, just laid there, his weight against Rod as his dick softened. He knew he needed to get out of him, so he pulled free, taking the condom off, tying it and tossing it into the trash.

He had an unfamiliar fullness in his chest, his body sated in a way he wasn't sure he'd ever felt. He ran a hand down Rod's back, watched Rod shudder…and realized that in this moment, coming wasn't the only thing he wanted from him. He wanted to know more about who he was, his past, and what he hid in those eyes of his.

Jesus, he was so incredibly fucked.

CHAPTER TWENTY-THREE

"I need to get cleaned up." Rod let the bullshit excuse roll off his tongue. Good sex was messy sex, so he sure as hell didn't care about dried come and sweat on him. What he did need was to put some space between the two of them, to mentally work through what had happened, which he really shouldn't need to do. They'd fucked. It wasn't the first time they'd fucked. He was the one who'd pushed Landon about it only being sex and how it wouldn't screw with their friendship, but now he needed space and to sort through his thoughts. There were too many red flags popping up and he didn't like it.

"Okay," Landon told him without moving from his spot on the bed, not even to look at him.

Rod rolled over, got out of the bed, thought about grabbing some underwear but then thought better of it. He wouldn't have felt the need to cover himself up with anyone else, and this was just like every other time he'd been with someone. Sex. Fucking. Using each other to get off and that was that.

The bathroom door felt like it echoed when he closed it. He

knew it hadn't, and wasn't sure why he was being so fucking strange about everything.

Jesus that had been intense, the way they'd kissed, and touched, and had sex. The way Landon almost felt like he was doing it for Rod, to give him something because he wanted to, and not just because it happened. Sure, Landon had said as much, but words and actions were two different things. People said things all the time, but this he'd *felt*.

The second he thought those words he had to bite back a laugh at himself. He was reading too much into things, that much was obvious. He'd had to pressure the guy to fuck him at all. Maybe that really was the *how* of Landon doing it for him. But then, that hadn't been what it felt like. Not at all, which meant Rod was feeling shit that wasn't there. Landon spoke his feelings loud and clear from the beginning, and now here he was turning it into the very thing he told Landon he didn't have to worry about.

Rod turned on the water, splashed some on his face and then looked in the mirror. "Get it together, Rodney. What the fuck is your problem?" he said softly.

Maybe it was talking about his dad that had screwed with his head. It didn't usually bother him. It was what it was, and he couldn't do anything to change it, the same way he couldn't change who he was for his father. He'd gotten over the fact that he wasn't enough for the man who raised him a long time ago.

He didn't really need people anyway.

Rod turned the water off and dried his face. He was cracking up, thinking about things he didn't need to think about, so he shut the door on all those things in his head, and opened the one that led back to his bedroom.

Landon laid in bed, his spent cock resting in a nest of dark hair between his legs. He had one of his legs bent, the other out straight, his head to the side so he looked at Rod, and damned if Rod's pulse didn't stumble. Christ the man was beautiful. He couldn't believe he had him in his bed right now. "Think I could get you hard? I'd be willing to go another round if you are."

Landon acted as though Rod hadn't asked him a question, and just continued to look at him with those dark eyes that made Rod think things he shouldn't. Landon looked at him as though he didn't know who he was right now. He couldn't have that. "Or you can use a toy on me. There's more in the closet. I—"

"Shut up," Landon cut him off.

"Aren't you supposed to be in a good mood after sex?"

"Who are you?" Landon asked, and the question made blood rush through Rod's ears, and his head spin.

"I'm the guy you just fucked the hell out of. The guy who's hoping you'll do it again." Rod sat on the bed, and then said, "So do you want to watch a movie or are you tired?"

"I want to know more about your past." Landon's voice was soft, coaxing.

Oh fuck. "Why? It's the past for a reason. Why worry about it now?"

"I don't know why." Landon's hand wrapped around his wrist, and Rod closed his eyes. Jesus, what was wrong with him? He wanted to spill his fucking guts to Landon like that would change anything. Like Landon really wanted to hear that. There was a tug on his wrist, and Rod went easily. He lay down beside Landon. He was such a sexy man—tanned, taut skin, dark hair, and firm muscle.

"I shouldn't have said that stuff in the living room. I guess I'm still feeling a little too free from our ride today."

"I asked." Landon rubbed his thumb over the wrinkles Rod knew were in his forehead. He liked the feel of Landon's hot skin. "Sometimes I feel like I know you. We're friends. We spend enough time together, but sometimes I wonder if I know you at all."

His gut churned, heavy and uncomfortable. "What you see is what you get. I don't hide much."

"I think you do and I'm conflicted on how I feel about it, if I'm being honest. There's a part of me that wants to know it all, wonders if anyone really knows you, but there's another part that thinks it's better to get up and walk away now."

The rolling in his stomach became harder, heavier. Walking away was never a problem. He'd done it; everyone he'd fucked had done it. That's just what happened, but the thought of it happening now made him want to reach out, hold tight. "What are you going to do? It's your call."

"We're friends," Landon replied.

"Friends who fuck." Landon didn't respond. He was still looking at Rod like he wasn't sure who he was. It made him want to turn away, to hide, but he forced himself to return Landon's stare. To show him there wasn't anything more to Rod than what was on the surface. Finally, when there was no response, Rod added, "We can just keep going the way we are. Hang out, get off. That's really all there is to do."

"Yeah..." Landon said softly. "Yeah, that's what I thought too, but...fuck, hearing you talk earlier? That shit you said about your dad? About who you are? It nearly fucking ate me alive. I wanted to *fix* it when I've never wanted to fix something for someone before."

Rod got it. Of course he would pity him when he gave him part of a sob story. Poor gay boy whose daddy couldn't love him. It was every book and made-for-TV movie come to life. And he wouldn't have that. Fuck pity. So Rod grinned at him, reached out and touched his arm. "With this ass, how could you not care?"

"I'm serious. Don't make a joke about it."

"I'm serious too. I have the best ass in three counties. Plus, I give good head, and I sell sex toys for Christ's sake. I'm the whole package." He paused a beat, then another, and another. When Landon didn't respond, he said, "I'm tired. Let's just go to bed." He reached over and turned out the light.

Landon didn't respond, and when Rod woke up the next day, he was gone.

CHAPTER TWENTY-FOUR

"Oh my God. You look so handsome, Landon. I can't believe how handsome you look." Shanen fiddled with his bowtie and then ran a hand down the arm of his tux. The light shined off the wetness in her eyes.

"Can I ask why I'm not doing this with your fiancé and the groomsmen?" He knew she would get emotional at the fitting. He guessed he was lucky their mom had to work. He wasn't sure he could handle the both of them together.

"Because I wanted to spend some quality time with my brother. Is that too much to ask?" There was a smile in her blue eyes, which were so different than Landon and their mom's brown. Shanen had their father's eyes.

"If you're going to cry, then yes, it's too much to ask."

She swatted his arm and he grinned at her. He sure as hell didn't feel like smiling right now. His head was still a mess from last night at Rod's. He didn't know what he thought about anything so mostly he tried not to think about it at all. Maybe it was a good thing he had this fitting scheduled with Shanen today. He doubted he or Rod would have been able to find any words between the two of them today.

"You really do look handsome," Shanen told him, and he could read the sadness in her voice. This had to be hard on her. He was glad he was here, that he could give Shanen away, but she had to wish it was her father doing it.

"I know, kid." He pulled her close, an arm around her shoulders. Shanen buried her face in his chest.

"You haven't called me that since I really was one."

"I haven't?" he asked, but he knew she was right. Their dad had called her kid and then Landon started doing it. When their dad left, he stopped.

"No, and you know you haven't." Just then Amanda the seamstress came back. Shanen pulled back and wiped her eyes, putting on a brave face the way they always did. He wondered how often they really felt it. How often Rod really felt the smiles and jokes he tossed out left and right.

"I think this works!" Amanda said as she wrote something down on a piece of paper. Shanen stood off in the background, a façade of a smile plastered on her slender face.

"Yeah, I think so," Landon replied to her. She excused him so he could get dressed in his clothes, and he heard her talking to Shanen about there only being one more month until the wedding.

Shanen had never dated much. He couldn't remember her

dating in high school at all, even though she'd been asked out, plenty. Then her life was all about college, and whatever she and their mom had going at the time. She'd always seemed content, happy. They'd talked about their parents enough in their lives for him to know Shanen struggled with the same feelings he did, but now here she was, getting married.

Landon got dressed again, and then came out to find Shanen sitting on a bench outside. Once he thanked Amanda, he made his way out to his sister. He knew her well enough to know what she needed. He held his hand out to her, "Come on. I'll buy you ice cream."

It had been too many years since he shared an ice cream with his sister. Guilt surged to life inside him again. He shouldn't have stayed away as long as he did. That was wrong.

"I thought you'd never ask." Shanen took his hand and stood. There was an ice cream shop two doors down, so they went in and each got a bowl—strawberry for Shanen and chocolate for him, before they made their way outside again.

It was a quiet July day, the humidity keeping people inside or in the water. "Can we walk?" Shanen asked, and he nodded.

They made their way down Main Street. He'd always loved this street. It reminded him of old movies he used to watch with his dad. This area was called Old Town and it definitely looked like it, with wood buildings and benches outside of each shop.

"Have you noticed anything different with Mom?" Shanen asked.

Had he? He didn't think so. Maybe he wasn't home enough to

notice. "She's been busy. She's gone a lot, but that's a good thing. She's creating a life for herself."

"Yeah... Yeah, I guess. It just feels...different. I don't know why." They were silent for a few minutes before Shanen finally asked, "Do you think Daddy forgives her?"

The question was like a punch to the gut. Sometimes he wasn't sure if he forgave her. Then the guilt would kick in and he'd think about his mom's depression and being alone all these years.

His instinct was to tell her who the fuck cared what he thought? Who cared if he forgave them? What he'd done had been worse. He'd walked away from his kids. Landon sighed. "I don't know, Shan. I don't know anything about what he could be thinking. He made sure of that when he left us behind."

"Are you still angry at him?"

"I will always be angry at him. I will always hate him for leaving."

"But they weren't happy," Shanen added.

"So?" They hadn't been. They'd made each other miserable. They'd hurt each other. Landon's biggest fear was doing that to someone he cared about.

"What if that happens with Jacob and me?"

"What? No. It won't happen." But did he really believe that? He didn't know.

She nudged him. "Are you all knowing now?"

189

"What do you mean now? I've always known everything."

Shanen giggled but sobered quickly. "It worries me sometimes. Remember all their stories? They were best friends most of their lives, and then they turned into something different. They started to bring out the worst in each other. I don't know what I would do if that happened to Jacob and me."

They walked by a trash can and Landon tossed his ice cream into it. His stomach suddenly felt sour, his sister's words reminding him of everything he felt. "Why are you marrying him?"

"What?" Shanen stopped walking and looked at him. "What do you mean?"

He nodded toward the sidewalk and they started walking again. A few cars drove by. People sat outside on the patio of a restaurant eating and laughing. Living. "If you're scared of what will happen, why are you marrying him?" He really wanted to know. Maybe he needed to know.

"Because he's worth the risk," Shanen said, as though it was the easiest answer in the world. "I love him. He's worth it. I'm worth it. You never know what's going to happen, Lando. One minute Dad was there, the next he wasn't. You can't go through life afraid of everything or you're not really living it. Actually, no, that's not true. You can be afraid. Fear means you're being honest with yourself. We can't really live without being afraid of something. You just can't let that fear hold you back."

He let her words swim around inside him for a minute. He hated the thought of being afraid of anything, but the truth was, he was scared shitless. But Jesus, he didn't want to let that fear get the best of him either.

"Are you serious about Rod?" she asked. He didn't bother to tell her they were just friends. Maybe in a lot of ways they were, but at the same time, he knew they weren't. It didn't matter what either of them admitted out loud.

"No…yes…I don't know."

"Finally, I get the truth at the third try!" She tossed her ice cream in the trash and weaved her arm through his. She held onto him as they continued to make their way down the cracked sidewalk.

"I don't know what I feel, Shan. I like spending time with him. I care about him, but honestly that scares the fuck out of me. I never thought I'd really give a shit about anyone, not that way. Then I start thinking about Mom and Dad and how much I like spending time with him now. I don't want to lose that."

"Being afraid is normal. But letting the fear win is no way to live."

Jesus, he felt ridiculous having this heart to heart with his sister as they walked down the fucking road. Hell, he didn't want to have this discussion anywhere. "Okay, that's enough of that."

"No! I don't think so." She held his arm tighter. "Does he feel the same way about you?"

Wasn't that a good fucking question? "How am I supposed to answer that when I don't completely understand what I'm feeling?"

"I think you do, you just don't want to admit it."

Landon sighed, not ready to discuss that with her. "I never would have thought it before, but I think he's more gun shy than I am." But then, that didn't really ring true. "I don't think he believes anyone really cares about him. The more I get to know him, the more I wonder how much he keeps hidden, maybe even from himself."

Shanen gave him one more squeeze and then let go. "Prove him wrong. That's all you can do, care about him, treat him well, and prove him wrong. Actions speak louder than words. He's lucky he found you. You may not realize it, but you have a big heart, Landon."

He wasn't so sure about that...but for the first time in his life, he thought he might be willing to put it on the line for someone else.

CHAPTER TWENTY-FIVE

Rod sat behind his work computer, processing online orders. The store wasn't very busy today, and that always worried him. He'd put everything on the line for this place. He loved what he did, but he knew small businesses often failed. The only thing he had going for him was his product. It wasn't as though there were a lot of places close by that sold what Rod did. His biggest competitor would always be the many online sites to choose from. He needed to advertise better, so that's what he'd spent his day thinking about.

Or trying to think about at least. Damned if Landon didn't keep squeezing his way in, which just pissed him off. He was dwelling. He didn't dwell, but he couldn't seem to evict Landon or their night from his thoughts.

At about five o'clock the store picked up. It was as though everyone was suddenly in the mood for sex, and needed to make a quick stop by Rods-N-Ends before they could make that happen. Not that he was complaining. He needed the business, and it helped the day go by faster, so it was a win/win for him.

Rod worked like crazy all day and when closing time finally

came around, he was fucking beat.

And he hadn't heard from Landon all day, which shouldn't matter in the slightest, but a quiet ache inside him told him that it did. That was a huge screw-up on his part, the caring, and he needed to find a way to lessen those feelings.

After taking care of what he needed to take care of at the shop, he jumped in his car and headed home. As he turned into the driveway he saw Landon's motorcycle. He felt his brows pull together as he looked at the bike sitting there.

He'd offered his house to Landon a hundred times, but he never took him up on the offer unless Rod had been there. Rod always left the back door unlocked, and Landon knew that. The lights in the house told him that Landon had taken advantage.

A low ache in his gut suddenly started to spread through him. He should have expected this. Hell, it made sense. It's what he'd planned on happening. They got what they wanted out of each other, good sex. It wasn't as if he really thought they were forming a life long friendship with each other. He'd told Landon he knew the score up front, and apparently Landon had decided that it was time to do the walking away part. There was no reason for him to be here unexpectedly like this, and he was probably right that the time had come.

Rod sucked in a deep breath and then got out of the car. He smiled as he opened the door and saw Landon sitting on the couch, his nerves playing off of each of his features. Showing in the rigidness of his body as he looked at Rod.

"We don't have to make a big deal about this. We're both grown men. We know how it goes." Rod walked into the kitchen and grabbed a bottle of water.

"What?" Landon frowned at him.

"This." Rod pointed at Landon and then himself. "We don't need any drama. I'm surprised you're going this route, though, I probably would have blown you at least once more if I'd have known we weren't going to hook up again."

Landon stood. He was only a few inches taller than Rod, bulkier, but in this moment, he seemed bigger, an angry force that Rod didn't understand. "What the fuck are you talking about, Rod?"

Rod opened his mouth to respond, but Landon cut him off. "Actually, shut up and just come here. Jesus, I don't know which way is up most of the time with you."

With him? Rod thought he was pretty easy to understand. Landon was the confusing one—pushing the friendship only, talking about his family, the way he'd taken Rod that last time, and also forcing Rod to talk about his own shit. Most of the time, he didn't have to worry about that. People accepted what he showed them of himself because they really didn't want any more than that.

"Get your ass over here before I drag you to me. Oh, and turn off the kitchen light."

The twisting in his stomach was different now, more confusion than the knowledge that this was ending. Rod took a step closer to Landon, and then another. He noticed a couple small speakers that he hadn't seen before, speakers that didn't belong to him. "What are you—"

"You keep asking me that and my answer is the same. I don't know what I'm doing. I'm just going with the flow. Come here."

And Rod went. He turned off the lights as Landon said, and then closed the distance between them. "We missed the fireworks. It was my fault so I thought we could watch them now." Landon pointed the remote at the TV and then a huge fireworks display came to life on the screen, the whistling and popping playing through the surround sound that Landon had hooked up.

Damned if Rod's hand didn't start to shake. He couldn't move, didn't know what to say, but knew he had to let something pass his lips. "Why are you doing this?"

The light from the television shone around Landon, and he shrugged. "I know it's not the same as the real thing, but I just wanted to do something nice for you. That's it."

He'd done nice things for Rod already, a big one being the way he'd let Rod drive his bike.

"When's the last time someone did something nice for you?" Landon asked.

The answer was easy. "The last time I saw you."

Landon shook his head. "That doesn't count. That was selfish. I want someone to ride with, and I like sharing my love of bikes. Unless you're talking about the sex, and then there's the fact that I came so hard I saw double."

But this was just for Rod... He tried to make sense of it, tried to work through how they'd gotten here. Landon was the one who made sure Rod knew what this was. It was Landon who didn't want to take the chance that Rod would read something into it that wasn't there and now here he was, doing things like this for him. The kind of thing no one had taken the time to do for him before.

"Come on, we're going to miss the show again."

When Rod didn't reply, when he couldn't reply, Landon continued, "Just ride it out with me. That's what I'm doing, riding it out. We're shifting gears, that's all. Not sure where we're going. Not even sure I know how to get there, but let's just try to enjoy the ride."

And he wanted that. Wanted it so fucking much, that the need ate him alive. It scared the shit out of him at the same time.

Still, Rod closed the distance between them. When Landon sat, Rod went to the other end of the couch, lied down, and put his head in Landon's lap like he'd done fifty times before.

Landon touched his hair, ran his fingers through it and neither of them spoke; they just continued sitting there together, watching the show.

CHAPTER TWENTY-SIX

"Craigslist, huh? I heard Grindr's a better option, though I never had to try either. Before Nick, I had to fight women off with a stick, and then there was no one but him."

Landon rolled his eyes at Bryce, not surprised by his joke. He liked Bryce a lot. He liked Bryce and Nick both. "Betcha had to fight Nick off too, at first. Hell, I don't know how I keep my pants on around you. The struggle is real. I want to drop my jeans around my ankles for you right now."

Bryce gave him a cocky grin. "Tough isn't it? Most people have that response to me."

Landon looked around the break room for something to throw at Bryce's head. When he couldn't find anything that wouldn't do serious damage he chuckled instead. "How does your boyfriend put up with you?"

Bryce winked. "I'm good in bed. That makes the rest of me bearable." He sat in the brown chair across from him, and Landon found himself eager to tell Bryce what he was really doing. Maybe

Bryce would have some connections to help him do this for Rod sooner rather than later.

"I'm looking for a good starter bike for Rod."

The expression on Bryce's face immediately became one of surprise. "No shit?"

"Yeah, I took him out on the Harley once. I don't mind letting him ride it, but I think it makes him nervous, because it's not his. He doesn't want to mess anything up. I want him to feel comfortable so he can just go for it, let go of the excess fear. It's already nerve wracking to learn to ride. I figure if I can find one for cheap, we can grab it and he can ride that. If he changes his mind, I can always sell it."

Bryce crossed his arms and eyed Landon. "You want to buy Rod a bike? What are your intentions with my friend?"

Laughing, Landon told him, "Shut the hell up." When Bryce smiled, Landon continued, "Really I'm just excited to have someone to ride with." He didn't have to buy it *for* Rod. Hell, it wasn't as if he could ever have enough bikes, but like he said, he could always sell it if Rod discovered he didn't like to ride. He liked buying bikes, fixing them up some and selling them.

"And what? I don't fucking exist or what? Unless it goes back to the whole *struggle to keep your pants on around me* thing, you have to know I'd be down to go with you. Nick likes to ride with me, but he has no interest in driving his own bike. I'd love to take a cruise with you sometime."

Landon nodded. He would definitely like to go out and ride with

Bryce sometime. That didn't change the fact that he wanted to ride with Rod too. He loved bikes, and really wanted to share them with Rod. "That'd be great. Let's plan something."

Bryce nodded and then said, "You know he'll lose his fucking mind if you buy him a bike, don't you? I've noticed that about Rod. He struggles with things that feel too real. He's good at playing it off, but there's something more to it. This isn't *a Hey, let me buy you lunch.* This is a fucking motorcycle. No matter how you play it off, saying you'll sell it yada fucking yada. You're buying him a goddamned bike. How would you feel if some guy you were fucking bought you a motorcycle?"

Landon closed his eyes and dropped his head back. Bryce was right. He sure as hell wouldn't be able to accept something like that from someone, especially a guy he was sleeping with. Instead of saying that, he asked, "How do you know I'm fucking him?"

Bryce shrugged. "Just figured. Find a bike, take him to look at it. If he wants it, he'll get it."

Jesus, he was losing his fucking mind. For the second time Bryce was right on the money. What had he been thinking? "Thanks, man."

With a nod, Bryce stood. He looked as though he wanted to say something, so Landon decided to make it easy on him. "Go ahead and say it."

"Just...be careful with him. I know that sounds ridiculous. It's sex, and I'm sure we all know Rod doesn't hide the fact that he has no problem with sex, but like I said, I think there's more to him than he lets on. And I think he has the potential to be hurt, though he would never let anyone know he was. Maybe he already has been hurt and we don't realize it."

He had been hurt. Landon had no doubts in his mind about that. Rod all but admitted it to him with what he'd said about his dad. The fucked-up part was he still didn't know what he was doing. He just knew how he felt, even if he hadn't completely worked through the why of it yet.

He liked Rod.

He wanted to spend as much time with him as he could.

He wanted Rod to be happy.

"I know. We're figuring shit out as we go along."

"None of it is my business, but I wouldn't be me if I hadn't said what I was thinking. Hey, you two should come hang out at the house sometime. You know, since you lied your way out of the last get together." He cocked a brow at Landon and he knew there was no getting around that he had in fact acted like an idiot.

"Yeah, sure. That'd be great. I'll talk to Rod."

He was making all sorts of plans for someone who didn't know what in the hell he was doing. Full throttle. He didn't know any other way.

***

"I was thinking we could play... There are some new products I want to try. Do you like nipple play?" Rod asked Landon the second he showed up at Rods-N-Ends. Landon stumbled and looked up at him in wide-eyed surprise that was sexy as hell.

"Um…yeah? I guess it depends. I'll use my tongue on your nipples all you want. You can suck on mine too. I'm not into the whole pain thing. No clamps or shit like that."

Well, that hadn't gone as planned. He'd expected to embarrass Landon. There were a few people in the store, and he hadn't exactly whispered.

"You were giving me shit. You're trying to annoy me, aren't you? Don't lie. I see it in your eyes." Landon set a bag on the counter. "I brought dinner when you have a break."

Landon really needed to stop it with this stuff, bringing him dinner, the fireworks surprise the other night. People didn't do this with him. People fucked him. Rod enjoyed it. The end.

"I'm going to help people have good sex, or at least help them masturbate better. I'll be back in a minute." He ignored Landon's questioning dark eyes and made his way to one of the couples shopping. He helped them. He sold some edible products, which he thought were ridiculous. He thought about Landon, about sucking his dick and licking his skin. When he had his mouth on someone, he didn't want to taste anything except him, the salty taste of his skin and the flavor that was unique to him.

Rod spent about thirty minutes helping people before the store cleared out. Landon still waited patiently by the counter for him, so he told Abigail that he was taking his break, before he led Landon back to his office. "Smells good. What is it?"

"Italian. I got you cheese ravioli. Is that okay? It's gotta be cold by now. Do you have a microwave in your office?"

"I do," Rod told him as he opened the door. Landon closed it behind them and he grabbed the bag from Landon's hand and set it on the desk. He turned back to Landon and rubbed his hand on his crotch. "I think I'd rather have some of you instead though."

He really would. He wanted Landon all the time. He pressed his palm against Landon's dick, and felt it start to harden immediately. He loved that he had that effect on him.

"Christ, you are a horny son of a bitch." Landon wrapped his hand around Rod's wrist. "As good as having my dick down your throat sounds, that's not what I came here for. We don't have time for that. You should eat."

Rod didn't move. "Well, shit. Are we back to that again?"

"Back to what?"

"Back to you not wanting to touch me."

Landon shook his head and stepped back. "Wanting to touch you isn't the problem. I just wanted to stop by on my way home. My mom's been running around like crazy lately. She's working herself to death, so I told her I'd come home and help her with a few things tonight. I'll take a rain check on the blowjob. Your mouth is fucking hot, but I like to spend time with you even when I don't get to come."

Maybe that was true before they'd been together, but since Landon had finally given in, he figured that would be all he wanted. It made him feel upside down and backward when Landon rejected him. It made him feel unwanted. Landon hadn't even fucked him after they'd watched the fireworks the other night. *Because he's losing interest already. But then...why is he here?*

203

"You wore the eyeliner. You know that makes me hot. You're too fucking tempting." Landon leaned forward and kissed him before he made his way around Rod, pulling food out of the bag and putting it into the microwave. "Sit down. I don't have long. Oh, hey, I found a few bikes we can go look at, if you want. And Bryce said something about having us over. What do you think?"

Rod didn't know what to think about any of it. The only thing he did know was that he was in over his head where Landon was concerned. Rod knew sex. Rod knew making people laugh. This other shit? He had no fucking clue.

CHAPTER TWENTY-SEVEN

They had to take Rod's car to look at the bikes. He'd borrowed a trailer from the shop, and hooked it up in case they ended up bringing one home. He'd made calls on three bikes. They'd looked at one already, but Landon didn't think it would work. It had obviously been ridden too hard. It was dirty, had sat for a while, and hadn't looked like it had been taken care of very well.

The second one, the guy wasn't home despite the fact that they'd set a time to go see it. Shit like that happened, but it still annoyed the hell out of him. "I hope this one works. It's an 883, which in my opinion is a perfect first bike for you."

"That means nothing to me," Rod replied to him from the driver's seat.

"The blue one."

"Oh! Yeah, I liked that one. I hope it works, but if it doesn't, there will be other bikes."

Landon looked over at him. "I'm not feeling your excitement. I need more excitement from you, Rod. It's a fucking bike."

Rod chuckled like Landon hoped he would. "Jesus, I don't know what I'll do if we don't come home with a bike today. I was awake all last night thinking about it—oh and the fact that I feel like I'm suddenly being forced into abstinence, but that's besides the point."

"Huh?" Landon didn't like the sound of that. He crossed his arms. "What does that mean?"

"It means I like sex. I miss sex. I want to fuck, Landon."

"I want to fuck too, and if I remember correctly, it was a week ago that I blew and fucked your brains out."

Rod glanced his way but then looked at the road again. "I'm a slut. Didn't you know that?" He said it playfully, but Landon heard the truth behind his teasing.

"I own a sex store. I've worked in one for years. I'm *gay*. We only care about fucking. Maybe it's different for you since you're bi?"

"Stop the goddamned car."

"What? I'm giving you shit. Ignore me. I didn't sleep well last night and—"

"Stop the fucking car. I'm not playing around with you." Landon had no idea where that had come from. Actually, scratch that. He had a pretty good idea where it came from, but that didn't mean he wasn't taken aback by it.

"Ooh, I like it when you're bossy."

"Pull the car over, Rod."

Rod sighed as he slowed down and pulled toward the side of the quiet road.

"Shit, I'm sorry. I don't know why I said that. My head is all fucked up right now."

"Why?" Landon asked.

"Sleep, remember?"

"You're lying. Be real with me. I deserve that."

"This. Us. I have no fucking clue what's going on, and I don't like it. I have sex with people, Landon, and then we go our separate ways. My head is all twisted up!"

"Is that why you pushed sex with me so hard? So I'd walk away afterward?"

"It's what happens. It would be easier that way."

Landon sighed, those words hollowing him out. Breaking his heart. "Do you think my brain isn't fucked as well? I don't do this either, Rod. Whatever we're doing, I've never done it, but I'm here, trying to work my way through it. I want to figure this out with you."

There were a few beats of silence in the car. Both men were breathing heavily. It was Rod who broke the silence first. "Well, obviously you're a lot better at it than me."

There was laughter in Rod's voice, but Landon didn't let it distract him. "I like you. Jesus, that makes me sound like I'm fourteen, but it's true." He liked Rod in ways he never imagined.

Landon looked over to see him gripping the steering wheel tightly. His fingers were discolored, and he didn't meet Landon's eyes. "I like you too. I guess we both sound like twelve year olds."

"Fourteen."

"Whatever."

"I'm the most sex positive person you'll find, Rod. There's nothing wrong with wanting sex. There's nothing wrong with hooking up, and blowjobs with people you know or people you don't know, if that's what you want. As long as they're both consenting adults, that's all that matters. If someone made you think otherwise, they have the problem and not you."

He nodded. "I know that in here." He tapped the side of his head. "It's here," Rod tapped his chest, "that the message gets lost sometimes. I thought I was over that shit. Jesus, I'm too old to struggle with daddy issues."

"You feel how you feel. That's all that matters." He reached over and stroked Rod's cheek. It was then that the younger man finally looked at him. "I love having my dick buried inside you. Know that...but I like spending time with you too—talking to you and riding with you. Being real with you. Can you handle that? Because if you need something different, tell me now. If you want to walk away, then tell me. If you want to fuck other people, then that's something we need to have a discussion about. I'm not sure if I can deal with that, but we can talk." They didn't have any real commitment between them. They were free to do what they wanted, but the idea of Rod with someone else made him see red. It made his gut clench and white, hot anger shoot through him.

"I don't want to fuck anyone else. Does that mean we're dating?"

Rod's eyes went wide. He had such expressive fucking eyes. It was all there in his blue orbs—the confusion, fear, and yeah, the excitement too.

"Um…I think so… Shifting gears, like I said. Strange, isn't it?" He'd never wanted to date someone in his life. He wasn't even sure how to do it.

"Absolutely. Damn, I did well. My boyfriend is hot."

Landon chuckled. Jesus, he liked this man. Liked the way he made him smile, the way he made him feel…like this right here? Like his life was enough. He'd never felt that before.

He wrapped his hand around the back of Rod's neck and pulled him forward. Their lips met, the kiss going full throttle, from zero to sixty in five seconds flat. Their tongues tangled, delved into each other's mouths as though they couldn't get enough. Landon's dick went hard and he was suddenly wishing they were somewhere else right now.

When they pulled away, Rod said, "I might fuck up."

"Me too. We'll take it slow."

"Okay."

"Now can we go look at this bike for you? I really want to see you on a bike. Or we can go home and ride mine. It gets me hard thinking about you and motorcycles." He winked, hoping his joke eased Rod's tension.

"Then I guess we better go get me a bike. Then we can go home and you can ride me."

Landon couldn't fucking wait for that.

***

Rod bought the bike. It was gorgeous—a deep, sparkling blue, that he really hoped he would be able to ride. Landon had test driven it first, then Rod. He'd only gone up and down the man's driveway, but he'd ridden with Landon when he really let loose on the open road. He'd told Rod it was a good bike and that was all the convincing Rod needed.

Now, they were on their way back home, but they were stopping by Landon's house first. This day was surreal as hell for him. He still wasn't sure what he thought about their discussion in the car. Dating? It was a foreign fucking language to him, but he felt a calmness inside him at the same time. A need that was too strong to walk away from. He liked Landon, and it seemed that Landon cared about him too. He wasn't sure quite how that happened, if they were both out of their fucking minds, or how long it would last, but he was going with the flow for now.

Landon gave him directions, and before he knew it Rod pulled up in front of the homey, yellow house. It was small, bigger than his own place, but a cute, little one-story house that he tried not to imagine a young Landon growing up in.

He leaned back as Landon opened the door. He looked at Rod, before getting out and said, "Are you coming?"

"I thought you were going to have a panic attack when your mom and sister stopped by the shop when I was there, so I figured it would be safer for me to wait here."

"I wasn't that bad." Landon nodded toward the house. "Get out of the car and come inside with me. Jesus, this is weird, coming to my mom's house before I go home with a guy. I need to get out of this house."

Rod killed the engine and then got out of the car. "It's not that bad. You just moved back a couple months ago. There's nothing wrong with staying here for a while. I'm sure your mom loves that you're here."

He was envious of that. He'd never know if his mom was the kind of person who didn't care that she had a gay son. If she would have just wanted him happy regardless. "I'm nervous. What if your mom doesn't like me?"

Landon stopped walking and looked at him like Rod was crazy. You'd think he'd be used to the look by now.

"She's already met you and she liked you."

"She did?"

Landon nodded, looking almost sad. "Yeah, she did. Of course she liked you. Now let's go."

"Wait, but that was before we decided to date. I'm dating Landon. We're dating. Landon and I are dating. I'm dating someone." When Landon's brows pulled together, Rod added, "Sorry, was testing the words on my tongue."

"You are so fucking crazy." Landon wrapped his arm around Rod's shoulders and pulled him toward the house. He opened the front door and Rod followed him in. He'd tried to sound as though he was teasing out there, but he really did worry. What if he was too much for her? What if she liked him fine as Landon's friend but didn't feel the same now that they were dating? Christ, there was that word again.

Landon's dark-haired mother scrambled up from where she'd been lying on the couch. "You didn't tell me you were bringing Rod by."

He stopped walking. "I can wait in the car."

Landon groaned.

Joy's brows pulled together the same way Landon's did. "Why would you do that? I'm just embarrassed that I'm vegging on the couch so late in the afternoon. Today is my lazy day. I might have at least brushed my teeth after lunch if I would have known you were coming over."

Some of the tension inside him suddenly loosened. "Thanks for the warning."

For a split second he wondered if he shouldn't have said it, but then she smiled and Rod suddenly felt completely relaxed. "I like you. You should come around more often. If you can put up with my son, that is."

"I'll see what I can do about that. He drives me a little crazy sometimes, but I've always been a good Samaritan. He only tests me sometimes."

"Me?" Landon nudged him. "I think it should be the other way around. And thanks, Mom. You're a traitor."

"I try my best." She smiled and stood. "What are you guys doing here?"

"We bought Rod a bike. I just had to stop by and get some of my tools. I want to mess around with it a bit when we get back to his house."

"Oh, great. Now I'll have two people to worry about on those death traps."

Rod's pulse slammed against his skin at her words. She didn't know anything about him, just that he was Landon's friend, yet she would worry about him riding?

Sure it was probably just something you said to be polite, but it still meant a lot to him.

"He'll be fine, just like I'm fine. Come out and see it," Landon told his mom, and then the three of them went out to look at Rod's new motorcycle. How in the hell had this become his life?

CHAPTER TWENTY-EIGHT

"Why are we working on a bike that I just bought? Since we just got it, isn't it supposed to be good to go? I want a refund."

Landon looked up at Rod from where he sat in Rod's garage doing a maintenance check. He grinned over at Landon as though everything he'd just said made complete sense, and Landon felt his heart rate hammer down. Jesus, this man did something to him. He exhausted him, yet breathed life into him at the same time. It was exciting and intimidating. These feelings shot into him, an injection he wasn't expecting, a quick burn that shot through his blood stream.

"You're looking at me funny. Why are you looking at me like I suddenly grew another head?" Rod asked.

"Another one? I can hardly keep up with the one you have. And to answer your question, *we* aren't working on anything. *I'm* working on your bike and you're complaining. It runs well, but it needs to be cleaned up a bit. We'll want to keep up on things like that so she continues to run well."

"He."

"Huh?" Landon asked.

"You said she. My bike's a male. Not that I don't love women. Women are great, but I only ride men."

Landon barked out a loud laugh, unsure why anything surprised him when it came to Rod. "You're right. He. I'll be done out here in just a bit. You can go in if you want to."

Rod stood. Landon thought he was going to walk into the house, but he came over to Landon instead. "You'll teach me to do that? Or to know when it needs to be done? I like to take care of my boys."

"You do, huh?"

"I do."

If he was being honest, he'd admit that he loved the fact that Rod wanted to be able to do things like this for his bike. "Yeah, sure, I'll teach you. I don't mind doing it for you though. That's the perk of knowing a mechanic."

"Yeah, but you won't always be around."

Landon fought to hold back his frown. "You planning on kicking me to the curb?"

"You'll get sick of me before that. I'm going inside to shower. I'll be waiting for you. Remember, you promised me a ride." Rod winked and tried to walk away, but Landon reached out and wrapped a hand around his wrist.

"Nothing in life is a guarantee, but right now, I can't see me wanting to go anywhere, anytime soon." Maybe that wasn't the best thing to say, but it was honest. Landon respected honesty. He wouldn't make promises he couldn't keep. People did that all the time, promised things they couldn't promise, but not him. "Right now, there's nowhere else I want to be." And there wasn't. He was taking a page out of Shanen's book, and going for it.

Rod's blue eyes stormed over, clouds of confusion rolling in. He didn't believe Landon, but Landon could understand that. It was hard for himself to make sense of it, too. He only knew how he felt, right here, right now.

"You've gotten sappy. It's cute." And just like that he knew that whatever he said, Rod would make a joke out of it. That he wouldn't believe him. Maybe Landon should try to fight harder, tell him, but hell, he couldn't make sense of it all himself.

"I'm not cute. Puppies are cute. I'm sexy as fuck."

"Speaking of fucking…"

Landon tossed the shop rag from his lap at Rod. "You're incorrigible. I'll be inside in a bit. Don't worry. I'll have your ass tonight."

"One of these days, I might want yours."

Landon nodded. "And I'll give it to you. Hell, you can have it tonight, if you want."

"No. I want that thick cock of yours filling me tonight. Maybe round two. We can watch a movie in between!"

Jesus Christ, Rod and his fucking movies. "Whatever you say. But you need a new hobby."

"Besides the fucking or the movies?"

"The movies. There can never be too much fucking. Now leave me alone so I can get this finished for you. I want you to go riding soon."

"Yes, sir!" Rod saluted him and then walked away, Landon laughing as he went.

*****

Rod loved showers, the feel of hot water beating down on his skin. When he had time, he often stayed in until the water began to turn cold, forcing him out.

With Landon in the garage working, he took care of what he needed to for their night, before jumping under the spray and letting himself relax. It had been one hell of a day, and while part of him wanted to run it through his head over and over until he could make sense of it, the other part of him knew it might never become clear to him, so he just needed to try and go with the flow.

So, that's what he did. He cleaned up, and then got out and dried off. He must have been in the bathroom longer than he thought because by the time he got out, Landon was in the kitchen.

He looked up at Rod when he came in. "I'm hungry. Are you?"

Rod nodded. He hadn't eaten since this morning. "Yeah, let me see what I have." He opened the fridge and started moving things around inside. There was a package of Italian sausage on the rack. "I have sausage. We can make spaghetti."

It was then that he felt Landon's chest against his back, his swollen cock pressed against the crack of Rod's ass. "Funny thing, I have sausage too."

"You did not just say that." Landon rolled his hips, pressing his hard shaft against Rod's ass again and rubbing. "Oh fuck," Rod added, his goddamned toes curling against the linoleum floor. Landon's hands were there next, squeezing his cheeks as he pushed his dick against Rod's crease.

"This ass of yours. I can't get enough of it. Want my hands on it all the time. Why haven't I tasted it yet?"

Rod's knees nearly gave out beneath him. He loved being rimmed. Loved the feel of a hot, wet tongue licking and probing his hole. "I don't know. Maybe you should get on that right now."

Landon's mouth came down on his neck. He bit into the muscle where Rod's neck met his shoulders. There was a slight burn, and then he licked it, kissed it, making him shudder.

"Maybe I should."

Rod gripped the door of the fridge, reminding him where he was standing. He closed it because it had to be all sorts of wrong to get his ass eaten while he stood in the open refrigerator. "The room..."

"Can't wait. I'm suddenly fucking starving."

A tingle raced down Rod's spine. Oh yeah. Fuck yeah.

Landon wrapped his arms around Rod's waist, pulling him flush against him, still fucking kissing his neck as he walked Rod to the table, a short distance away.

"Put your hands on the back of the chair." Rod did, gripped it so hard his fingers hurt in anticipation of what Landon would give him.

He heard Landon's knees hit the floor when he went down. Pushed his ass back toward him when Landon started to pull down his basketball shorts. He palmed the globes of Rod's ass, squeezed them and then pulled them apart. "Spread your legs for me." Rod did and Landon growled in response. Fucking growled. "Jesus, you have such a nice, tight hole. Your legs are shaking. You're eager for my tongue, aren't you?"

"Yes," Rod hissed out because he really fucking was. "You know I love my ass to be played with."

"I do," Landon replied, his voice hoarse with what sounded like lust. Rod wanted more of it.

"Shh, I need to concentrate. Wanna eat you until you're out of your fucking mind."

Rod already was, but he didn't say that. He wanted more, wanted to be taken to the edge over and over before Landon finally let him career over it.

When he felt the first wet lash of Landon's tongue on his asshole, he nearly lost it right there. Rod gripped the chair tighter, bent over farther, giving his ass to Landon, who devoured it. He ran his tongue back and forth over Rod's pucker. Each rasp of his tongue sent pleasure soaring through him. His whole body felt sensitive. He trembled, savoring the feel of Landon's strong hands parting his cheeks and his skilled tongue licking him like his life depended on it.

"I'm leaking in my pants. I knew you'd taste like a fucking dream." He ran his hands down Rod's thighs. "I love this, hairy fucking men. So goddamn sexy." And then he spread Rod's cheeks again, his tongue probing at Rod's asshole.

Rod looked down to see a string of pre-come a few inches long leaking from his dick. He reached down and wiped it. Was going to lick it off his own fingers, but then Landon said, "Don't you fucking dare. That's mine. Rub it on yourself."

Jesus fucking Christ, the man was trying to kill him. Rod reached around, wiping the pre-come on his sensitive asshole, and then Landon went at him again, moaning as he ate Rod's hole.

Rod held the base of his dick to keep himself from coming. "Fuck me. I need something inside of me."

He heard Landon spit, and then what had to be two fingers pushing inside his hole. It was as though his body sighed in relief. He relaxed, savored the stretch of Landon's fingers spreading him.

"Christ, that is sexy, watching your tight, greedy hole swallow my fingers. What else can I put in there? There were anal beads in your drawer. I want to play with you."

"Anything," Rod gasped out as he pushed backward, fucking himself on Landon's fingers. "Anything you want."

"Later. I can't even make it to the room right now."

Rod gasped when Landon pulled his fingers free…but then his tongue was there, pushing inside Rod's hungry asshole.

It felt like everything.

It also wasn't enough.

Landon licked up and down his crease, went between Rod's legs and licked his taint. He felt Landon's hot breath against his balls and nearly fucking lost it. "I need to come."

"Jesus, me too. My nuts feel like they're going to fucking explode. I don't have condoms or lube out here, though, so we're going to have to make do." Landon licked him again, wetting his hole and the crease of his ass. He stood, pulled down his own pants, not even taking them all the way off. They rested below his ass, the denim rubbing the backs of Rod's legs as Landon spit.

He rubbed his bare cock up and down the crease of Rod's ass. "Jack off," Landon told him, and Rod did, jerking his aching dick with strong pulls. "You're so fucking sexy, I could come just like this. Just rubbing my prick against your ass and thinking about that hot, hole of yours."

That was enough for Rod right there. He came in two long spurts, groaning out Landon's name as he did. And then Landon's hand was there, jerking with him, gathering up his come before his hand was gone. When Rod felt the slick rubbing of Landon's shaft again, he knew he was using Rod's spunk as lube.

Landon's arms were around him, holding him as he thrust once, twice, three times and then hot jets of his come squirted onto Rod's back and ass.

They both stood there, breathing heavily for a long moment before Landon said, "Sorry. I didn't mean to do that right now. I really did want to eat, but you looked so damn sexy, I couldn't help it. Everything about you is addictive. I can't get enough."

The words filled Rod's chest. Made a home there, pushing blood through his heart. He wanted what Landon said to be true. "Then why are you apologizing? That was…" Incredible. Different. Every-fucking-thing. "Hot." Did he really just settle on hot?

Landon chuckled. "You can say that again. Take another shower with me, then we can make some dinner and eat."

The fullness in his chest spread out, filled him. "Okay…yeah, that sounds good."

It sounded better than fucking good.

CHAPTER TWENTY-NINE

"Holy shit. I think I'm in love. Mind if I move into your spare bedroom?" Landon looked around Bryce's set up in his garage. The space was a wet dream come true. He had three bikes, two of his own and one he apparently bought to fix up. It looked like a mini shop with everything you'd need to sit and play with bikes all day. Bryce lived in motorcycle heaven.

"Beautiful isn't it? When Nick and I first moved in, and I finished the garage, I slept out here. Jacked off twice to the scent and visual of tools, bikes, and all that fucking metal. Nick epoxied the floor for me as a surprise."

Landon had no idea if Bryce was serious about the jerking off thing, and he didn't care. Hell, if Bryce wasn't here, he just might have to rub one out himself. It was incredible. He wanted his own set up like this. "I was serious. I'm moving in. I do dishes."

"You do?" Rod cut in. "Why haven't I seen that yet?"

Landon wrapped an arm around his shoulder, pulled him close and kissed his forehead. "I washed dishes this morning." He'd spent the last week at Rod's place. When his mom was home, he sometimes went and spent a few hours with her between the time he got off work at the shop and Rod was finished at the store, but he always ended up at Rod's at some point. He liked sharing a bed with the man. Liked being able to fuck him every night, to watch movies with him, and talk to him, so that's what he did.

"You're right. I'll have to find something else to complain about then."

"Do you want to borrow some of the annoying habits Bryce has?" Nick asked, and all four men laughed.

They finished their tour of Bryce's garage before they made their way back into the house.

"I got steaks. They've been marinating all night. Bryce is going to throw them on the grill in a bit. I made some pasta salad as well. I hope that's okay." Nick looked over his shoulder as they walked.

"When he says pasta salad, he's not talking about that shit most people make. Nick has his own recipe. It's fucking incredible just like everything he makes. I'm surprised I haven't gotten fat yet." Bryce put his hands on Nick's shoulders and squeezed. "It'll be good. You guys will love it."

"Sounds perfect to me. I'll eat anything," Landon replied. When he rubbed his thumb against fabric, Landon realized he had his hand on Rod's back. That he'd reached out and touched him the same way maybe Nick and Bryce would do. It wasn't something he'd ever really done, just hold someone like that or to touch them for no reason, but now it was a reflex when it came to Rod.

They went to the living room and hung out for a while, before Bryce announced that it was time to put the steaks on, so they made their way to the backyard. It was a beautiful yard, with a large deck and two outdoor tables. "Think you have enough space?" Landon nodded toward the tables.

"We both have big families," Bryce replied and it reminded Landon of what Bryce had said about one of Nick's sisters before. He couldn't believe he'd forgotten to ask about it. He wanted to now, but wasn't sure if it was appropriate. If things hadn't gone well, he didn't want to bring up the painful memory.

"How are things going with that, by the way?" Rod asked, looking at Nick with a sad smile.

"Okay. I saw my sister Michelle, once back at the beginning of the summer. It was the first time I met her youngest child. I've tried a couple times since, but she always makes up an excuse. It's a start, I guess."

Landon could see the tension in Bryce as Nick spoke. It killed him that Nick was going through the situation, that much was obvious. Landon couldn't fathom what that was like, how it would feel not to have support that way. His heart went out to Nick and Rod both, because he knew Rod had suffered more than he'd told Landon about as well.

"It'll get better. I know it, but Christ it pisses me the fuck off." Bryce's hands were in tight fists as he spoke. "Nick is the best person I know. Don't like me. Don't be around me. That's fine, but not him. That is not fucking fine with me. Anyone who doesn't want to spend every fucking second with Nick can't know him, not the way I do."

Landon could feel the passion in Bryce's words, feel the love that dripped from them, the love that gave them life. Jesus, to feel that...to have that...he looked over at Rod who sat in one of the chairs. He was looking toward the back of the yard, away from them all.

"Hey," he heard Nick say to Bryce, but Landon kept his eyes on Rod. "We're good. It'll all be okay somehow. All I know is I have you and I wouldn't change that for anything. I don't want anything to do with someone who doesn't see how incredible you are or how our love is the realest fucking love there is."

At that Rod looked up and turned toward Landon. He was transfixed with him, with the way Rod's serious blue eyes held him. He put on a front for the world. Landon saw that. Not that he didn't like to laugh and have fun, but he had buried pain that he only showed in glimpses like he did now. They hid in the shadows of his normally happy eyes, and Landon felt the need inside him build. The need to evict anything that had ever hurt Rod from his memories and to leave nothing but happiness in their wake. He wanted to protect him and care for him, and let Rod do the same things for him. He wanted Rod to prove his past thoughts to be false. Wanted Rod to show him how to not be afraid to love. Wanted Rod to show him people could be happy, that maybe they could be happy together.

"I love you," he heard Bryce say softly in the background. The words were like a pebble thrown into a lake. They made small waves, little echoes that floated out and into Landon, making him wonder if that's what he felt for Rod.

Before he could say anything, or do anything, not that he knew what he would say or do, Rod stood up, putting on that sham of a smile he wore when he didn't really feel it. "Bryce is fucking amazing. Nick is fucking amazing. Anyone who doesn't see it doesn't know what they're talking about. Oh, and me. I'm pretty amazing too."

"Hey! What about me?" Landon asked. "Everyone is amazing except for me?" He tried to lighten the mood because he knew that was what Rod needed right now. Later he would get the man to talk to him, though.

Rod winked at him. "You're all right."

Somehow, all right was exactly what he needed.

***

Rod couldn't remember the last time he'd laughed so much. They'd cooked, eaten, talked, played a couple games of poker, and now as the sun was going down, he sat on Landon's lap in one of the outside chairs while they visited some more with Nick and Bryce.

"You should have seen Nick's face the first time they came into the store," Rod told Landon as Nick gave him the evil eye from across the table.

"I don't think he needs details," Nick said before Bryce continued.

"I think he does need details."

"I thought he was going to run out. Either run away or vomit all over himself." Rod told Landon who laughed with his arms around

Rod's waist. It was such a foreign feeling, having someone hold him as he sat with friends. Rod wanted to savor all of it. He didn't want it to go away.

"Can you blame me? The way Bryce just spit it out like that? He told the whole store about our sex life." Rod could tell that Nick tried to sound frustrated, but really he didn't mind the conversation.

"I told Rod about our sex life, and his shirt told me to." Bryce responded.

"Huh? His shirt told you to?" Landon sat up straighter, pulling Rod closer against him.

"His shirt said *Ask me about my favorite products.* Considering we were new to the whole thing, and were in need of some products to help us out, I thought it was a good idea. You should have something like that at Rods-N-Ends. I liked it."

"Hmm... I'll see what I can think of. It sparked some really interesting conversations, and even got me a phone number or two." The second the words slipped past Rod's lips, he'd wished he'd swallowed them down, because the truth was, he didn't want anyone else's phone number. Not now. Now while he had Landon.

"Hey," Landon nipped the back of his neck and Rod shivered. That drove him fucking wild, feeling Landon's teeth against his skin.

"Not that I want any phone numbers. Wow, that's the first time I've said something like that."

"Crazy, isn't it?" Bryce asked. "Threw me for a fucking loop when I fell in love with Nick and realized I wouldn't ever want anyone but him."

Rod's heartbeat stumbled at the word love. Landon wasn't in love with him and he wasn't in love with Landon. Landon couldn't be in love with him. They'd only recently decided to date. Hell, Rod had practically had to bribe the man to get him into bed in the beginning.

"My how the tables have turned. Who looks like they're going to vomit all over themselves now?" Nick asked.

"Aww, I'm crushed," Landon said playfully. "The thought of me makes you sick?"

Nothing about Landon made him sick, and the truth was, not wanting phone numbers felt okay too.

"Don't worry, Landon. You'll wear him down eventually. I did with Nick," Bryce teased.

"I'm working on it," Landon replied, and Rod sat there dumbstruck yet again by Landon Harrison.

CHAPTER THIRTY

"I need to throw in a load of laundry. Do you want me to wash anything for you?" Rod asked when they got home late that night. He'd forgotten to wash any of his work clothes before they left earlier today.

Landon came around the corner to their room—shit, Rod's room and replied, "Yeah, I'll gather up a few things. Colors or whites?"

"Does it matter?"

"What?" Landon's dark eyes held a spark of surprise. "Yes, it matters. You wash your colors with your whites?"

"Doesn't everyone?" His father had never taught him to separate his laundry before doing it. He'd heard people talk about it, but thought it was one of those things people spoke about but didn't really happen.

"You're crazy. Sit down on the bed. I'll take care of the laundry."

Rod sat and Landon went to the pile of clothes in the corner of the room. He began making different stacks, splitting the piles between dark colors, whites, and light colors. "How old were you when you lost your mom?" Landon didn't look at him, just continued to toss clothes into different piles.

Ah hell. Were they really going to do this? He preferred staying in the present. The past wasn't his favorite place to be. "Eight. Nick and Bryce are great, aren't they?"

Landon glanced at him then and frowned. "They are. Not sure how we got from your mom to Nick and Bryce."

"How did we get from laundry to my mom?" Rod countered, and Landon sighed. He was upsetting Landon, he realized that, but he wasn't sure he could do anything about it right now.

Landon began working with the clothes again. They were washing their clothes together—Landon's mixed with Rod's. He wasn't sure why that hit him like a ton of bricks all of a sudden, but it did.

"Let me in, Rod. We're friends first and foremost. But we're also lovers. I spend ninety percent of my time with you, my nights in your bed. This is new for me too, but I'm here, I'm trying. I'm not running or hiding. Let me in."

Landon spoke the truth. Rod knew that. He also knew that Landon deserved more than he gave him. Hell, he deserved more than Rod all together. Still, anger lit a fire inside of him. "You're in. You've been in every fucking night! I just don't see why we can't leave the past in the past."

"Because you don't leave it there!" Landon's voice vibrated loudly through the room, as he repeated, "You don't leave it there. You may think you do, but you don't, Rod. It affects you. It affects us, and you turn everything we talk about into sex every damn time." Landon dropped Rod's work shirt from his hand. He was pissed. The anger blazed in his eyes, in the sound of his voice.... And there, inside Rod was this ache, this desire to open himself up to Landon. To tell him how much he hurt, and how fucking scared he really was every damn day of his life.

He didn't think he could do that though.

"What do you want me to do? Tell you that every fucking day from fourteen until I left home, my father looked at me with hate in his eyes? That I disgusted him, and that he had no problem telling me? That the older I got, the worse it got? That he told me he was glad my mother died so I couldn't break her heart? I was a disgrace, Landon. A faggot, a queer. I wanted to wear makeup for God's sake! There had to be something wrong with me!"

He sucked in a deep breath, knew he should stop, but didn't. "He said I would never feel love and no one would ever love me because I was wrong and sinful. I was dirty, especially when I started fucking, because yeah, I'm an asshole and I didn't hide it from him. He knew when I let men use me and he knew I fucking loved it, so yeah, he was right in some ways. I like being dirty. I like fucking. No amount of talk and dragging up the past is going to change that."

Now that he'd started, he couldn't stop. Memories built in his head, water in a tub filling higher and higher until it spilled over.

Rod shoved to his feet. "I was so fucking scared when I realized who I was, Landon. Scared and confused. I needed him. I needed my father. I thought he could fix it, or that he would tell me that the mixed up feelings going on inside me were okay. I was fourteen years old, a fucking kid, and I spilled my goddamned guts to him. With tears pouring down my face I told him what I was feeling, begged for him to tell me it was okay, and he pushed me away. Told me that as long as that's who I was, that I would never be okay. There would always be something wrong with me, and I wasn't a son of his. I haven't depended on anyone since that day. I haven't needed anyone since that day. I don't know if I can change that."

His chest hurt. His gut clenched. He was pushing Landon away. He realized that, but he couldn't do anything about it. He had to be honest. This was who he was. The sooner Landon realized that, he could be on his way and leave Rod behind.

He waited for Landon to speak. Waited for, and maybe hoped that Landon could somehow make him believe he was wrong. When no words came, Rod took a step, then another, and another. He made it all the way to his bedroom door before Landon's voice stopped him. "I think I'm falling in love with you."

Rod closed his eyes. Sucked in a deep breath...and wished Landon was right. *I can't...I can't love you if you're like this. No one will.* If his own father couldn't love him, how could anyone else?

"You think wrong."

He heard him exhale deeply. "Fuck you, Rod. Don't tell me how I feel. You're this pulse in my chest that doesn't go away. Even when

I'm not with you, I feel you there. The traces of you are imprinted inside me. Your father was wrong and I'm going to prove it to you."

Rod couldn't move, couldn't breathe. He wanted that, Jesus, he fucking wanted it. Even if it couldn't happen, no one had ever wanted to attempt it before. But Landon did. This gorgeous, sexy, fucking man wanted to try, and he just didn't understand how that was possible. "Thank you. For this, whatever we are. Whatever happens, thank you for everything."

"I'm going to prove you wrong, Rod. Maybe it can fix what's broken inside of me too."

Rod wanted to be wrong. He'd never wanted anything as much as he wanted to be wrong about this. He turned, and this time the measured steps he took were to Landon. When he reached him, Rod dropped his forehead against the other man's shoulder. "I'm sorry. I was a dick. It's not easy for me."

Landon wrapped an arm around him and kissed the top of his head. He'd never known how fucking incredible a kiss to the head could feel. "I know. Hey, my sister's wedding is in a couple weeks. We want you to go too. I'm going to need a date and since we're dating..."

"Okay," Rod said softly, still leaning his forehead against Landon's shoulder.

Landon pressed another kiss to his hair and then said, "Can I finish showing you how to do laundry the right way now? Seriously, you're fucking killing me with this shit. My mom would lose her mind if I told her."

Rod couldn't help but smile. "Don't tell her. I think she likes me, and I don't want to fuck that up." He pulled away. "Finish. I'm watching. I'll even take notes."

They continued separating the clothes and then Landon threw the first load in the washer. Then they stripped and climbed into bed together.

"When I hear things like what you just told me, it makes me feel like my own shit is so fucking petty. He left...so what? But it's hard." Landon rolled to his side, and Rod did as well. They lay there facing each other, the pain etched in lines on Landon's face.

"I hate him. I fucking hate him for what he did. Don't leave." Landon's arms wound tightly around him. "Don't leave."

They didn't part the rest of the night.

CHAPTER THIRTY-ONE

The next couple weeks were crazy. Landon was back and forth between work, Rod's, and helping his mom and Shanen with the wedding.

Weddings were no fucking joke. He didn't realize how many last minute things there would be to do, and he could see how much it wore on both Shanen and his mom. Especially his mother though. She looked exhausted, with heavy bags under her eyes. She wasn't sleeping either. The few nights he stayed home, he heard her up doing things halfway through the night.

It worried him. She seemed to be okay though. She was taking her medication. She wasn't overly stressed. From what he could tell, she was just a mom who wanted the perfect wedding for her only daughter. The marriage she never had herself.

When she made her way into the kitchen, looking half asleep, Landon said, "Maybe you've been overdoing it with your group, work, and the wedding. You need a day off. What can I do to help you?"

She waved a hand at him as though he was being ridiculous. "You have to work. What can you do?"

"I can try." He watched as she took her medication.

"I'm just going to be home most of the day. I'm putting together the centerpieces and a few of the other decorative pieces. I'll be fine."

"Is Shan coming over to help?" Landon stood, went to the coffee pot and poured her a cup.

"She'll be here later this afternoon. She really wants to come, but she has to work. Plus, Jacob's parents just got back into town. Shanen didn't say much, but apparently there's some kind of drama between Jacob and his brother."

Landon nodded, wondering if there was a way he could call Bryce and take the day off. He didn't like the slump in his mom's body, or the tiredness in her voice. "What about Rod? Is it something he could help with? He's off today. I know he wouldn't mind giving you a hand."

His mom looked at him as though she didn't know him, her eyes pinched and her nose wrinkled...and then an ear-to-ear smile pulled at her mouth.

Oh shit.

"You're serious about him, aren't you, Lando?"

He'd wanted to avoid this. Honestly, talking with her about it was one of the last things he wanted to do, but lying about Rod, didn't feel right either. "I care about him. He's important to me." He was falling in love with him. He was also afraid to let Rod down. Like

Landon had told Rod, he was there and he wasn't hiding, but that didn't mean he didn't worry this was a mistake, that it could go wrong or that they would just end up hurting each other. He'd seen it happen before, and now, especially after he learned more about Rod's past, the thought of hurting him was a constant fear threatening to pull him under.

"But?" she asked, and again, he really didn't want to do this. It didn't feel right to talk to her about things Rod was dealing with and he sure as shit didn't want to talk about his own issues. Bringing up his dad, especially now when she was so tired and had so many things going on, was a bad idea.

"But nothing. We're taking it slow and will see what happens. I don't know where we're going, if I'm being honest. I just know that he makes me happy and I want to do the same thing for him." He made Landon feel things he'd never felt. Made him want things he never thought he'd want.

Landon turned to get the creamer out of the fridge. When he looked at his mom again, he saw the tears in her eyes. Oh hell. He definitely hadn't wanted this. "Please don't. I don't want you to get excited or to get your hopes up."

"Funny because I just want *you* happy, Landon. That's all I've ever wanted. You haven't been truly happy since you were a kid and neither of us should pretend otherwise."

She was right about that. He and Rod had that in common. They both hid behind their pasts, both liked to pretend it didn't affect their lives, but it did. How could it not? "I'm fine, Ma. I've always been fine, okay?"

She sighed. "I'm so afraid of hurting you. Of hurting you and Shanen both. I don't know what to do sometimes. I've messed up, Landon, messed up a lot. My actions have hurt you and Shanen, but I love you both. I love you more than anything. I hope you know that."

Landon tried to stamp down the anger burning through him like a wildfire. "It wasn't your fault. You didn't do anything wrong. He left. It was his decision."

"Your father loves you. I know he does. No one is perfect."

"No offense, Mom, but fuck him. He doesn't love us. He abandoned us." And Landon was afraid he would be just like him. "Listen, I need to go. Do you want me to call Rod to see if he can help you today? I think he'd like it." Landon knew he would.

"No." She shook her head. "I'll be fine. Call me after work and let me know if you're coming home or heading to Rod's, would you? That way I don't worry."

"I'll come home. I can try to help with whatever you haven't finished."

She nodded, opened her mouth as though she was going to say something, but then just hugged him instead.

Landon stopped his bike when he got to the end of the driveway, and pulled out his phone. Rod answered with, "My bed is lonely without you. I'm not sure if that's a good thing."

"It is," Landon told him, because he liked sleeping with Rod too. "I can't talk long. I'm going to be late for work, but I wanted to ask you a favor. Shanen won't be able to help my mom until late today and she has some centerpieces or something like that she has to put together for the wedding. I have no idea what in the fuck that means, but I was wondering if you could maybe come and help her... I'm a little worried about her. I don't want her to be alone." It was so hard to tell if she was going to go through one of her dark periods again. He hadn't been through one with her in years, because he'd left, just like his father.

"You want me to go and spend the day with your mom?" Rod asked.

"Yeah...fuck, I'm sorry. I know that's putting my shit into your lap. If you can't, I understand, but I—"

"Yes," Rod cut him off. "I'd love to help her."

They were both quiet for a moment, somehow having a silent conversation through the line. *I trust you. I need you. Thank you.*

It was Landon who broke their silence. "I appreciate it."

"Of course. Let's just hope it doesn't make your sister hate me! Crafts and I don't mix. They might look scary when I'm finished with them."

Landon laughed at that. "Just visit with her and that will be enough. She's determined that she's fine. She doesn't know you're coming. Blame it on me, okay?"

"Oh hell, what in the fuck did you get me into?" Rod asked.

Landon shook his head. "You'll be fine, I don't have a doubt about that." With a smile on his face, he hung up the phone and drove away.

***

It took Rod nearly two hours to get to Landon's mom's house. He'd gotten out of bed, showered and changed before heading out, and of course there had been a car accident that had a road closed. He'd had to turn around and go back a different direction.

He was nervous as hell. He hadn't been joking when he told Landon he wouldn't know the first thing about helping her put together centerpieces. What in the hell had he been thinking sending Rod?

And that was besides the fact that spending time with the mother of a guy he was fucking was so far out of his reality, that it might as well mean he could fly. *Dating...the guy I am dating.* He still couldn't get used to that word. It was another fucking mystical experience that was made for fiction.

But he wanted to go. Wanted to go so fucking badly it was probably a little pathetic.

Rod turned down the driveway that he'd only been down once before. As soon as the house came within view, he was surprised to see Joy standing by a car, with another man leaning against it. Both their heads snapped up at the same time, two sets of frantic eyes watching him.

Oh fuck. Something was up here. He could tell by their expression, could tell by the way the man tried to hurriedly get into the car, but Joy held on to him.

For a brief second, Rod considered backing the hell out of there. Something was up, but then Joy raised a timid hand to wave at him and he figured he had to keep going. "Gee thanks, Landon. What did you get me into?" Of course, he'd go help out a guy he was dating for the first time and pull up to see something he was pretty sure he wasn't supposed to be seeing.

Rod turned off the car, and got out. "Hey... Sorry to interrupt. Landon asked me to stop by and..." Holy hell. Holy fucking shit. The closer he got, the more he was able to make out the man who stood next to Joy. He knew that face. Knew that same curve to the jaw, the same dark hair, and the same dimple under the left side of his mouth. The only difference was he was thinner, gaunt, unhealthy.

He was looking at Landon's father. The man he hadn't seen in years. The man he hated. The man who Rod was pretty sure was dying.

Joy sighed. "Rod, this is Landon's father, Larry. Larry, this is your son's boyfriend, Rod."

Larry coughed, cleared this throat and then held out his hand. "It's nice to meet you, Rod. Joy's told me a bit about you."

Rod couldn't make himself reach out, couldn't make himself shake Larry's hand. Not at first. It felt like a betrayal to Landon. "He doesn't know?" Rod asked, standing still. Of course he didn't know. Landon would have said something. He had to believe that.

"No." Larry shook his head. "Not yet."

Fuck. How in the hell was he supposed to do this? How could he know that Landon's dad was not only back, but sick, without telling

242

Landon? "Don't ask me to lie to him. I can't lie to him." Jesus, how could he keep this from Landon? It would fucking wreck him. It would wreck Rod to see him hurt so badly.

"Maybe we should go." Following the sound of the voice, Rod looked down for the first time to see a man in the driver's seat. A dark-haired man who looked a whole hell of a lot like Landon and Larry for Rod's comfort.

Acid burned his esophagus, making its way down to his gut. A brother? Jesus, fucking Christ. A brother? "No. I should go. I can't do this." Every second he stood there he felt as though he was stabbing Landon in the back, shoving the knife deeper and deeper, so deep that Rod himself bled. Because Landon bleeding meant he was hurt too. Landon's pain would be his own.

Rod turned and started walking back to his car. Oh fuck. He was in love with him. He'd let himself fall in love with Landon.

"Rod, wait! Please, don't go. Let me explain." Joy's broken voice made him halt, but he couldn't turn around. If he didn't he could deny what he saw, deny knowing something that would break Landon. Maybe even deny that Rod was in love with him.

"Please, don't go," Joy said, stopping next to him. "Let me explain. I need to explain."

He heard a car start, watching as Larry, and the brother who Landon didn't know he had drove away. When the car was out of sight, Rod nodded. "This is going to kill him."

Joy closed her eyes, and a tear rolled down her cheek. "I know. Please, come inside with me."

Rod went.

CHAPTER THIRTY-TWO

"Do you want something to drink?" Joy asked Rod as they made it inside.

"No, thank you. I don't think I can keep this from him. Not Landon." Landon was the only person who was always there for him. Landon made him wish for things he never thought he'd have.

Joy gave him a sad smile. "Does it sound crazy that I'm glad to hear that?"

Rod wasn't sure how to respond to that so he didn't.

"You love him, don't you?" He did. God help him, he fucking did. *I can't...I can't love you if you're like this. No one will.*

Rod closed his eyes, trying to quiet his father's voice in his brain. He hadn't thought about the things he used to say in so long. Not until Landon came into his life. Not until someone made him feel.

"Don't answer that. You don't have to answer it for me to know. I'm glad. Landon deserves to be happy. He loves you too."

"No." Rod shook his head. Maybe he thought he might, but he

couldn't.

"Have a seat." Rod opened his mouth to tell her he couldn't, but before he could, she said, "Please."

He nodded once and then sat in one of the chairs at the kitchen table. "I assume Landon had told you about his father and I?"

"Yes."

"See? He wouldn't do that if you weren't important to him. I know my son."

He's important to me.

"I got a phone call from his father a few months back. It was right before Shanen moved out and Landon came back. It was the first time I'd spoken with him since he left. I was shocked and angry. I didn't understand why he was coming back into the picture now. And if I'm being honest, I was afraid. I was just about to get Landon back and now here Larry was, threatening that. It killed Landon when his father left, and I know part of him has to be angry at me for it, too. He would never admit it, but how could he not be?" She wiped her eyes.

"Anyway, I wouldn't listen to Larry the first time he called. It was selfish and I know that. I was just getting Landon back, and I didn't want anything to come between that."

"He loves you," Rod told her. "You're his mother. He wouldn't do that."

She nodded before continuing. "From there I got another phone call. It was from Justin. He's Landon's half brother."

They looked too close in age for Rod's comfort. Landon's dad left when Landon was twelve. There was no way the two men were over twelve years apart.

"I can see you working it out in your head. That was a hard pill for me to swallow. Larry was a truck driver for a few years. He met Justin's mom on one of those trips. They had a one-night stand, and he came home to us. She found him after Larry left us and told him about Justin. He's been raised by their father since he was eight. Do you know what that's going to do to my son? The fact that Larry was the father to him that Landon needed?"

It was Rod's turn to close his eyes this time, the pain in his chest almost too heavy to bear. "Yes, I know what it will do to him." He already felt unwanted, similar to the way Rod did. It wasn't that Justin didn't deserve his father...both men did. Rod had, too.

"Justin told me he was sick—lung cancer. He's dying. That's what changed things for me...that and the fact that I still love him. Despite everything I have always loved him. I will always love him."

"Why doesn't Landon know he's back?" When Joy winced, he said, "I don't mean to sound unsympathetic, but—"

"You're thinking of Landon as you should be. Larry asked me not to tell them yet. With Landon just moving back, and Shanen getting married, he thought it was better to wait until after the wedding. How can he spring the fact that he's back, dying, and that they have a brother right now? Maybe we're selfish and looking for an excuse to put it off, but it felt right to Larry, and I agree with him on that."

Rod didn't know if he agreed or not. Hell, it wasn't his place to agree or not.

"I've been helping take care of him. Justin has a lot on his plate. He's losing his father. Larry is dying. He's receiving chemo to prolong his life, but the truth is, he's going to die. That brings a lot of clarity to a person. He has a lot of regrets. He's trying to make up for them. He wants to get to know his children. We're going to tell them. Shanen and Jacob will be gone for a week on their honeymoon. When they get back, we're going to tell Landon and Shanen both."

Rod rested his elbows on the table, and looked at her. Jesus, how could he do this? "How can I keep this from him? How can I look him in the eye and know the father who abandoned him is back, sick, and that Landon has a brother he didn't know about?"

He was surprised when Joy reached over and held his hand. "Please. I know it's wrong and I know it's a lot to put on you. Let us have this time to figure things out, and then we'll tell him. It might not sound like it, but we really want to do what's right for our children. Maybe we're wrong. Maybe we're not, but we're trying."

Conflicting thoughts warred inside him. Rod didn't know what to do, what to think. What the fuck was the right thing?

"I'll respect your decision whatever you decide. I can see how much he means to you. That's all I've ever wanted—a better life for both Shanen and Landon than I had for myself."

She squeezed his hand again and then stood. "You don't have to answer me. Just do what you think is best. I'll understand either way. Now, can you help me put together these damn centerpieces? The wedding is in a week and we still have a thousand things to do."

Rod had no clue what he was going to do. Still, he got up, followed Joy to the living room, and got ready to fuck up some centerpieces.

***

Rod had been acting strange all week. They'd gone out riding on his new bike once, and Rod had practiced driving it again. It was the only real time they got to spend together besides the couple nights Landon had stayed at his place, and that time was mostly spent sleeping.

Now, it was the day of the wedding and they were getting ready to go. Rod was lagging behind, and they needed to leave in about ten minutes or they were going to be late. He couldn't be late for his sister's wedding. She'd threatened him with bodily harm at the rehearsal the night before. Every time Landon mentioned the time, Rod blew it off like things were fine, but they really fucking weren't. Rod had already skipped out of the rehearsal dinner with him last night. Yeah, he'd had to work, but couldn't he have tried to rearrange the schedule? Landon didn't know if he was asking too much for wanting that or not. They were both so fucking green when it came to the relationship thing. He felt like they were screwing up at every turn. "If you don't want to go, all you have to do is say so." Maybe it was too much expecting Rod at his sister's wedding. All he knew was that he wanted him there.

Rod looked over at Landon from where he stood in front of the bathroom sink, putting toothpaste on his toothbrush. "What are you talking about?"

"This is the second time you've brushed your teeth. It never takes you this long to get ready. You've been acting distant all week. If you don't want to go, tell me. If this is too much, tell me. I don't know what I'm doing here. I've never done this. Half the time, I'm afraid I'm going at you full fucking throttle and need to back up, the other half the time I think I'm being too lax. It's like I'm on a one-way street going the wrong direction. I'm fucking lost in all of this, and if you don't tell me what you're thinking, we're going to crash and burn."

"This is really the second time I've brushed my teeth?" Rod asked. There was silence and then the both of them started laughing. Landon's cheeks hurt he laughed so hard. It was Rod who settled down first, and said, "I want to go. You have to know that. There's just a lot going on up here." He tapped the side of his head. "Even more than you know, and I'm just trying to figure it all out. Hoping like hell I'm doing the right thing, but I want to go with you. It's frightening how much I want to be there with you. I'm nervous though. That much I can't deny."

Immediately it felt like Landon could breathe again, like he caught breath that had eluded him. "Shifting gears, remember? That's what we're doing. And I want you there, too. Now would you hurry the hell up and finish getting ready so we can go? Shanen will kick my ass if I'm late. She's already under a lot of stress with Jacobs's family. His brother Andrew skipped out on the rehearsal dinner last night. I'm not sure what's going on there."

Rod rinsed his toothbrush off and tossed it in the cup. After taking a deep breath, he turned to look at Landon, the nerves clear as day on his face. "Let's go. I'm ready. I don't want to make you late."

Jesus, they acted like they were going to war or something. It was a wedding. There was no reason they should be this unsure. He wanted Rod relaxed. Wanted Rod to know he could be himself. Landon didn't move from the doorway. This wouldn't do. "You're ready?"

"Well, Christ. I thought I was. Is there something wrong with the way I look?" He glanced back in the mirror and started to finger his short, dark hair. "I think I look fucking hot. I'd do me." He ran a hand down his long-sleeved, button-down, white shirt. It covered the tattoos he had on the front of his forearm. His suit jacket lay on the arm of the living room couch with Landon's.

He was fucking gorgeous. That was a fact. He loved the way the suit hugged Rod's frame, which was slightly smaller than his own. Loved that his short hair was mussed from his hand. "You do look hot. I'd definitely fuck you, but I think something is missing." Landon picked up the black eyeliner from the counter. He had a feeling Rod wanted to wear it, but maybe he didn't because of the fact that they were going to Shanen's wedding. "I'd do it for you, but I don't know how."

"You don't want me to wear that to your sister's wedding. They're getting married in a church for Christ's sake." Rod shook his head.

Landon stepped closer. "People can't wear makeup in a

church?"

"Men can't."

The steely distance in his voice told Landon this was what part of the problem was. Maybe it reminded him of his dad, or his past, but they were here and now, and he wanted to keep them in this place. "I beg to differ. I really fucking do want you to wear it, and who gives a shit if we're going to be in a church? You are who you are and not a person at that wedding will care and if they do, fuck them."

When Rod didn't look completely convinced he added, "One of the things I love about you the most is that you are who you are. You earned that right, Rod. Put the fucking eyeliner on before I try to do it for you."

"You'll make us late."

He smiled. "It will be worth the bodily harm inflicted on me. You can save me the pain and just do it. I want you to wear it. It makes my dick hard. You know that. Put it on."

He practically saw the switch click in Rod, saw him make the decision to do what he wanted. "Christ you're fucking bossy." Still, he reached out and grabbed the eyeliner.

"When I want something, I'm determined."

Rod rolled his eyes at Landon and then Landon watched as Rod put a black line on the top and bottom of his lids. He tossed it to the counter, and then asked, "Better?"

Goddamn he was fucking sexy. "Perfect. Now let's go. I'm telling them it's your fault if we're late."

CHAPTER THIRTY-THREE

Rod sat in the first row feeling incredibly out of place. They had assured him that they wanted him here. They'd said Landon and Shanen didn't have much family, and that he belonged.

Belonged. Family. Those were two words that he hadn't felt since he was fourteen. Hell, maybe even since before that, when his mom passed away. He and his father had never been close. Rod had never been the son he wanted; coming out at fourteen had only cemented that. His dad had probably always known who Rod was.

But this was different. He was sitting here in the front row, watching as Landon gave his sister away. Sitting where Landon's family should sit. Where Joy and Landon would be in a moment. Where Larry and Justin should be, only Landon and Shanen didn't know that one was back and the other existed. The guilt from that was eating him alive every fucking day.

Landon deserved to know, and Rod should have told him...he thought. Fuck, he didn't know. No matter what he did it felt like it would be the wrong thing, so he'd kept his mouth shut ever since he found out.

He watched the ceremony, feeling strangely comfortable in his own skin, on one hand, and that was because of Landon. Thinking of that made the guilt steamroll him again. Because the other part of him felt like he was betraying Landon every day.

Rod kept his eyes firmly on him. He was so goddamned beautiful it almost hurt to look at him. His tall, muscular frame. His strong hands, and the way they flexed in nerves. Rod still couldn't believe that this man wanted to share his bed, that he continued to share it, to be there...Rod was starting to believe that maybe this could be real. That maybe Landon could feel for Rod a fraction of what Rod felt for him.

A moment later, Landon was sitting beside him, his hand on Rod's thigh as they continued to watch. Soon the pastor told Jacob he could kiss the bride, and everyone was standing and clapping as they walked back down the aisle. Rod felt a tightening in his chest. Felt the truth settling in there, making space for itself, carving out a spot for it to call home.

He didn't know if he ever wanted this—the whole marriage thing, but it became fiercely obvious that he did want one thing, that he did have one thing. Love. He loved the man standing beside him right now. Loved him in ways he didn't think were possible, ways that he'd been told he would never have.

Landon's strong, calloused hand was suddenly against his cheek. "Hey, you look lost in thought. Are you okay?"

Rod looked at him, and for the first time in his life, he one hundred percent was okay. He was doing the right thing, he told himself. He loved Landon and he only wanted what was best for him. He should let his family be the ones to talk to him about his dad. "Yeah...yeah, I'm good."

Landon lowered his hand. "I'm glad to hear it because I have a feeling things are about to get really fucking crazy around here."

"Oooh, do tell! I'm curious about the Jacob family drama. The brother has some serious heartache going on."

Landon looked on the other side of the aisle where Jacob's family congregated. "How do you know?"

Rod took in the other man. He was tall, sinewy, with blond hair, and a scowl. "I know because I'm good."

Landon wrapped an arm around him. "You're mine."

***

"The centerpieces are gorgeous. You did these?" Jacobs's mom asked Landon's. He felt like an ass, but he couldn't remember what the woman's name was.

"Thank you," his mom replied. "I had some help from Rod. He saved me because they were a lot harder than I thought they would be."

Landon felt Rod tense up. He frowned at him, silently asking what was wrong. But then, that was Rod, wasn't it? He loved attention but he liked it on his terms, and didn't do well with compliments.

"That was nice of you, Rod." The woman smiled at him, but then returned her attention to Landon's mom. Jacob's family had a lot of money. His parents traveled most of the year, which was why Landon hadn't met them until recently.

"I was happy to help."

They'd made their way to the hall Jacob and Shanen rented for the reception about two hours before. Landon was already exhausted and wanted to go home and crawl into bed, but this was his sister's wedding, so obviously he couldn't.

"Do you want to go sit down for a minute?" Landon asked and Rod nodded. They moved toward their table. Everyone else milled around talking and eating. "Broken heart, huh?" Landon nodded to the corner where Jacobs's brother Andrew sat alone, wondering if Rod was right about him.

"I don't know. He's obviously not happy to be here."

"I got lucky with Shanen. She was always a great sister. She would have done anything for me. I don't think Andrew and Jacob are close. Makes it easy that it was always just Shan and me."

Rod tried to hide it, but Landon saw him flinch, and he immediately felt like shit. Rod had grown up without a sibling. He'd grown up alone even though his father was there the whole time. He didn't mean to remind him of that.

It was then that they announced the first dance. He wrapped an arm around Rod's shoulders as they watched his sister dance with Jacob for the first time as a married couple. The next dance, Shanen called him up with her.

He squeezed Rod's shoulder and then walked up to Shanen. He

held his hand out for her, and she smiled before taking it and Landon pulled her close.

This should be their father here doing this with her. It wasn't that Landon didn't want to. He wasn't lying when he told Rod he was incredibly lucky to have her, but he just wished she had more. "I'm sorry I'm not him," Landon whispered as they danced.

"I'm not. Even if he was here right now, I'd want this dance with you. You're my best friend, Lando. The best brother a girl could ask for."

He didn't feel like it. He hadn't felt like it since he was a kid. "I'm sorry I left."

"Why? You had every right to leave. I chose to stay. You lived your life. There's nothing wrong with that. And you're back now." He squeezed her tightly, silently thanking her. After a moment, she asked, "Are you in love with him?"

The answer came swiftly, with confidence. "Yes."

"Does he feel the same?"

This part he couldn't answer with the same assurance. "I think so, but I don't know."

"I do. I don't know why I even asked. He hasn't taken his eyes off of you. He looks at you like you're his center, his compass. He's so in love with you I don't think he knows how to deal with it himself."

Landon's chest squeezed, his pulse thrummed rapidly. He didn't tell Shanen how much he needed to hear that. Instead he quietly chuckled. "Look at you. You didn't used to be such a romantic."

"Love does crazy things to you, Lando. I'm sure you could vouch for that now."

He nodded. Yes, he definitely could.

CHAPTER THIRTY-FOUR

Rod just finished filling his glass of punch when Joy approached him.

"I just wanted to thank you. I appreciate the fact that you haven't said anything to Landon yet. I know it can't be easy, but I think it's important that it's us."

Rod set the glass down deciding to grab another and fill it for Landon. "It is important. Please, tell him soon. If not, I'll have to."

"Have to what?" Landon stepped up beside him.

Rod stood there like an idiot, not sure what to say. Finally, Joy said, "He's threatening to show me how it's done on the dance floor. I haven't danced in years! I don't even know if I remember how."

Landon smiled and grabbed her hand. Jesus, he looked happy. Rod wasn't sure he'd ever seen him look so happy, so content.

"Come on, Ma. I'll show you. I'll be back in a minute," he told Rod before dragging Joy to the dance floor.

Guilt gnawed on his bones while he stood there watching Joy

and Landon dance. He spun her around, smiling as she threw her head back with a loud laugh. They were happy, so fucking happy. They'd been dealt a shit hand with his dad leaving, but they'd made the best of it by loving each other. Rod wanted that so fucking much.

"Rod! Come out here before this son of mine wears me out."

He didn't move for a moment, and then Landon jerked his head in a nod that said come here. Rod went but when he approached, it was Joy who took his hand and danced with him. Soon the dance floor was filled with bodies and people dancing to fast-paced wedding music.

He'd always loved dancing. Shanen was suddenly beside him, Jacob beside her. Shanen's dress kept getting in the way and tripping people as they moved to the music.

Sweat dripped into his eyes, a continuous laugh on his tongue. Rod's heart pounded as they continued on dance after dance.

It was Landon who stopped first, breathing heavy. "I'm done. I need a drink. I'll be back." He leaned in to kiss Rod, but he shook his head.

"I'm going with you."

"What? Can't keep up with an old lady?" Joy asked. He could practically feel the energy vibrating off of Landon.

"You're a machine! Keep it up," Landon told her before the two of them sought out the table with the punch. "It feels good to see her happy. I was so worried about her, but I think she's good. And she likes you a lot." He nudged Rod with his arm. The truth was, Rod really liked her too. She loved her kids. There wasn't a fiber in his being that doubted that.

"I like her too."

They found a quiet corner to stand in and finish their drinks. Just as their cups were empty a slow song came on. "Dance with me?" Rod asked him.

Landon nodded. He set their glasses down and then Rod led him to the dance floor. They wrapped their arms around each other, their bodies close as they swayed to the music. "This is the first time I've slow danced with someone," Rod admitted. He'd never had the opportunity before.

"This is the first time I've slow danced with a man." Landon's hand ran up and down his back. "I'm glad it's you."

Rod rested his chin on Landon's shoulder, holding him so tight, he wondered if he hurt him. "I'm glad it's you too."

***

It was late when they got home. It had been such an overwhelming, hectic day, that part of him wanted to just fall into Rod's bed, and pass out. But he also needed to get cleaned up...and he needed Rod, as well.

"Wanna take a shower with me?" Landon asked, wagging his eyebrows at Rod, trying to sound more relaxed than he felt.

"Yeah, I do. Give me a minute first though, okay?"

Landon nodded at him, and Rod disappeared into the bedroom. Landon got a drink of water, emptying the glass before he made his way to the bedroom. He took his time getting out of his clothes. He heard the shower turn on and then before he knew it, Rod opened the bathroom door and called him in.

The shower was small, too small for two grown men, but they didn't need much room anyway. He liked having their bodies close as they each soaped off, cleaning the day from their skin.

"Do you want more tattoos?" Landon asked, fingering the symbol for happiness on Rod's forearm. Really it was an excuse to touch him.

"I don't know. If it happens, it happens. I got my first one to piss off my dad."

Landon laughed. "That doesn't surprise me. If I ever get one we can go together. You can hold my hand in case I cry."

Rod rolled his eyes at Landon. "You're crazy."

"Hey, that's my line for you!" These were the moments he'd been denying himself, the moments he'd never had with someone else. The quiet, everyday moments. Talking, laughing, just being, but he didn't find himself wishing he'd had them before. He only wanted them with Rod.

"You left your bracelet on." Rod fingered the chain on Landon's wrist. His sister had given it to him at the wedding.

"Shit. I forgot about it." And then Landon pulled him close. "I don't know what in the hell you've done to me," Landon told him.

As though Rod was inside his head, he replied, "I don't know, but you did the same thing to me."

"Yeah?" he asked.

"Yeah."

They got out of the shower in silence. They bumped into each other as they dried off in the too-small bathroom. "We need more space."

Rod cocked a brow at him. "Do we now?"

He touched Rod's muscular stomach. "We do," and then he turned and went into the bedroom.

Rod was right behind him, and when they stepped into the middle of the room together, naked, Rod's hand wrapped around his wrist. "Did you mean it?"

"Mean what?" Landon replied.

"That you think you're in love with me. Did you mean it?" There was nothing but sincere honesty in Rod's eyes. It nearly fucking broke Landon's heart.

"You really don't know, do you? You don't see how fucking incredible you are. You don't believe it."

"I'm trying."

Landon pulled him close. He wrapped his arms around Rod, one on his back, the other on his ass. He held him close, tried to fuse their bodies together as tightly as he could. Rod's face went to his neck, burying it there.

"I am so fucking in love with you," Landon told him. "No one has ever been worth that risk until you came into my life."

"You're the first person who ever has. I tell myself my mom must have, but I don't really remember. I'm so fucking scared of losing that. Of messing it up."

"Hey, you won't," Landon told him. "Not a fucking chance, okay?"

"You can't know that."

"I do."

Still holding each other, Rod answered with, "I love you too."

"I never thought you'd say that. Thank you." And then their mouths met. The kiss started slow but accelerated quickly. Before he knew it, their lips and tongues were frantic. They ate at each other's mouths, Landon's left hand still firmly at home on Rod's ass.

Rod kissed a trail down his neck. "I want your dick in my mouth. Want to worship you. Want to suck you like I need you to stay alive. Hell, maybe I do."

Rod wrapped a hand around Landon's dick and stroked. He hissed and then Rod dropped to his knees in front of him. His mouth ravished Landon's prick as he sucked it deep in one long pull.

"Fuck yes." Landon wrapped a hand in Rod's hair, as he continued to work Landon's erection with his skilled mouth. He'd never been so fucking hard. His balls ached to spill, to empty down the back of Rod's throat.

Rod went lower, his tongue lashing over Landon's sac as he ran a finger up and down the crack of Landon's ass.

"Gimme your finger. Wanna feel more of you inside of me."

Because part of Rod was already fucking there.

Rod sucked a finger into his mouth. Landon spread his legs as Rod's mouth went to work on his straining prick again. He didn't tease, just pushed his spit-slick finger in Landon's hole.

He groaned out Rod's name. It had been a long time since he had someone inside of him. "Jesus fucking Christ you're killing me. Get up here before I ruin this too soon."

Rod's finger pulled out of him and then Landon jerked him to his feet. As he did, Rod put his finger to his mouth and sucked. "Haven't gotten to taste you there yet."

Landon's balls burned. His dick flexed against his stomach. He squeezed it, holding off his orgasm. "You are so fucking sexy. I want to come all over you right now, but I want this to last, too."

With a sexy rasp to his voice, Rod said, "Make it last."

Landon intended to do just that.

CHAPTER THIRTY-FIVE

Rod's legs trembled as Landon pulled him to the bed. He grabbed the lube and a condom, tossing them to the bed before he sat down. Rod stood between his legs as Landon wrapped his arms around him, cupping his ass. He squeezed his cheeks before parting him. "Jesus, this fucking ass. I don't know if I want my tongue or my dick inside it more."

"Both?" Rod asked, because honestly, he didn't know which he wanted more either.

"Get on the bed and show it to me. Let me see your hole."

Rod didn't hesitate for a second. He got onto the bed, kneeling before he lowered his upper body, offering his ass to Landon. "Jesus, you're beautiful. I can't wait to make love to you."

Rod's hole clenched, but it was more than that. Hearing Landon say he wanted to make love to him made his chest full, his heart pound. The man was determined to kill him tonight.

"You're more than that though. More than just sex. I love you." Landon rubbed his ass, placed his thumb against Rod's hungry pucker and rubbed it. "You're more than that. Tell me."

Rod closed his eyes and Landon continued rubbing his thumb against his asshole. He felt Landon's lips on his left cheek, kissing him there, and then his right.

"Tell me," Landon said again.

"I'm more than that. Now hurry the hell up and give me something before I have to do it myself."

They both laughed. "Who's the bossy one?"

And then Rod couldn't reply. Landon's tongue took the place of his thumb as he kissed Rod's hole. He tongued it, moaned against it as he spread Rod's cheeks, his face there as though this was his last meal.

Rod pushed back toward him, trying to get as close as he could, wanting Landon all over him.

A tingle started at the base of his spine. The dull burn in his balls got more and more intense as Landon worshiped him.

"I need you, fuck, I need you, Landon." He'd sworn to himself he would never need anyone, but Landon had changed that.

"I'm right here." He kissed his way up Rod's spine. "I'm not going anywhere."

***

"On your back. Open your legs for me." Landon looked down at Rod as he did what he said. It was so strange, feeling this way, looking into someone's eyes and feeling like they're your whole fucking world.

And Rod felt the same way about him. It was there in the intensity of his stare.

"I've never made love before," Rod told him and Landon touched his lips, his hair. He just needed to touch him.

"Yeah you have. We just didn't call it that before. We knew though." He reached over and grabbed the lube and a condom.

Rod spread his legs for him, as Landon lubed his entrance. His body burned to be inside him, ached to burrow himself as deep as he could go.

He rubbed Rod's pucker, pushed the tip of his finger in and then Rod said, his voice hoarse. "Just take me. Make love to me."

Landon shook as he opened the condom. His eyes didn't leave Rod's as he rolled it on.

After liberally lubing himself, he pushed Rod's legs back, and started to press in.

"Fuck." Rod gave a guttural moan as Landon eased into his tight heat. His body was on edge. He wanted to slam into him. To rail him, fuck him into the mattress, but he wanted to make love to him too.

He felt raw, cut open, on display.

"Me too," Rod said as though he read Landon's mind. And then Landon thrust forward, buried himself balls deep. He wrapped a hand around Rod's steely length as he started to pump inside him, the tight fist of his ass, squeezing Landon's prick.

"Fuck yeah. You feel so goddamned good. I'll never get enough of you."

He pulled almost all the way out, the head of his dick rubbing Rod's opening before he slammed in again. Over and over he took him, made love to him.

Rod's hand replaced his as he jerked himself off. It wasn't enough for Landon so he bent closer, let his tongue make love to Rod's mouth the same way his dick did.

Rod arched forward, heat radiating off his body. "Oh fuck. I'm gonna come Landon. Shit, I'm gonna come."

And then his ass muscles clenched around Landon. They kissed again. Landon's hips smacked against him as he watched the come shoot from Rod's slit. It went up his chest, hit his chin as his ass kept constricting around Landon.

His balls burned, drew tight and then he shot, filling the condom, but he didn't stop thrusting. He couldn't. He rode out his orgasm, Rod's nails digging into his back, until his balls were empty and then he went down, Rod's legs wrapped around him.

He never wanted to leave this spot. This was home.

***

Their bodies were slick with sweat. The room smelled like sex. They both had come all over them. Rod wanted his spunk to dry into Landon's skin. The room was thick with their heavy breathing as they held each other. There were too many thoughts in Rod's head and even though he tried to hold them in, he couldn't help but let some escape. He'd go crazy if he didn't. "I felt like I had a family today... Your mom and Shanen. They made me feel welcome."

Landon rolled onto his stomach and looked down at Rod who lay on his back. "You are welcome and you do have family. I want it to stay like this." He rubbed his thumb over Rod's bottom lip. "I don't want us to ever hurt each other, to ever ruin each other. Promise me."

Rod's heart seized in his chest. "I promise."

Landon kissed his neck, his chest, flicked his tongue over Rod's nipple. "Just be real with me. Always be real with me."

Tell him warred with *it's not your place.* He wanted what was best for Landon, wanted that more than anything. He just hoped like hell that's what he was doing.

Landon rolled on top of him, settling between his legs. He kissed his way down Rod's chest.

"Landon...?" Rod said, not sure if he was going to tell him or if he just needed to say Landon's name. "Would you ever want to see him again? If you had the chance?"

Landon stopped kissing and looked at him, hovering over his navel. "No. I don't want to see him. I don't want to know anything about him. He made that decision when he left."

Fuck. He didn't mean that. They were just words, Rod told himself as Landon stuck his tongue in Rod's belly button. "Landon...I..."

"Think I could suck you hard again? I didn't get to eat your come and I really fucking want it. I know it's crazy, but I can't get enough of you."

He pulled Rod's soft dick into his mouth and all thought was lost. Tomorrow, he'd talk to Joy tomorrow and tell her that if she didn't tell Landon, he would. He couldn't handle the thought of losing Landon when he'd just found him.

CHAPTER THIRTY-SIX

Landon met Shanen in the driveway of their mom's house. She'd called him and asked him if he could stop by after work today. Shanen had just gotten back from her honeymoon the day before, so he hadn't expected to see her here.

"Did Mom call you here too?" he asked as they walked toward the front porch together.

"She did. What's going on?"

"No clue." Discomfort slid down his spine. He didn't like this, didn't like it at all.

Landon took the stairs two at a time, before he opened the door, and signaled for Shanen to walk in. She made it two steps before she stopped dead. "Daddy?" she said softly. It was like a kick to Landon's gut. His eyes shot forward and he saw him there, his father sitting at the kitchen table with his mom.

"Daddy? Is that you?" Shanen asked and then she ran to him and threw her arms around Larry.

Landon's stomach rolled. Heat scorched him, incinerating his insides. Still, he found himself closer, and getting closer to them.

"Dad, what are you doing here? Mom...I...I can't believe it."

What the hell was Shanen doing? "You have got to be fucking kidding me." The man had left them.

"Landon, I know it's a surprise," Joy said, "But please, sit down. Let me explain."

"No thanks. I don't need to hear anything." He turned to the door when his father, his fucking father's voice stopped him.

"Landon, please, wait."

"Fuck you!" He turned on the man. "You don't get to request anything from me. You left. You fucking abandoned us. It doesn't matter what happened between you and mom. You had a commitment to us and you walked away. Now you can see what it feels like."

He turned for the door, made it all the way there before the man's broken voice stopped him again. "I'm sorry. I was wrong. I know that. Please listen to me, Lando. I don't have much time left."

His hand shook on the doorknob. He didn't remember grabbing it. Hell, he didn't even remember closing it when they'd come in.

He heard Shanen and his mom begin to cry. "I'm sorry. I didn't mean to tell you that way," he said to her. Still, Landon couldn't make himself turn around. He was sick. One look at his gaunt face and deep-set eyes told him that, but hearing it was a different thing.

"I know I don't deserve it, Landon, but hear me out. Please. If you want to walk away after that, I won't blame you. Hell, I don't blame you now, but I'm asking anyway. I always was a selfish bastard."

Landon laughed humorlessly. "That you are." He turned, didn't take a step toward them and leaned against the door. "Talk."

It wouldn't change anything. He knew that right now. The man had left him and Landon couldn't forgive that.

"I won't make any excuses for leaving. There are none to be made. I fucked up. Nothing I can say will change that...but I can tell you both, I never stopped loving you."

Landon huffed. "Funny way of showing it."

"Maybe that's hard for you to believe, but it's true. It's easy to feel as if you have forever, as if what you're doing makes sense. It's easy to lie to yourself, and that's what I did. A whole hell of a lot of clarity comes with dying. Your whole life plays out for you, every mistake, every time you hurt, every *person* you hurt. And I hurt you both, all three of you. But I love you, and I'm here. I want to get to know you. You're mama says you still ride, Landon. I'd love to see your bike."

"Fuck you," Landon told him. It was childish and he was fully aware of that, but he couldn't hold it back right now.

"Landon," Shanen said and he turned his attention to his sister next.

"Don't. Don't tell me not to be angry. You can accept his apology and pretend nothing happened if you want, but I can't. He fucking abandoned us, Shan." *I needed him. I called him when I was scared and he walked away and didn't come back.*

"I know." She stood. "You think I don't know that? I felt it too. I stayed, even when you left, Landon. I know what he did, but he's still our dad. He's here and he's sick."

I stayed, even when you left, Landon.

"Shit, I didn't mean that. You didn't walk away from us," Shanen tried to assure him. "I know that. I just... We can have our family back."

"What if I don't want it?" Landon asked. He'd finally moved on. Moved past it. He didn't want to go back. He didn't want to forgive.

"Then you don't have to accept it," his father said. Landon closed his eyes, tried to fight off the pain that engulfed his chest. It was as though he stood in a quicksand of hurt, and it slowly continued to pull him under.

"Hate me if you want. I deserve that. I understand it, okay? Just don't ever let yourself feel guilty about it."

"Don't fucking play me. Don't try to make me feel like I will regret this!" He looked at his mom who sat quietly, tears running down her face. "You accept this? You've been alone since he left. You've blamed yourself. You're just going to let him come back into your life because he doesn't want to die alone?" He couldn't do that. Even if he wanted to, he couldn't.

"He's your father, Landon," she said. "I love him. I've always loved him, and he's sick."

So many things made sense now—the time she spent away from

home, the food, all of it.

His father interrupted his thoughts, "That's not why I'm here. I wouldn't be alone, but I wanted you too. I wanted all of you."

Landon was an inferno of anger. He felt like he was burning alive. "What do you mean you're not alone?" He fought the need to clutch his gut, to lose his fucking mind.

His dad's eyes shifted to his mom's, and hers to him.

"Tell me."

"I made a lot of mistakes when I was with your mother."

"No shit."

He ignored Landon and continued. "I was contacted by a woman I'd..."

Jesus, he knew. He fucking knew what his dad would say next. "Slept with while you were with Mom?"

He nodded. "We eventually married. My wife and I are separated now but... I had a son with her. He was eight the first time I met him. His name is Justin. He's looking forward to meeting you. He came back with me."

Landon couldn't move, couldn't think. His head spun. He felt like he was going to lose it right there. "You had another family."

"Yes," he answered simply.

Landon had to grab ahold of the wall to keep himself up. He had another son. "Did you stay? When you and his mom separated, did you take care of him?"

His dad closed his eyes, let out a deep breath, and Landon knew the answer. "Yes," he replied. "Yes, I did."

His hand shook. His heart broke. He couldn't do this. He couldn't hear this. Couldn't be in this place with these people. He needed to get the fuck out of here before he lost it. *He left you, but stayed for him...* "I can't do this. You made your bed, you can lie in it. I'm going to Rod's." Somehow even his name soothed him. He needed Rod. Needed to hold him, to tell him what happened. Needed Rod to bring him back to reality.

Landon pulled open the door.

"I love you, and I'm glad you have him. He seems like a good man."

Landon's insides crystalized, broke apart, an icicle falling and crashing to the ground. "What do you mean by that?"

He heard his mom sigh. His dad cursed.

"It was an accident Landon. Don't be angry at Rod. I asked him not to tell you. I thought it would be better if your father and I did it."

He knew. Rod fucking knew and he hadn't told him. He'd asked him to be real with him, asked him that they didn't do this to each other, didn't hurt each other. He knew how Landon felt about his father yet he'd known he was back and didn't tell him.

"Fuck you all." Landon walked out, slamming the door behind him.

CHAPTER THIRTY-SEVEN

Rod hadn't heard from Landon since about noon. He'd expected him to stop by when he got off work, not because Landon told him he would, but because he usually did, and if he didn't, he called instead.

Today, he'd heard nothing though.

From about seven on, he started to worry, because he had a pretty good theory as to why. He must know about his dad being back. He knew Rod betrayed him.

The knowledge had been in the back of his head all day, but the later it got, the more he knew it was true.

For the third time, Rod picked up his cell and called. When Landon didn't answer again, he shot him a text. **Hey. Worried about you. Call me.** He really was. He knew something like this hitting out of the blue, had to hurt. That's what had made him keep his mouth shut all week. That's what told him it was best to let Landon and his family deal with it. It was only one week. What could it hurt to wait one more week?

Rod set the alarm and then locked up the store. As soon as he turned around, he saw him, Landon leaning against Rod's car, his motorcycle parked next to it.

His shoulders curled over, his head down, and even from the distance, Rod could see the extra weight he carried in his bones.

"Hey…" He stepped up to Landon, who turned to look at him. The street light above felt too bright, stinging his eyes. Or hell, maybe he was just fucking weak and couldn't handle to look at Landon, knowing what he'd kept from him.

"You knew?"

Rod could hear the profound pain in his low, hoarse voice. He closed his eyes, sadness searing his chest. This was it. He'd fucked it up. He would lose him. There had never been a doubt in Rod's head that this would happen. "I did. It wasn't my place to tell you. It wasn't my business."

Landon's head snapped up at that. "What happens to me is supposed to be your business, the same way it would be mine if something would hurt you! That's what this is supposed to be about, Rod, being fucking there. Having each other's backs. Taking care of each other, instead of letting each other get hurt!" he spewed venomously.

"I didn't know what to do! It wasn't my place! I wrestled with it every fucking day, Landon. It was like acid eating away at me. Jesus, I told you I wouldn't be good at this. We were supposed to fuck and that was it, fuck and then you'd walk away. You're the one who wanted to shift gears." He felt like his chest was cracking apart, all his vital organs spilling onto the ground.

Landon shoved off of the car. "Are you fucking kidding me right now? You're going to give me shit for giving a damn? Sorry I cared. Obviously, you don't. No worries. The error has been fixed. I don't give a fuck anymore."

Landon's feet hit the ground with heavy steps as he walked to his bike, threw his leg over and got on. That wasn't what he was saying, it wasn't what he wanted, just what he knew would happen, but the words got tangled up inside him. People didn't love him. They never had, and he hadn't expected it to be any different...but he'd wanted it. Wanted it so fucking much he ached. He'd made himself believe it would happen.

Landon started the bike and put on his helmet. He turned to look at Rod, watched him, waiting, but he didn't know what in the hell to say. *I'm sorry. I love you. I never wanted you to walk away.*

Before he could settle on something, Landon sped away.

***

Four days later Rod heard a banging. At first he thought it was inside his head, the result of too much fucking alcohol the past four days. When the pounding happened again, he realized it was the front door. He wanted to ignore it, Jesus, he wanted nothing more than to ignore it, so he rolled over, covering his head with the pillow, but the thumping kept coming.

"Fuck, hold on!" He shoved out of the bed, shuffled into the living room and pulled open the door.

The sunlight burned his eyes, no doubt another result of the nights he'd spent partying at a club.

"You look like shit."

Rod's sight narrowed in on Bryce as he shoved his way into the house. Nick was right behind him. "Thank you."

"Usually I'd try to find a way to soften whatever Bryce says, but he's right, man. You look like hell." Nick closed the door behind them.

Perfect, just what he needed. His asshole friends to come over and make him feel worse. "I'm suffering a broken heart here. Thanks for the support. You should be trying to make me feel better, not worse. Oh, I know. The two of you can finally—"

"Don't even say it," Bryce cut him off. "This isn't a joke and this isn't about sex. Christ, the scent of alcohol is leaking out of your pores. What the hell have you been doing?"

Rod would have thought that was obvious. "Drinking." He went to the kitchen and started coffee. Nick pushed him out of the way and Rod let him take over. He finished preparing the coffee pot as Rod took a seat at the small table across from the kitchen. "I have a headache. Can we do this quickly so I can get back to sleep? I have to go to work in a few hours." It was early as hell. "What are you doing here, anyway?"

He looked at Nick who turned away. Rod let his eyes find Bryce next. "Tell me."

"Landon called. He hasn't been to work, and he asked me to check on you."

Rod hated the fact that his pulse sped up. "Well, that was nice of him. Does that mean we really had an amicable break? We parted as friends who still love and respect each other?"

"What in the hell happened with you two? Last time I saw you, he couldn't keep his eyes off you." Nick brought a mug of coffee over and set it in front of him.

"Exactly what I knew would happen, happened. That's why I wanted nothing to do with it—well the fucking I did, but not the relationship outside of friendship. He kept fucking pushing and look what happened." Rod rested his elbows on the table, his head in his hands. His fucking head was killing him...it had nothing on the pain in his chest.

The truth came slamming into him then, a wrecking ball turning the wall he tried to build inside him to rubble. "He made me want it," Rod said softly. "He made me believe we could work. He made me believe he could love me."

There was a hand on his shoulder. Without looking he knew it belonged to Nick. He squeezed in support as Bryce quietly cursed on the other side of the room.

"If I see him again, I'm going to fucking kill him," Bryce said. "I told him. I fucking told him to be sure he was real with you."

Rod's head snapped up at that. "What? Why would you do that?"

Bryce's brows furrowed. "Because I'm your friend, dumbass. Because we care about you."

And they did. Logically, Rod knew that. Sometimes the connection between what his brain knew and his heart felt got severed. Nick and Bryce were his friends.

"You sold us our first butt plug. We love your crazy-ass." Nick squeezed his shoulder again and Rod couldn't help but let out a sharp laugh. He could imagine Bryce saying something like that, but not Nick.

"He's rubbing off on you."

"I rub off on him often," Bryce replied. "Nick likes it. There's a lot you don't know about him. He's a closet freak."

Nick groaned and both Bryce and Rod laughed again. It felt good to laugh. It was an honest laugh, the kind he'd felt often since Landon had come into his life. "There's a part of me," Rod looked down at the green coffee mug, running his finger along the rim so he didn't have to look at Nick or Bryce. "There's a part of me that says, *I told you so.* Part of me knew this would happen. No one in my life has ever stayed there."

"Did you ever think it's because you don't let them?" Nick asked. "I don't know your past, but I know what I see. You're the funny guy, the guy who's up for anything, but do you really let anyone in? Sometimes I feel like there's a façade there, the real you and the you the world sees. It's even there with Bryce and I. I'm not saying this is the case with Landon because I don't know what happened. I just know what I see when I look at you."

"Yeah," Bryce added. "What Nick said."

Rod couldn't find it in himself to laugh, so he continued circling the cup with his finger.

They were right. Another one of those things he knew but didn't always believe. When his father rejected him, he'd vowed to never let anyone in and he hadn't. How could he make real relationships and friendships when that was the case?

"I let him in." He'd wanted Landon there, inside him. He belonged there.

"I'm angry at him," Rod admitted. "I'm fucking pissed. He's hurting, I get it, but I did the best I could. He owed me the right to explain. He owed me more." Because Rod would have given it to him.

"Good." Bryce walked closer and Rod looked up at him. "Months ago, would you have been angry at him or would you have taken the blame? Hell, maybe even weeks ago. What would you have done?"

There wasn't a question in Rod's head about that. He would have taken one hundred percent of the blame. He wouldn't have been angry at Landon. There was the quiet voice in his head that tried to pull him that way now, part of him that doubted himself and his choices. Maybe that devil inside him would always be there, but the self-doubt was quieter than it used to be.

He wasn't perfect, but he'd done his best with what he'd been given. Maybe he should have told Landon, but Landon shouldn't have just walked away either. He didn't deserve that.

He didn't answer Bryce's question out loud, but he didn't need to. He knew the answer. Rod knew the truth, and despite the crack in his heart, he felt a little bit of pride squeeze in. His father hadn't been right about him. His dad's rejection wasn't his fault. He deserved more than he'd always allowed himself to have.

And damn did he want Landon to have a part in that, because Rod deserved to be happy. He deserved to be loved, and he wanted

Landon to be the man to do it.

CHAPTER THIRTY-EIGHT

Christ, he looks like me.

Landon stared hard across the hotel room at his brother...his fucking *brother.* The man his father had taken care of...the man his father had stayed for, even after it didn't work out with his mother.

"Thank you for agreeing to see me." Justin leaned against the door with his arms crossed. His brown hair was the same shade as Landon's.

"You wouldn't stop calling. You didn't give me much choice." He'd called at least five times a day since Landon walked out of his mom's house. He was relentless, Landon would give him that. It didn't mean he liked him. It didn't mean he wanted a brother.

"Nice place you have here." Justin's eyes skated over the older hotel room with floral blankets and a crooked painting on the wall. Sarcasm sparked off each of his words.

"You're funny. Did you get your sense of humor from him?" Landon asked and Justin shrugged.

He pushed off the wall, and paced the room. Landon was quiet, waiting for Justin to say whatever he came to say. He was the one who'd wanted to talk. He was the one who'd forced himself into Landon's life. "I'm gay too," is what Justin settled on. Landon didn't bother to correct Justin and say he was bisexual.

"Congratu-fucking-lations. Is that supposed to change anything? Are we supposed to bond now, the gay queer sons of an asshole dad?" Though he had to admit, it was a surprise. He wondered how often more than one sibling was gay or bi.

Justin looked at him, anger in his dark eyes. "Fuck you. I'm trying to figure out how to deal with this too. I get that you're pissed. I was too, but what I don't get is why you're pissed at me. I didn't make him leave you. Did you ever think about how it felt for me to find out? For the man who raised me, who I respected more than anyone in the world to tell me he had a son and daughter I never knew about? That I had siblings I knew he sure as shit hadn't taken care of. I was fucking devastated!"

Landon's hands balled into fists. He wanted to hit something. He wanted to hit Justin. "Am I supposed to feel sorry for you?" he spewed. "He stayed for you! I was alone! I wanted my father and he was with you!"

Justin looked down. His hands were tight. Veins sprang to life on his arms. "I will never look at him the same. How can I? Every memory I have of him is tarnished. Everything good has a black cloud over it because I know you didn't have it. He robbed me of something too. He took you and Shanen away from me."

He was right. Fuck, he was right, and Landon knew it. That didn't make it any easier to deal with. "You're here. That makes it easier to be mad at you."

"He's there for you to be mad at as well. I punched him in the jaw when he told me."

Damned if Landon didn't feel his lips tug into a small smile. If the situation were different, he thought he could like Justin. "No shit?"

"Knocked his ass on the ground. Felt good. I wish you could try it. He's a little sicker now than he was then."

"Lucky bastard."

Justin laughed and damned if it didn't sound like his own. Landon found himself chuckling too. Maybe that made them both sick, but he couldn't help it. It was laugh or hit something.

A moment later they were both silent again, the heavy kind of silent that was louder than any noise could ever be. Landon sat on the edge of the bed, his leg bouncing up and down. "I don't know how to do this. I don't know how to have a brother. I don't know how to stop myself from holding what he did to my family against you." Maybe the words were harsh, but they were true.

"This might make you hate me more, but there's a part of me that feels the same way about you. I had an amazing father. He went to my games, and taught me how to play catch, and now he feels like a fraud."

The pain in Justin's voice was too powerful, too broken to ignore. He was a victim too. He was aching just like the rest of them.

"How did you do it? How did you forgive him?"

Justin frowned at that. "Who said I forgave him? Half of the time I think I hate him, the other half he's the dad I always loved. I don't know how in the hell to deal with any of this any better than you do. My head is just as fucked up as yours is...but I just keep asking myself, will I have regrets if I turn my back on him? How will I feel five years from now if I let my anger ruin the time he has left? How would I feel when he died, if I left him alone the same way he left you?"

His words fractured everything Landon thought he knew, what he thought he felt. He'd worried about being like his father. How would he feel if he walked away from him now? If he turned his back on Justin, the brother who would likely be just as scarred as the rest of them.

Landon would never forgive himself. He'd hate himself. This wasn't something he could run from without it changing his whole fucking universe.

He had a brother.

His dad was back.

His dad was dying.

He hurt, fucking hurt in ways he didn't know were possible. He'd dreamed of having his dad back for years...then he'd never wanted him. Landon had wished him dead, and now he would get that quiet request he'd made as a broken-hearted kid...and he didn't want it. No matter what, the man was his father. He didn't know how to deal with all of those conflicting thoughts so he did what he'd wanted to do for days, stood up, and swung, his fisting connecting with the wall. Pain shot through him. "Fuck!" He grabbed his hand, cradling it.

Swelling began immediately.

"That was stupid," Justin said.

Damned if he didn't like the guy. "Hey! You punched something too."

"I didn't break my hand though."

Justin had him there. Landon sighed before grudgingly saying, "Take me to the hospital."

"Sure. We can do that brotherly bonding thing on the way."

Landon nodded as they headed toward the door. "How are you at relationship advice? I fucked up with the only man I've ever loved."

Justin held the door open for him and Landon walked out. "Good luck with that one, man. Relationship advice I can't do."

Well hell, it looked like Landon would have to figure out how to fix his life on his own.

***

Rod stood in the back of Rods-N-Ends stocking the shelves. He had one employee here with him today. She was at the register, taking care of the steady, but manageable string of customers who trickled in and out of the store.

It was nearly time for his dinner break, but he'd told her he wanted to finish what he was doing before he went.

"Do you have any Easy Ride?" Rod tensed up at Landon's voice from behind him.

"No. It's been recalled. They discovered that whoever used it became an unruly bastard."

"At least I now have an excuse for my behavior," Landon said and Rod sighed.

He hadn't expected this. He'd wanted Landon to come back, but hadn't expected it. "In a way, you do. Your dad coming back is life changing. I get that." *So why couldn't you let me in?*

"I don't have an excuse for the way I treated you."

He closed his eyes, let the words seep into him. He'd needed to hear that. He wasn't sure if that was a good thing or not, but it was true.

Rod turned to look at him—at his dark hair and painful eyes. The downward curve of his lips and his strong jaw. He was so damned beautiful it hurt.

"I know I was too big an asshole to deserve this, but I'm asking for it from you anyway. Talk to me. Let me explain." He held up a pizza box. It was then that Rod noticed the cast on his right hand. "I brought you dinner. It's cold. I've been waiting in the car until your employee let me know you'd be going to dinner. I didn't want to miss you."

What the hell? "You called and spied on me?"

"I did. I told her I was an asshole, but an asshole who was in love with you. That I wanted to talk to you and asked that she let me know when it was your dinnertime. Don't be mad at her. It was my fault."

"I know," Rod told him. Landon's eyes dimmed, the frown deepened. "Let's go."

He led Landon to his office, closing the door behind him. "What did you do to your hand?" he asked. He wanted to kiss it, to make sure Landon was okay.

"Punched a wall. I don't recommend it." He set the pizza down. "I'm sorry. I'm so fucking sorry for walking away from you. For not understanding the position you were in. Jesus, that had to be a struggle for you, but I was so damn angry at him. So scared and confused. When he came back, I felt like my world was crumbling and all I could think of was you, that I needed you to put it back together again. I need you to hold me together."

Rod started, "I—"

"No, please let me finish. I needed you because I love you. When I realized you knew, I shut down, because I'm a fake. I've told you how many fucking times to let me in? To give us a chance? But really the whole time I think I was waiting for it to fall apart too. I was waiting to become them. Waiting for us to become those people who hurt each other over and over, so I did it the first chance I got. I became them and I walked away and I'm so fucking sorry for that."

The tremble in Landon's voice echoed in Rod's head. He was open and honest in his raw pain. "Your world had just been tipped on its axis. I understood that. It was eating me alive to keep that from you, but I didn't know what to do, Landon. I don't always have the answers. None of us do. Sometimes we just have to do our best and hope like hell it's the right thing."

Landon nodded. "I needed you. I just wanted you to hold me. To tell me it would be okay, but you couldn't. All you said was you knew this would happen. I didn't know what to do with that. I still don't."

Rod sighed, fighting every single fiber of his being that wanted him to go to Landon, to hold him. To forget everything that happened. "I believed that. Maybe a part of me still does, but I'm trying not to. We're going to learn as we go. We're doing something we've never done. We're opening ourselves up. It's not going to be perfect."

Landon opened his mouth to speak, but Rod held up his hand. It was his turn to get out what he needed to say. "I went out. I was out almost every night you were gone—drinking and clubbing."

Landon leaned against Rod's desk, gripping the edge with his good hand. Fire blazed in his eyes, but he just nodded, waiting for Rod to continue.

"I told myself I was going to party, fuck who I wanted, when I wanted. I'd show you I didn't want you. I'd show you I didn't need you. I'd go back to being alone and not needing anyone, but I couldn't do it. I realized I didn't want anyone but you, so I just got drunk every fucking night. And then I got angry at you, because I didn't deserve to hurt like that. Neither of us did. But Jesus, that's life isn't it? It's like you said, all we can do is ride it out, live it and see what happens. I realized I want to do that living with you, because I deserve to be happy. I deserve to be loved. The question is, did you realize you deserve the same thing?"

"I did. Christ, I fucking did. Come here." Landon grabbed Rod and pulled him close. Landon's ass rested on the edge of the desk, Rod between his legs as they held each other. "I felt like I was in neutral without you. I could pull the throttle, but I couldn't take off."

Rod smiled. "Oh, motorcycle talk. I like it. We can do it together. We'll get a feel for the clutch just like you said. We're just shifting gears. That's it."

"Jesus, that was hot. I didn't know I'd like motorcycle speak on you, too."

"Baby, you ain't seen nothing yet. I printed out a whole list of motorcycle terms. Studied for the test too. I was going to show you what you were missin' if I saw you again."

Landon laughed, but his typical happiness wasn't there. He buried his face in Rod's neck. "Will you go with me? When I go to talk to my dad for the first time, will you go? I...I need you there."

Maybe a part of Rod needed to be there as well. Needing someone didn't always mean you'd get hurt. Sometimes, it built you up, too. "Yeah...yeah, I will. I think it's important, Landon. I wish I had the chance to see my dad, to prove him wrong about who I am. To show him that someone could love me." But he would never get that chance. He just had to work through it all himself...with Landon by his side.

"I know. You're right. I'm so fucking sorry."

Rod leaned back. He grabbed Landon's broken hand, kissing

each of his fingers. "I know. We'll be okay. I love you."

Landon's arms encircled him, the cast rubbing against his back. "I love you too. I missed you. I almost lost my mind when you said you'd gone out. I can't handle the thought of anyone touching you but me."

Rod smiled. "Nope. I had to do all the touching while you were gone. It's not the same anymore. You've ruined self-enjoyment for me. I don't know if I can forgive you for that," he teased.

He pulled back enough that he could look down at Landon, who rolled his eyes at him. "I'll make it up to you. I can't wait to go home with you. I'm going to hold you all fucking night."

Rod cocked a brow at him. "I hope that's not the only thing you plan on doing with me."

With a smile tilting his lips, Landon shrugged. "Guess you'll have to wait and see."

Rod crossed his arms, feigning annoyance, but really, he couldn't fucking wait for this and everything else the future held for them.

#

His dad and Justin had been renting a small, one-bedroom house. They'd needed a home base when Landon's dad had decided to come back for Landon and Shanen.

His brother, Christ that was still weird to say, slept on the sofa in the living room.

From what Landon's mom told him, his dad was okay for now. The chemo gave him the time he needed to get his affairs in order and apparently getting to know Shanen and Landon was part of that.

It wouldn't work forever. They weren't sure how much longer his quality of life would be as good as it was now. Soon, he would likely stop treatments, which would make him feel better in the time he had left.

Jesus. How fucking fair was that? He'd just gotten his father back, but it wouldn't be for long.

He was still angry at him. Still hurting. He didn't know if he could forgive him, but he needed to try. He needed to try for himself, and in a roundabout way, for Rod, because it wasn't something he could ever do. Landon thought a part of Rod might need Landon to fix his relationship with his father, since he never could.

"This is it, right? This is the address Joy gave us?" Rod asked him as they pulled up in front of the small complex. He'd spoken to his mom and they made their peace. He didn't agree with her decision to keep Justin and his dad away from him, but he'd gotten over it. Sometimes you just had to force yourself to get over shit in your life, or it would rot away inside you until you couldn't be saved.

He did worry that she'd forgiven him so easily, and was so involved with helping take care of him, because of her fear of being alone, but he'd told her how he felt, and that's all he could do. She had to decide what was best for her.

"Yeah," Landon answered him. "This is it."

Rod parked and they got out of the car. Landon took a few deep breaths, trying to prepare himself for this. It helped when Rod grabbed his hand.

Justin stood at the door waiting for them. He nodded at Landon and then walked away, leaving him alone with their father.

No, not alone. He had Rod.

"You can do this," Rod whispered, and he could. He knew he could.

They walked into the apartment to see his dad sitting on a chair. He had an oxygen tank, and somehow looked even skinnier than the last time Landon had seen him.

"Thank you for coming," he said.

"Why?" That was all Landon needed to know. Why?

He looked like his bones couldn't even hold him up, the sadness weighed him down. "I don't know. I was young, and stupid. I thought I had forever. The longer I stayed away, the harder it became to think about coming back. Eventually, I told myself it was too late, and that you were better off without me. It's all bullshit. I fucked up. I was wrong. I was a coward, and I will die knowing that. I will regret walking away from you and your sister every day of my life."

Somehow...that was enough. No, Landon didn't forgive him. He didn't know how close they would ever be, but it was his answer, and he wouldn't let himself dwell on the past forever. He wouldn't let himself rot from the inside out. He wouldn't have the same regrets his dad did. "I don't know if I can forgive you. I don't know how much of myself I can give...but I'll try. I accept what you said, because there's no changing the past, and I'll try. Is that enough for you?"

His dad nodded. A tear leaked from his eye and rolled down his cheek. "I'll take whatever you can give me."

He returned the nod and damned if he wasn't crying too.

Landon pulled Rod closer. "I'd like to formally introduce you to my partner, Rod. Rod, this is Larry." He wasn't ready to call him his father yet.

Rod stepped forward, and they shook hands. "It's nice to meet you again, Larry."

"You as well. Thank you for being there for my boy." He nodded at the table. "Would you like to sit down? Maybe we can get to know each other a little bit. Can you tell me about your bikes, Landon?"

That he could do. He and Rod sat at the yellow, square table with the man he never thought he would see again.

"I have an R1 and a Switchback. We bought Rod an 883. He's just learning to ride." Landon paused, unsure. It wasn't until Rod reached over and put his hand on Landon's that he found the courage to continue. "What about you? Did you still ride after you left?"

It wasn't perfect, but it was a start. That's all you could do sometimes, jump in and start somewhere. The pieces would fall together, or they wouldn't. Life was funny that way. The only thing you could do is keep going because as short as it was, life was also pretty fucking incredible.

No matter what happened, as long as he had Rod by his side, he knew everything would be okay.

THE END

KEEP READING FOR BONUS CONTENT

BONUS CONTENT

Dear Reader,

Considering Rod's job and that fact that he's a self-proclaimed lover of toys, I'd originally planned to have a scene in the book where they got to play around with a few things. I thought it would work for both Rod and Landon, but as I wrote their book, it just didn't fit anywhere inside their story. There was never a good time for another love scene, and the extra play didn't really fit into their current scenes.

I'm a huge fan of a good love scene just like the next person, but it's also important to me not to throw random sex within the content of the story, just to have another sex scene.

So, I decided to add a little bonus content in. I hope you don't mind. LOL.

That way those who want to read it, can, and those who are content without it, won't be missing a vital part of the story if they don't read.

Here's a little fun between Rod and Landon! It takes place after the end of the book.

***

It wasn't a secret that Rod liked ass play, and today, he was in the mood to play.

He'd faked a need for pizza flavored chips and chocolate milk, and while Landon groaned and complained about it, his guy had still gotten up to go for him.

The second Landon was out the door, Rod jetted for the en suite and got ready as quickly as possible. He finished off by adding black eyeliner to his eyes, before racing back to the bedroom. As he laid out everything he wanted to use for them to play, he heard the front door open. "Shit, shit, shit," he mumbled to himself, before lying naked on their bed.

"I have your stuff, you weirdo!" Landon called from the living room, laughter in his voice.

"Come here!"

"No, you come here. I went to the store for you. The least you can do is walk out here to get it."

Great. Of course. Leave it to Landon to fuck up his Rod's display. "You're going to want to come in here. At least, you better want to come in here. I have a surprise that's probably no longer a surprise." He heard the rustling of a bag before Landon's heavy steps sounded down the hall. It was only a few seconds later that Landon stood in the doorway of their bedroom, gripping the frame tightly with one hand. "I want to play. Will you play with me?" Rod stroked his hard shaft, as Landon practically growled at him.

He didn't wait for Landon to respond before he rolled over. As though all he had to do was snap his fingers for the man to appear beside him, Landon was suddenly right there, standing beside their bed. He ran his hand down Rod's back, circled the dip at the base of his spine before he finished the journey down his ass. Rod trembled in response to Landon's gentle touch, coupled with the calluses on his fingers.

"You are so fucking beautiful. How did I get so lucky?"

Rod looked over his shoulder at Landon and grinned. "I don't know. I'm still trying to figure that out. You really scored with me."

Landon playfully rolled his eyes. "So fucking cocky. I guess I better hurry up and serve his majesty so he keeps me around."

"Oh. I like that. Maybe we should use His Majesty instead of Hot Rod."

"You're crazy."

"So you've told me."

"Be quiet so I can take off my clothes and play with you."

That Rod could do. He watched as Landon kicked out of his shoes. He went for his pants next, pulling the faded jeans down his muscular legs. His long, thick cock sprung free and Rod almost said fuck the toys and just asked for Landon's dick in his ass instead. They'd get to that later, though. There was nothing wrong with playing a bit first.

"Put a pillow under you. I want your ass is a little higher, but don't want you to be on your hands and knees for too long."

"This gonna take a while?" Rod cocked a brow at him.

"If I'm going to play, I'm going to play right."

"You always play right."

Landon smiled down at him, then cupped his cheek. "I love you."

He still wasn't used to hearing those words. Landon said them often and there wasn't a part of Rod that doubted them, but he figured years of doubting himself couldn't be wiped away in just a few months. He was working on making sure he consistently felt worthy of Landon's love and that wasn't something Landon could give him. It was something Rod had to give himself. "I love you too."

He shoved a pillow under himself the way Landon told him to and then waited for him to do his thing. He didn't have to wait very long.

Landon kneeled between his spread legs. He started out by peppering kisses along Rod's ass, rubbing the globes as he did so. Already he wanted to thrust, to rub his erection against the pillow for the delicious friction it would give.

Landon's tongue started at the base of his spine, and then he ran it down the length of Rod's crack. "Oh fuck," he gasped out as he pushed forward just a little, feeling the fabric rub against his cock.

"Such a pretty ass. I love that it's mine," Landon said before tracing his tongue back up Rod's crack. "Now I get to decide what I want to do with it first."

Sex had always been this strange struggle for Rod. He loved it, craved it...but he'd used it as well. Used it to feel, but it was so damn different to be with someone you loved. To know there was more behind it than orgasms. It was almost as though he got to rediscover sex all over again with Landon. Or he guessed, now he was learning the difference between just sex, and making love. They could still get down and dirty, still fuck, still play, only now, it was about love.

"Do something." Rod wiggled his ass and Landon chuckled.

"Always so impatient. I'm going to start with the beads. I've always wanted to watch them slide out of your ass."

Rod trembled in anticipation. He heard the lube open and squirt before what felt like two of Landon's fingers probed his hole. He groaned, loving the feel of Landon and again he considered forgetting the play, just to have Landon.

It was only a couple seconds later that Landon's fingers were gone. He heard the lube again, and on reflex, Rod spread his legs more and lifted his ass higher in open invitation.

"Such a pretty fucking hole." Landon rubbed his thumb against Rod's sensitive anus and then he felt the first bead pop inside. They ranged from half an inch to an inch and a half, the sizes staggered, six beads attached with a couple inches between each.

"I've never done this," Landon whispered as Rod felt the second bead pop inside of him. He could tell by the way it felt that it was one of the bigger ones.

"Never?" Rod closed his eyes, pushing his ass back farther. Landon's other hand came to rest on the cheek of his ass.

"No. Just you. It's so fucking sexy watching them slide into you."

There was a slight stretch and then another bead popped inside. Then another, and another, the last one stretching him more than any of the ones before it. He started to feel full. It was fucking amazing, even more incredible because when he opened his eyes, he got to see that it was Landon doing it.

"You good?" Landon asked before he leaned over and kissed Rod's ass. He was better than good. He was perfect.

"Yeah. Getting full but you can keep going. I can take them all."

Landon nodded at him, before he pushed another bead inside Rod's ass. They were heavy, and so fucking good. Landon's brows were pulled together, his eyes intense as he watched his work, watched himself filling Rod's ass. "I like watching you," Rod told him.

"I like your eyes on me. I like watching you, too."

There was a burn and stretching before Landon inserted the last bead inside him. "Oh fuck," Rod groaned out, his eyes practically rolling back in his head. "Pull them out slowly. Christ, this is so fucking good."

***

Landon's dick was angry at him. It wanted to fuck. He wanted to fuck with it...but he liked this too. He more than liked it. He'd always been up for this kind of thing, but he hadn't thought he would get the pleasure out of it he did. His balls ached. Pre-come dripped from him.

Yeah, this was good for him too.

He began pulling, watched Rod's pink hole stretch and then a black bead pulled free. "I like watching it stretch you, seeing you let it go."

Rod was moving now, gentle thrusts as he no doubt rubbed his dick against the pillow.

"I love how it feels."

Landon got the sudden urge to feel it himself. Maybe one day Rod could try this on him... Though Rod was the ass man, he had fucked Landon a couple times by now.

He tugged slowly and watched Rod open, watched the next bead and then the next as they popped out of his tight pucker.

He rubbed Rod's ass as he pulled them free. Watched him shudder and listened to his gasp. Jesus, he loved this man.

Deciding to switch things up, he inserted the bead that just came out, and then pulled it free again. Rod moved faster now, moaned louder.

One by one he popped each of the beads free. Watched Rod stretch and give them to him. His dick was fucking twitching.

"Jesus, that was beautiful. Why did it take so long for us to do that?"

"I don't know. I also don't know how long I'm going to last with the next one."

Landon winked at him. "We'll figure it out." He picked up the black, curved, vibrating plug and prostate stimulator. He squirted a little lube on it, before positioning it at Rod's hole.

He didn't turn it on at first, just watched it disappear inch-by-inch as he inserted it into Rod's ass.

Rod's fingers were clutching one of their pillows, his hips moving as short, quick breaths fell from his lips.

Landon wanted to make this last...but he also wanted to see Rod lose it too.

"More," Rod rushed out and Landon pushed it all the way inside before turning it on. "Oh fuck!" Rod cursed. Landon moved the stimulator, rubbing Rod's prostate. His hips were jackhammering against the pillow now and Landon knew it wouldn't take him long to explode.

"Oh God, Landon. I'm not going to last."

"Then don't," Landon told him as he rubbed what he knew was an aching spot inside of Rod.

The man thrust, his thighs shook and then he called out as he no doubt spilled his seed all over the bed. He kept pumping against the bed, as he reached back, grabbing for Landon's wrist.

It was so fucking beautiful, Landon felt his own orgasm creeping up on him.

"Finish...I want you to finish too," Rod gritted out, his voice heavy with post-orgasm bliss. Landon pulled the toy out and lay on top of Rod. He didn't even have to fuck him. His balls were already heavy and tight. He rubbed his cock up and down the crack of Rod's ass, letting it cradle him. It was less than ten thrusts later that his nuts let go, come jutting out of him and pooling in the small of Rod's back.

Landon fell on top of him; their deep, heavy breaths mixed. Landon kissed the back of his neck, his cheek, ran a hand through Rod's hair. He couldn't stop touching him.

"I love you," Rod said softly.

"I love you too....and I can't fucking wait to do that again."

A HUNDRED THOUSAND WORDS

Riley Hart writing as Nyrae Dawn, available now.

CHAPTER ONE

It was my best friend's older brother who made me realize I'm gay. Sure, I'd wondered before. I mean, a part of me had to have known, but it was Levi who made me admit it to myself. Or rather, it was the fact that when I really started jerking off on the regular, it was to thoughts of him. It didn't matter that he was an asshole—a straight-as-straight-could-be asshole—he was the star player in a whole hell of a lot of my fantasies growing up.

But then I went away for college and made all of those fantasies and more come true. Not with Levi because of the whole being a straight asshole thing, but once I was out of Coburn, the small town in Oregon where I grew up, I didn't need to pine after the guy I'd never have. I was in San Francisco for fuck's sake. Home had a shortage of gay guys to choose from, but San Francisco was an all-you-could-eat buffet.

Now it's winter break and I'm home from college, so of course the Levi-factor is in effect again. His family is throwing a holiday party and I'm sitting on their living room couch watching Levi do what he does best: charming a group of women. He must be telling some kind of joke or something because they're laughing and smiling, all eyes pinned on him. He was always the golden child—straight A's in school, popular, good at sports. Maybe that's why I wanted him so much. He was everything I wasn't. Not that I want to be those things, because I don't, but on him they're sexy as hell.

He flashes a smile at his admirers that gives me a tingle in my balls. Groaning, I try to look away but can't. He's always had this magnetic energy that sucks me in.

His hickory-brown hair has grown out since I saw him last. It's hanging in his face, almost blocking his dark eyes. When he grins, big and bright, his thin lips stretched wide, the group does the same. It's like when someone yawns and you're powerless not to yawn yourself. Sometimes it's as though he lends you some of his confidence, or at least I tell myself that. I'm pretty sure I'm not the only one who feels that way as everyone looks at him like he's teaching them to hang the moon. But then he has to go overboard when he puts his arms out, flexing his biceps. That's when I roll my eyes and look away.

"What a fucking idiot." My best friend Chris sits next to me on the couch. We met in fifth grade and we've been tight ever since. I was the quiet kid before I met Chris. Take after my dad that way, I guess, but Chris pulled me out of my shell.

We were always doing something stupid when we were kids. Nothing too outrageous: got caught drinking and smoking a few times, missing curfew. He stole two Playboy magazines for us to jack off to, which was when I first realized there was something different between the two of us. Naked girls and tits did nothing for me. I pretended to come as hard as he told me he did, and then a few months later, I was forgoing the magazines in favor of mental images of his brother.

"Eh," I reply, because talking about Levi with Chris never goes well. He's always had issues with his brother.

"Watch them, though—women eat him up. I don't fucking get it. I swear to God if Gemma falls for him I'm going to beat his ass."

Laughing, I look at Chris. His hair's the same shade of brown as Levi's but it's shorter. Chris has always had this jealousy thing with his brother, which I guess is probably normal. I don't have siblings so I wouldn't know. His concerns aren't too farfetched, though. Every girl who spends more than five minutes with Levi ends up falling for him. I can see why Chris would be jealous, especially because Chris had been in love with some of them. Or at least, he'd wanted to screw them. There was one girl in particular who Chris had been into. They'd fucked around a few times and the next thing we knew, Levi was taking her out. Chris hasn't forgiven him for that one.

"I'm sure your girl isn't going to fall for your brother." If I don't change the subject, he'll go off on all the ways he can't stand Levi, and I'll want to stab my eardrums so I don't have to hear it all for the millionth time. Nudging him, I say, "It's kind of good to be home for winter break. I missed this."

This being his family. My dad was around and he tried his best, but it wasn't easy for him to support us. He worked all the time to make ends meet, and Chris's family let me pretend like I belonged there because Chris and I were close. It made things easier on Dad. He misses Mom more every time he looks at me.

"When will Gemma be here?" I ask. Chris went and fell in love our sophomore year of college. Since I'm in San Francisco and Chris's school is back East, this break will be the first time I meet her.

Before he replies, loud laughter erupts from the other side of the room and I glance over to see Levi sitting by the table with his head tilted back, letting out belly laughs. I watch his throat move. He has a really sexy throat I wouldn't be averse to kissing...and I really need to shut my goddamned brain down and stop lusting after Chris's brother. Even if there was a chance in hell I could bang Levi, I'm pretty sure Chris would lose his fucking mind if I did. Chris is the best friend I've ever had, my only real one, and I wouldn't sacrifice that for anything.

"A few days. She's incredible, Toby. You'll love her. I can't wait for you to meet her." Chris nudges me the same way I nudged him a minute before, so I pull my attention away from Levi and back to him. "What about you? You said there were all kinds of dudes to choose from at school."

While I'm glad he feels comfortable talking to me about this, discussing my sex life with him isn't something I'm in the mood to do. With Chris it's all roses and hearts and love. With me it's ass and hands and mouths. Big difference in what we're looking for.

"There were plenty of guys." I wink. "So many, in fact, I feel like I'd be doing them a disservice if I got serious about any of them. Who buys the first car they test drive?" That's what going off to school was about for me. Yes, there's the education, but I really wanted to *live* and experience all the shit I couldn't while at home. I'm the only gay guy in my small town—the only one I know of, anyway—and I never had an opportunity to experience much of anything before leaving for San Fran.

Portland, which isn't far away, has a great gay population, but it wasn't always easy for me to get there when I was younger.

Chris has always been sympathetic to my situation in Coburn, but my brand of loneliness isn't something he can really understand. It's easier not to mention it much.

Still, he's really the only person I have in my life who wants to be there for me. He never gave a shit that he was hanging out with not only the only gay kid in town, but the only black kid, too. He was my boy from the start and I was his. Reason number two I need to end my obsession with the oldest Baxter son. They're like family to me, or at least they've always accepted me as such.

More laughter from the other side of the room. Nearly everyone at the party is congregating around Levi and he's making the holiday party all the merrier, soaking up being the center of everyone's universe.

"He's such a fucking bastard. Always has to be in the middle of everything," Chris says, each of his words making me feel guiltier and guiltier, because as much as he can't stand his brother, and as much as I love Chris, I understand the draw of Levi. There's something about him, and even after all these years, I have to grudgingly admit that it's still pulling me in, too.

***

It's a couple hours later when I'm sitting in the yard on a two-person swing. We got lucky and ended up with a few hours of sunshine—something that doesn't happen often during December in Oregon—so I'm soaking it in.

We ate a while ago. The party has thinned out a bit, and Chris went to the store with his mom. My dad isn't here. The Baxters invited him—they always do, and he always appreciates it—but he likes being alone too much. He has ever since Mom left us. He never got over losing her, and if that's what losing someone does to a guy, count me the fuck outta ever being in a serious relationship.

There's movement on the side of the house, a flash of color, and I look up and see Levi kneeling, his back against the house and his face buried in his hands.

What the hell?

It almost looks like he's rocking, like his hands are knotted in his hair. Then, just like that, he pushes to his feet, straightens out his clothes, and turns around.

His eyes land on me instantly. And then...he smiles, his body language one hundred percent different than it was a minute ago.

In long, confident strides, Levi makes his way to me, making me wonder if I misjudged what I'd seen.

He's wearing a long-sleeved shirt that hugs his chest and arms and a pair of loose jeans riding low on his hips. Dude, I love that.

Love seeing the edge of a guy's boxers sticking out over his jeans and rubbing my tongue along the seam.

"How's it goin' T-Rex? Enjoying your sophomore year?" He plops down onto the seat beside me, his arm, hot and hard, brushes against mine. He doesn't move and I sure as hell don't move because he's gorgeous and I definitely don't mind a gorgeous guy touching me. I do, however, wish he didn't call me T-Rex.

"Don't call me that."

"Dinosaurs, man. That's all I have to say. You were what, ten or eleven when we met you? I think you were obsessed with dinosaurs until you were at least sixteen."

"Fuck off." But what he's said is pretty close to the truth. I used to want to be a paleontologist, which is funny considering I'm now an English major. Plus, those aren't the kind of bones I'm into anymore, but it was a good aspiration for a kid.

"Embarrassed?" he teases, his voice a little softer than it usually is.

"No. And I was fourteen when I stopped liking dinosaurs. You can give it up now." There's nothing like the object of your fantasies seeing you as nothing more than a kid who he calls T-Rex.

"Aww, but I like to call you T-Rex." Levi wraps an arm around my neck, and then pretends to ruffle my nonexistent hair. I keep it cut short enough that his attempt is impossible. And yeah, did I mention he treats me like a fucking kid?

"Get off." I shove his arm away and Levi lets me.

"I'm just giving you shit. It's good to see you."

First, if he wanted to see me, it wouldn't be hard considering he's at Stanford School of Medicine and I'm thirty miles away at San Francisco State University. And second, I wish he was thinking it's good to see me naked, but hey, I'll take what I can get. "Yeah, it's good to be home."

Levi laughs humorlessly. "If you say so."

At that, I turn to face him. That's not something I would ever expect Levi to say. Yeah, everyone's always known Levi's too big for Coburn, but I thought he'd always loved home, too. Ever since he was a kid we all knew he'd grow up to be a big-shot doctor like his dad. Levi's the guy who has everything and everyone loves him, so I'm not sure why he would hate being back here temporarily. "What's that supposed to mean?"

He doesn't answer right away. As he runs a finger over a seam on the swing's arm, he's almost subdued—like he's a different guy than the one who was laughing and joking earlier, a different guy than the one I've always known. "Nothing. Ignore me, T-Rex. I'll catcha later, yeah?" Without waiting for me to reply, Levi gets up and walks away, and I'm still sitting here trying to figure out what in the hell happened.

Acknowledgments

Do you ever wake up surprised that your life, is your life? I do that every day. I am blessed beyond belief with not only an incredible husband, and awesome kids, but also because I get to wake up every day and do what I love. I love words. I love romance. I love writing. I love happily ever afters. I'm able to write because of you—my readers. There are not enough thank yous in the world for what I owe you. But I will continue to try and find them.

Thank you to Riley's Rebels members for making my days brighter.

To the new crew at The M/M Daily Grind—both authors and members—for jumping on board and making it such a fun place.

To Hope Cousin and Jessica de Ruiter for moderating Riley's Rebels so well, and for your friendship, and all our chats. You make my days easier and happier. Seriously, I don't know how I'd survive without either of you.

Theresa Golish, I owe you big lady. Thank you for helping me think of the perfect title for Rod and Landon's story.

Thank you to Hope, Christina Lee, Jessica, Judy, Prema Editing, and Manda for helping me make Rod and Landon's story everything that it is.

Thanks to Felice Stevens for being awesome, and for letting me talk your ear off all the time.

I am so lucky to be surrounded by such incredible people.

About the Author:

Riley Hart is the girl who wears her heart on her sleeve. She's a hopeless romantic. A lover of sexy stories, passionate men, and writing about all the trouble they can get into together. If she's not writing, you'll probably find her reading.

Riley lives in California with her awesome family, who she is thankful for every day.

You can find her online at:

Twitter

@RileyHart5

Facebook

https://www.facebook.com/riley.hart.1238?fref=ts

Blog

www.rileyhartwrites.blogspot.com

OTHER BOOKS BY RILEY HART

Blackcreek Series:

COLLIDE

STAY

PRETEND

Broken Pieces Series:

BROKEN PIECES

FULL CIRCLE

LOSING CONTROL

Rock Solid Construction Series:

ROCK SOLID

Made in the USA
Middletown, DE
01 July 2022